<u>Series Dedication</u>

To all the imperfect people of the world.

THE JODE
PART 1:

General Ygl
& the Genie

PJSELAROM.COM

• Available on Kindle, Amazon.com, and other retail outlets.

All characters are fictional unless otherwise seen in a hallucination. The creatures (i.e., unipegon, asegafians, archeornyx; parashad) are his proprietary property.

Epic Adventure. Mystery. Romance.

2nd Edition Revised

THE JODE: Part 1: General Ygl & the Genie

ISBN-13:
978-0692066270 (PJ Selarom)

ISBN-10:
0692066276

Printed in the USA. Layout by PJ Selarom.

<u>Special Thanks to the ILLUSTRATORS:</u>

<u>Final interior & map</u>: Corey McNaught
(MCNAUGHTILLUSTRATION.WIXSITE.COM)

<u>Cover & interior art</u>: Apple Qingyang Zhang (APPLEQZ.COM).

<u>Final interior</u>: Robert Curet (ARTOFCURET.TUMBLR.COM)

<u>Acknowledgements</u>

Thank you, Gloria (Auntie G), for always encouraging me to get this initial book done for my series before you left this mortal plane.

Thank you, Laura, for choking me while saying, "You've got a novel." nearly thirty years ago.

Thank you, life, for permitting me to get this wonderful crazy series started.

DIALECTS

MAN	Father/Mother	Husband/Wife	Son/Daughter	Day/Night	Year, Life	Death
LOREL ELF	Bloodfather/mother	Mate	Bloodson/daughter	Sunday/Moonday	Season	End of seasons
KHUN ELF; SPRITE; GNOME	Bloodfather/mother	Mate		Sunday/Moonday	Season	End of seasons
NIXY	Bloodfather/mother	Chosen/Bonder	Spawn	Sea blanket/Great Pearls	Season	End of seasons
GIANT; FAIRY	Trunk/Stem	Seed/Earth	Sprout	Cloudnoon/Starmoon	Growth	End of growths
DWARF	Jewel/Gem	Brace/Charm	Nugget/Trinket	Great Light/Deep Cold	Ring	End of rings
OGRE	Boulder/Rock	Vitamin/Mineral	Stone/Pebble	Light/Dark	Shift	End of shifts
PIXY	Boulder/Rock	Vitamin/Mineral	Stone/Pebble	Light/Dark	Shift	End of shifts

DIALECTS

MAN	Emperor/ess	Prince/cess	General	Advisor	People	Old Person	Home	School	Doctor
LOREL ELF	King/Queen		General	Advisor	Kin	Elder	Home	School	Doctor
KHUN ELF; SPRITE; GNOME	Leader				Clan	Elder	Home		
NIXY	Ocean (female)	Lake/Pond	Reef	Tribune	Schools	Elder	Grotto	Ripple	Algae
GIANT; FAIRY	Tree/Flower	Plant/Fern	Thorn	Leaf	Roots	Twig	Hollow	Ring	Chloro
DWARF	Grand Diamond/Coal	Diamond/Coal	Stalagmite	Tar	Ore	Fossil	Core	Matrix	Crystal
OGRE	Mountain/Hill	Butte/Mound	Crag	Sand	Sediments	Dust	Cavern	Ion	Resin
PIXY	Lord/Lady				Sediments	Dust	Cavern	Ion	Resin

The Divinity

ELVIN:
ACHAL: Lorellian goddess of memory and history. Wielder of the psionic sword.
MIREDO: Khunian god of nature. Wielder of the bow of storms.

MAN:
ISTRATOS: God of magic and games. Wielder of the staff of power.
WELNA: Goddess of the arts. Wielder of the shield of creation.

NIXY:
JEBLE: God of the sea and logic. Wielder of the trident of waves.
NUMR'C: Goddess of dreams, fertility, and peace. Embodiment of the island.

GIANTS:
LOLUNG-COR: God of war. Wielder of the lance of strength.
PYTY: Goddess of the grain. Embodiment of the mountain. Wielder of the sickle of sustenance.

OGRES:
FALVANCH: Goddess of the earth. The Great Sculptor. Wielder of the club of order.
HOGAR: God of resilience. Embodiment of the desert. The Rock Shaker. Wielder of the pick of chaos.

DWARVES:
HENC: God of wealth. Wielder of the axe of winter.
PARIOT: Goddess of invention. Wielder of the hammer of sacred magma.

FAERIE (including Gnomes):
ETHNEL: Essence of preservation and small creatures; Wielder of the dagger of luck.

Salutations.

I am Achal, Elvin goddess of
memory and history.
Welcome to Inner Earth.

A WORLD IMBUED WITH ADVENTURE AND MUCH DIVERSITY—
DIFFERENT CULTURES AND DIFFERING IDEOLOGIES.
AHEM... ALLOW ME TO ABSOLVE MYSELF OF MY LOFTY STATUS
and narrate to thy... your... level... is that better? Good. Let me continue...

The continent of Zaendara, one of the prevalent masses in all Inner Earth,
is where Man has taken refuge in the Quirmean Empire, a vast empire
encompassing nearly half of Zaendara and ceasing at the extensive Wall of
Quirm. The wall borders to the east of two Elvin estates—the forests of
Lorel and Khun.

There are many other estates in Zaendara. A long chain of grasslands,
renowned as the notorious Dark Plains, detaches the Ty Desert in the east
from the forests. The Ogres thrive in the Ty. Along the southern border
stretches the proud Cory Mountains, residence of the Giants, as the region
looming over the Dwarf **Grand Diamond**om and across the Nesia Ocean
toward the Nixies' three **Ocean**doms. You are encouraged to pore over the
map in this book's terminal pages.

You may query these terms "Grand diamondom" and "Oceandom." They reflect the varied cultural dialects these races harbor amongst themselves. Of course, if you are a dissimilar race, you may articulate a different vernacular, and so it is consistent on Inner Earth. Moreover, in this book's preceding section are charts entailing these dialects if you get confused interpreting the excerpts. Man's dialect courses across the summit of each column to use as a reference to the other idioms.

Take your leisure construing this story about to be related. A tale of much gallantry, heartache, and love.

What is a story devoid of love?

It is important for me to note that ethnic multitudes exist within each race pertaining to each region. For instance, in the desert, dark-skinned ethnics thrive.

Also, note that the residents of Inner Earth age twice as long as you, though, for purposes of contingency, they will remain of the common age. For example, a sixty-six-year-old man would look thirty-three in age, therefore, thirty-three will be the relevant age. Moreover, those of Elvin/Nixy lineage will always be of youthful appearance while Khunian Elves mature far longer than the rest.

A final note, two points of views will relay this story: Ygl's and mine. General Ygl of the Lorel Elves will address in the first person, the "I." Whereas, I, Achal, will communicate the story in the third person, as any storyteller would. When I relate this adventure to you, I will indorse the participants to speak in their native vernaculars. Their initial dialects will be in emboldened print. Upon Ygl's narrative, the initial dialects will be emboldened and exotic royal titles will be capitalized anywhere to lessen confusion. I hearten you to embrace a dissimilar culture.

CHAPTER 1: The Nixy

Exuberant droplets of water trailed across the leveling pond, shooting stars against the evening's declining milieu.

Sama inhaled a dosage of air as her webbed feet dug sleek holes into the embankment's mud she ascended. The lagging sun's rays comforted her miniscule scales, but the Forest of Lorel's spacious land—its mundane trees—conveyed a certain vigor. Sama understood why, but she did not understand why, as well. This enigma tickled her senses, snared her memory, and ran away like a wicked child heckling her.

"Ryl!" She knew her spawn could swim well, no thanks to the Lorellian Elves. Meanwhile, she wondered where his father had gone.

As a livelihood, Ryl and she relied on their instincts to survive consuming the great fish from the isolated pond and the nourishing berries. Freedom called their names aloud, and she welcomed the autonomy with engaging arms.

The sensible Lorellians thrived in makeshift grass huts and elaborate treehouses in southern Lorel closer to the more expansive Lake Ban, with a small detachment guarding the north. They hunted furry animals for food while many meditated. Nixies did not believe in that way of living.

"Nixies?" she thought as she basked. She touched her sea-green skin with webbed hands. Water seeped from her pores. "I wonder what they are." Oblivious to the answers presented to her.

Ryl surfaced at the pond's eastern end. Though drenched, he conducted his small timber frame well. His hair, a mesh of luscious vines, bounced against his flesh made of bark.

"**Bloodmother**, the water feels nice so. Please swim to me," he giggled, gills flexing in his neck. "It has been **sea blankets** many since winter has passed, and we did not have to steal from Man." He skipped with no effort upon the stones up to the muddy embankment, the fibrous roots excellent padding on his soles.

Sama often wondered why he had peculiar feet like that and she did not. And her hair, though very fine and a light green, was not a bundle of bouncing vines; her skin, not made of bark. Who was Ryl's father, anyway? Where was his father?

"We did not steal much." Her confidence in her son never wavered. "We had enough to forage for the winter. The Elves have a selection better of fruits and vegetables."

Ryl darted across the viscous embankment to his mother like a spear lacerating through a gusty wind. The land resonated stronger to him. "Ah, but Man grows food when all the Elves need to do is pick the food." He laughed with a prance here and there.

"That is not true. Elves grow some, and we do not have to worry about fences."

Without warning, a sudden coldness crept… The land failed to sing anymore. A young spawn, Ryl was not as adept emoting with the land as his Nixy mother.

Sama, astounded, could sense the grass moaning. She coveted the trees to provide a better answer, but they never spoke. Did they ever?

Charismatic spring had manifested, yet this speedy coldness clambered up to them through the land as if winter never left at all. She blinked and noticed Ryl digging his roots into the land, endeavoring to discover the source of this recent feeling. A strange milky mist crawled from the profusion of firs behind him, exhibiting a slight bluish-yellow glint.

The grass wailed…

"Ryl!" Clutching her dagger in midleap, Sama sprinted to her spawn's defense. Her sartorial lattice of interweaving lianas performed a best effort to affix her bosom and garb her more alluring aspects. What magic of Man was this? Did Emperor Rondo have vengeance against a forlorn female and her child? Did Man finally acknowledge her little family's existence when Man hunted in these permissible parts?

Faces sketchy floated within the lithe miasma... Demonic faces... Demonic figures.

"Bloodmother!" Ryl knew how to defend himself from anything, a testament to years of survival. Lengthy thorns sprouted from his mahogany skin. Like a medusa, his hair of vines reared to protect its distressed master from the hissing pale miasma. Ryl cast his thorns before the mist engulfed his last cry.

"This cannot be." Sama slipped on the embankment's pebbles, overtaken by fury. Her buoyant flesh could not cushion her skull from fracturing upon a nearby boulder. She skidded underwater baffled about the disconcerting shadows slithering along the pond's surface.

CHAPTER 2: Rondo & Werkle

Gablen, the capital of Quirm.

Emperor Rondo brooded upon his oaken throne delineated in gold. A man in his early fifties, he slouched within his thick velvet robe's lavish fabrics. Athletic legs obtruded from the robe, adorned within an appealing pair of slacks and fitted slippers. To the emperor's right, an identical throne garlanded with silver rested upon the wide dais, vacant and glistening with pureness.

Three other thrones aligned near the base of the platform's quarter step, slighter in stature. They were established on either side of an extensive gray carpet, facing the carpet from a judicious distance, angling toward the larger chairs. The left gilded throne aligned with the emperor's while the silver laced chairs aligned opposite; and, all were unoccupied as well.

Exquisite paintings adorned the marble walls exploiting images of other royalty and him. Enormous aged statues of previous emperors and athletes stretched high fortifying the polished ceiling. Each statue enhanced with a lengthy profuse tapestry of unknown origin relating a significant story weaved in rich materials, including silks, golds, and platinum blends. Amongst an assemblage of couches, chairs, and small tables, a nearby hearth crackled. Once a locale of much fellowship, the well-kept chamber ceased such dynamic.

The emperor half muttered and half dreamt to himself as his crown tilted upon his brow. The crown's seven prongs signified the major cities; the largest anterior prong being Gablen. An etched asterisk aligned beneath each prong's point. Gablen's eight-point asterisk exhibited a lengthy horizontal and vertical axis. The horizontal axis, the lengthier of the two, extended farther toward the left. Small dots, positioned on particular spots on the asterisk, idealized the major cities' sites. The other cities' asterisks possessed a single dot matching the city's locale on Gablen's emblem. A centralized diamond was pinpointed on each asterisk aesthetic to size.

Not even Rondo's monstrous Demonguards comprehended what he was ruminating—not that they would, anyway. Their steel armor ensconced them quite well from head to toe; however, their large size became an unambiguous giveaway. Gleaming pupils peered or jagged incisors jutted out of their hefty helmets; some of their armor couldn't conceal the coarse hairy tufts or prominent scales.

Rondo slouched anticipating someone's arrival. The individual's delay unnerved him a bit—not a good sign if a herald wanted to mollify a summons.

The Demonguards reacted with drawn swords, their preemptive movement, inhuman. At last! A knocking arose from the oaken doors' exterior, breaching silence's hold.

"Come in, Werkle," Rondo commanded wryly.

A stout man, thirty years of age, wobbled through the rectangular archway. He appeared much older than Rondo, maybe because he was balding with much more gray—a product of much stress. Werkle's lengthy robe swathed his round belly exposing a modest pair of slippers with hearty soles within the hem's drag. In his hand he possessed a sheet of paper.

"You called, Sire?" He felt so awkward. Though he asserted himself before Rondo in a straight posture, he conceded he detested beholding his Emperor's rage.

"Of course, I called you, you imbecile. There are moments, I think, when I picked you to be my advisor that it should be me advising you. In any case, what took you so long?"

"I was out in the courtyard receiving a dispatch by Spenz stating they've captured the Dwarf **Diamond**om," Rondo's adviser sneered. "Ilinor, their general, and Eifner, their advisor, have been captured as well."

Rondo scowled. "What a silly word, 'diamondom.' Is Spenz heading back up?"

"Yes, Sire, he is going through the Dark Plains so his army will not be spotted by the other estates. He also left behind a large part of the army to place law and order in the Dwarf Diamondom, as you insisted, upon my advice."

"I want you to send him a message. I want it to say he will not go directly to Gablen. Instead, I want him to pick up reserves in Fumi and to head toward the Forest of Lorel. The Elf kingdom must be captured or else they will be a nuisance to my plans. I want them put into enslavement, but," he paused a moment, "their royalty will go to Skavir."

"But it's insane just to go barging into the Forest of Lorel. It just isn't like the attack on the Dwarves. The Dwarves didn't know of it; the Elves can see our army marching from the city just by looking out from the forest."

The emperor's smile returned. "Not if I assist our forces with this."

He tugged on a chain enfolded about his neck. An indescriptive item uncovered from his beard's trim confines. The article, credibly cut to fit the single-windowed case, drooped from the chain. Sporadic darkness obstructed the article's multicolored appearance; multifaceted maybe. An oddness with a tantalizing crook. "Trust in me, Werkle. It already worked last."

Once Rondo's advisor ascertained the enigmatic item, Werkle beamed with nervous approval.

CHAPTER 3: Ygl

We commemorated spring on its first **sunday** in the Forest of Lorel and my **kin** did what they had done in past– they danced. They danced in honor of our goddess, Achal. They danced in honor of the first great warmth that had come from the twin suns, Los and Num. Now, the **moonday** exalted our celebration with the twin moons, Nus and Anul. The reeds pipes blew...

Delicate little blossoms poked their petal heads from everywhere after hibernating during winter's visit, some adorned as a headpiece for celebrants. Light green coloring returned to our foliage marking a promising beginning.

Dancing was rather not the usual pursuit of my kin. We were a race preoccupied with meditation; however, around the bonfires my fellow Lorellians rejoiced with **season**'s initial signs introduced to our forest, a tradition shared with our Khunian allies with little difference. Our movements were rather sedated, almost trancelike, amongst the majestic oaks and maples bordering our vast dance area.

Winter's frosty breath left us for another passing, yet, somehow, I sensed another coldness approaching this part of our kingdom unlike any other. An eerie coldness not even my hooded cloak and lavender ensemble could grant me warmth from.

I tried scanning northern Lorel with my telepathy, but could not sense any feedback from our exterior defenses. This worried me. "*Guards, if you have arrived to the dance, let me know. This is an order.*"

I, alone, felt uneasy about this eerie coldness while affixing my bandanna to keep my hair away from my line of vision.

Steadfast, my majestic unipegon, felt a bit uncomfortable, too. I patted his waxen mane. "*Steady, Steadfast, steady.*"

Upon his rugged spine, I could admire his horned face and physique. A reptilian gaze scanned in all directions sensing nearby danger. His sturdy frame, similar to a dragon's, meshed with a unicorn's exterior appearance. An extended snout flared a smoky puff. Soft fur coated him just as impenetrable as any dragon's hide. Slender draconian wings, spattered with a thin veil of random feathers, tensed within their folds. His serpentine tail tried to remain in control protruding from a waxen cluster of horse hair; ending with a tassel of the same cluster from a spiny knob. A bold rare creature with an air of chaotic order, Steadfast made me a proud general. A wonder to care for and cherish.

Faint telepathic calls reverberated again, originating from the kingdom's northern part, but now they felt like a figment of my imagination. King Methelo, my **bloodbrother**, posted me down here with a small unit to safeguard the spring dance. Surveying the jubilant faces, I felt reaffirmed about Methelo's orders, but these unfamiliar warnings seemed so real... my thoughts would not disavow them.

Thalla, my beautiful mate, frolicked amongst the attendees. A bit lighter than our kin's color, her elegant olive gown bounced with every jostle of her wavy curly hair. She was a couple of seasons older than me—a benefit on my behalf. Maybe I should tell her about my suspicions. She would understand, "*Thalla.*"

My mental intrusion startled her. The back of her hand hit an attendee by accident, knocking the attendee over.

She turned with a scathing glare to attend to her victim, fixing her matching hair dress. "*Ygl, can you not give me some sort of telepathic warning before your telepathic sendings?*"

"*Sorry...*"

"*That is okay. I love your little surprises.*" She winked. "*Is your bloodbrother still having his stomach problems? Is the Britbert ginger root helping out?*"

"*King Methelo is doing fine, Thalla.*" I winked.

General Ygl & The Genie

"Funny, I still do not see him out here, or Prince Rolando and Sylvia. Maybe everyone is still pondering the stomach problem away?"

"Your sarcasm knows no bounds, Thalla. This sunday no one ponders."

"**Bloodfather**," my zealous **bloodson**, Limbus, pulled at my leg. He wore his best hooded tunic, a nice pair of tan slacks, and leather shoes to stay warm. At fourteen seasons old, I guess he wanted to dress similar to me. "Is it okay if Steadfast allows me to leap on him along with you?"

Enthusiastic Snip, Limbus' asegafian cat, squatted by his master's side staring with glossy eyes akin to translucent orbs. Snip had beige fur with big frilly ears; a dark brown face and tail tip. Interesting enough, his smaller domestic counterparts appeared relatable to the wild asegafian.

I started laughing. "Of course, he will allow you, Limbus." I loved Limbus. His perseverance separated him from other **bloodchildren**. While they ran around and played their games, he went to each of my soldiers and asked how to use the sword in combat, for example. He even seemed to better some soldiers. I hoped one sunday he would take my place as general of Lorel.

"Do you still have the present I gave you?"

"Yes, I do." He stretched out his leg to reveal a gold leg bracelet, a leglet, molded as a facsimile of my steed's wings. Upon the leglet's face, the relief of a unipegon galloping the winds.

"Remember, it can be a weapon as well. All you need to do is detach it and it acts as a boomerang."

"Yes, bloodfather."

"Where is your dagger?" He extended his other leg to reveal my gift resting in its sheath. "Good."

I bent over to help Limbus climb atop when I noticed Snip arching, his fur standing at end… a scream hit the moonday air. I shivered.

The Elves stopped their frolicking around the bonfires and trees, looking north where the scream originated. Other fellow Lorellians ran out of the underbrush in great fright.

I peered farther into the forest to witness a paleness engulfing my kin. A fog… No, a mist… a light mist, if any, somehow difficult to peer into. A bluish-yellow twinkling blazed all through the phenomenon. My kin should be able to pierce this absurd mist with their infravision, our ability to perceive warm objects as red in difficult settings and cold objects as blue. I used my infravision and could not perceive anything at all.

This thing, this pale mist, kept engulfing my kin, nearing the dance area. The Lorellians panicked and ran away from its inscrutable intrusion. More cries came from the east as I witnessed more Lorellians scrambling from that direction with this same mist hounding them. Still more screams came from the west followed by more Lorellians running from that direction. We were being surrounded! Was this Achal's trickery? Her absurd gratitude playing this strange game?

An elder male yelled. He struggled with someone, something, from the invasive mist's boundary. "Demons! Demons!"

The mist answered with a clean sweep of crude sword cleaving the poor elder's head from his neck. Before the elder embraced the **end-of-seasons**, a majority of Elves heeded his terrible warning. When his words struck me, I began to feel a long forgotten loathing and fear. I had been taught of Demons as being nothing but myth, but these invaders...

Lorellians scampered everywhere.

"*Limbus!*" my bloodson did not answer. In all this turmoil, he must have gotten scared and ran off. On second thought, if I knew my bloodson the way I did, then maybe he stayed. *"Limbus!"*

The mist crossed the dance area's outskirts. I could not wait any longer. If Demons had returned, they would not take the Elvin Kingdom without a fight.

Defiant Steadfast spewed scorching flames from his extended snout. The crowd scattered from our path as my unipegon galloped to the dance area's interior.

With my right hand on the reins, I reached for my back scabbard. Out Welbern, my broadsword, flashed. "Welbern, this is the moment for you to depict your namesake, 'Demonslayer'... *Guards!!*"

A dozen or so of my warriors sprang into action upon their horses; not enough to confront the coming threat. I needed more.

"Quickly, each of you form a perimeter and defend the area. Try to arouse some of the kin as you go along. Hurry! There is not a moment to waste! Let this not be our last stand! For Lorel!"

My kin tried to fight, but when the skulking mist absorbed them, I could not tell who was triumphant. Other kin ran faster, stumbling everywhere in panic.

The mist, now a towering goliath, encroached upon my very spot. I noticed a band of male Elves cowing around their mates and bloodchildren as if their bodies alone would act as an impervious barricade—most heads bowed in deep meditation.

My heart boiled. "*Cowards! Draw your swords! Arch your arrows! Quick, last defenders of Lorel! The mist is upon us!*"

And the lithe invader engulfed us. My infravision attempted to define the demonic figures popping in and out through the sea of paleness. Even my telepathic sweep had limited range, sifting through what felt like a thickening psychic sludge, instead of touching mental obstacles. We were supposed to have good hearing, yet sounds were muffled. None of my wits or abilities had any effect here. Oh, to have the Khunians' better senses now!

A couple of adversaries nearby took advantage of my mishap. I got swiped on my left side. Not a big swipe, but enough to bleed.

I struck out with Welbern knowing that every sweep would hit their mark; relying upon my blade's legendary purpose to decimate those of Demonic aura. The clashing metals' clanking increased within my proximity despite the auditory issue.

Magnificent Steadfast fought with nature's ferocity. My unipegon swung his reptilian tail trying to kill Demons with the spikey bulb's impact. He reared on his lizard-like legs to attack our invaders with his triple clawed hooves exposing his scaly underbelly. His head struck down through the mist plucking a Demon through the gut with his horn to lob the gorged parcel at expectant targets.

Steadfast's head shook, for the mist began to impair his vision as well. Another stream of fire spurted from his muzzle. I could have ordered him to stop before he hurt any of our kin, but… too many end-of-seasons had already occurred because of my failure… I did not need a telepathic readout to realize our horrible losses… too many horrible losses.

"*Limbus! Thalla!*" I did not care about this challenging mist, my mate and my bloodchild needed my protection.

Another Demon attacked me sideways, Welbern sliced through it.

<hum...>

"*Die, Elf!!*" Even in my thoughts the Demonic dialect churned.

I tore the monstrosity's mind apart with a telepathic blast. He should have not attempted his attack so close. This mist did have a weak link, at last. However, we were still losing. I started to get weary. I struck down many adversaries, but their assaults became endless. A painful sting conveyed an oozing wound on my right leg.

With a mighty flap, Steadfast needed no order to fly us out to safety despite the circumstances.

<hum...>

A massive fist bowled us over. Steadfast's solid body crushed mine upon the fall. My blood rushed... images spun.

Did Steadfast rear up against the brutal Demon? My mount missed the smaller grinning Demon standing above me with crude sword uplifted.

<hum...>

That humming?

"No! Leave him alone!" the female voice demanded. Blurry hands reached out for the Demon's sword arm; then the Demon fell with a growling gurgle. More Demons emerged from the mist pouncing upon my rescuer.

The scent of olives...

"*Ygl!*"

"*Thalla...*"

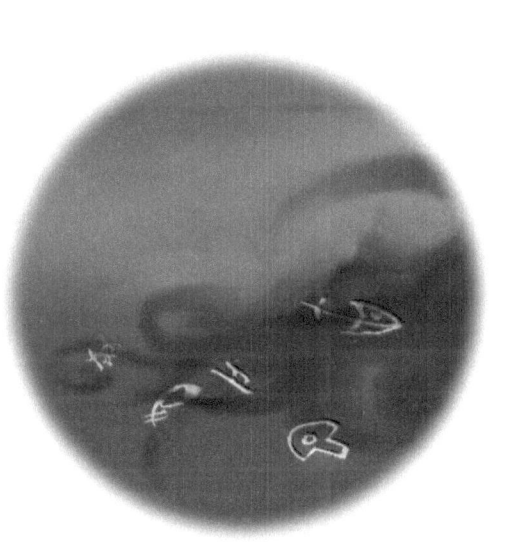

CHAPTER 4: Flower Juna

I awoke not in the Interim, but in a familiar place I had been to in previous **seasons.** The grass itself felt welcoming during the **moonday**'s progression. Mountains to my right in this locale indicated this smaller forest inherent to my kingdom.

I winced ahead. With the scenery still unclear, my infravision could distinguish something out there; definitely not a mist.

I tried to stand. A sharp pain from my right leg pierced through me equal to the pain on my left. A low tree limb acted as much needed support.

Farther out, a road of dirt led somewhere, but where? I remembered riding a hippogriff bareback with my bloodfather, Scall. How elated we were looking over the fresh grassland to admire Lake Ban on a visit to some place. Other Elves resided there... different Elves.

"Khun. This is the road to the Forest of Khun." But how did I get here and who brought my body to this destination?

This part of the forest did appear subdued, except for the light to my left. The source, a slow dimming campfire. Two figures, glowing pinkish to my infravision, slept flanking the flame. Wrapped in fleece skin, the huge sleeper overshadowed the smaller husky partner. I spotted a great gray wolf with white markings awake beside the husky individual.

A couple of large horses were strapped to another tree limb near me.

"These are not Elves," I whispered, astonished.

"Of course, they are not Elves. Who did you think they were?"

A bit startled, I sought in the tiny voice's direction. A small female, maybe three to four inches in height, hovered beyond me. She wore knee-high boots made of a taut spider webbing and a short auburn dress. Unlike any seen, the dress promoted a fashionable, yet conservative appeal. The outfit buttoned up to her neck with crystals; a few square-like glints tantalized the campfire's glow. Another set of stringed crystals pinned up her hair, glinting into braided buns similar to mouse ears—an exquisite headdress.

"Who are you? Are you with those two who rescued me? If you are, all I can do is thank you."

"No need to thank me," she giggled. "All I did was guide them up that hidden road. I am Juna, **Flower** of the Fairies. I would still be at my post guarding the camp, but I heard you awaken."

"You are not a Sprite?"

"No."

As her tiny figure hovered closer, I noticed the difference. Though pretty, she would appear quite plain against the visage of a Sprite. Her ornate clothing, not as elegant or wispy. However, her wings were the most damning. Unlike quadrupled fluffy wings, Juna displayed a pair of transparent insect-like filaments with much lackluster. Interesting, as she neared, the air released to a buoyancy. I could almost breathe better. Odd... the iris of her eyes contained no color.

"You are a Flower?"

"I am my **roots**' superior."

"Root's superior ... a queen?"

"I believe that is what your roots may call it." A miniature dagger laid in her hand, detached from a thick belt.

She turned her attention to her companions. "As for those two, the big one you may recognize. He is Kute, **Plant** of the Giants. The smaller one is known and despised by the Dwarves as a thief. His name is Ding."

"Plant? He is not a plant."

"A Plant would be below a **Tree** and my status."

"Oh, uhm, like a prince? He is a prince?"

"If that is what you call it."

"Trees, Plants, and Flowers. Ugh! We are very different."

"Of course, we are, silly."

"Yes. Why did you come to save Lorel?"

17

"I do not know about that. All I know is that Kute came to my treedom and asked my **seed**, Ood, if anyone would come along as a guide since they could not fly over because of Redfang, and I volunteered. I know I must have hurt Ood, but I sensed there was something wrong, so I went along with them to see if I could help.

Oh, well, I better let you get some sleep before I talk your pointy ears off. How cute! I love your ears! Not as cute or pointy as mine, but I love them, anyway. See you in the early **cloudnoon** and maybe you will get some answers from Kute, or even Ding."

She zipped up into the branches, gone.

The warmth of my green cloak provided me tangible security for the rest of the moonday. My headband replaced the bandages on my leg wound, but not my left soreness, forcing me to wrest away to another position.

My back scabbard pressed upon me with a reassuring firmness confirming Welbern's whereabouts.

How could I be so stupid to let our defenses down believing Man would be so trusting? I should have visited more with Methelo to understand better—our king. More logical than me, so I trusted Sylvia and him more. How could I be so dumb?

I let so many down.

CHAPTER 5: Plant Kute & Ding

The new **sunday** arrived, and I awoke with the smell of food circulating my nostrils. Beside me sat Kute on a log, preparing a big meal for the group near the campfire, but his namesake did not fit his facial attributes. His youthful face seemed worn far beyond his seasons, as if he enjoyed too much activity and not enough sleep. Maybe his left eye appearing bigger than his right gave me this impression. A scruffy head of blond hair matched a small stylish goatee targeting thin lips on a jutted chin.

An underbite... who has an underbite?

While he sat on the log, he imposed a much bigger height than any Elf. Being a prince, he exhibited much strength with a commanding presence. A contoured bearskin vest and gray leather pants flaunted his toned physique. Deer skin boots, his choice for knee-high footwear.

A hefty club, melded of brown and black stones culminating into a knobby batch atop, positioned to his other side. The dense club had a handle that mimicked a closed bear claw.

I must admit, for an unattractive man he maintained flawless skin. Who knows? Maybe all Giants were unattractive creatures. What did it matter in the greater scope of things?

A rustling in the underbrush produced Ding feeding the dark gray wolf. The bulging muscles all over his smaller bulky body demonstrated a ruddy tint from seasons of hard labor in the mines. He wore a dingy cotton shirt with a draping hood, pants and shoes sewn of a substantial bearskin. A diamond double-headed axe leaned against the tree near him. A unique weapon of peculiar craftsmanship with a thick spikey endpoint crafted out of iron. An exotic brown wood composed the axe's handle. His reddish brown mustache and long beard illuminated his apparent hatred when he glared up at me. His hair exhibited sparse braids.

"Lo!" Kute's deep voice startled me. "I am glad you awoke. I was beginning to think you were really at the **end-of-growths**."

"End-of-growths? Would that be the same as end-of-seasons?"

"If it means the moment you expire from this world, yes." His cheerfulness was resounding. "Well, are you not a handsome little creature?"

"I... uh... uhm... I am not homosexual."

"Well, neither am I, but one male can compliment another, can they not?"

"Well, yes, I guess..."

"Great!" He tasted the stew he brewed. "By the way—"

"Yes?"

"I am bisexual."

I felt a bit uncomfortable, however, quite grateful. "I am only glad I did not meet the 'end-of-growths,' as you say. Was it too much of a hassle saving me from that glittering mist, **Plant** Kute?"

"Just call me Kute. We are miles away from the treedom. To tell you the truth, it was not us who saved you, my handsome Elf."

"General Ygl."

"General?"

"As in superior of an army."

"Oh... oh, like a **thorn**. Well, if you do not mind, I would like to call you 'General', General?"

"That would be fine, Kute.

You were not the ones who saved me?"

He gave a booming laugh. "You saved yourself from it! When Ding and I came out of the mountains, we thought we were too late to warn your tree about the mist—"

"My tree?"

"Uh, yes, the one who rules you?"

"Oh, Methelo. King Methelo."

"Yes, yes, King Methelo. Tree Methelo. We thought we were too late to warn your king about the mist. We were too late, but we also saw you crawling away. I picked you up and here we are."

"But, why are we here and what happened to the Elves of Lorel?"

The Giant Plant's sordid face turned sullen. "The Elvin **roots** are now slaves of the mist. Do not ask me why this is so, but Ding knows. Ding appears to keep everything confidential even from me. If I were not so friendly with roots, I would take my club and entice some answers.

It is funny how we crossed through Khun without any incident. **Flower** Juna is a good guide."

"I feel like my season is over."

"If you feel it is over, I suggest you look underneath and see what is there. You might find a pleasant surprise."

"Then, let us get moving. The faster we get to Khun the better."

"You go by your title very well, General, though I fear we will not be able to go until we all ate our fill. Oh, I believe this is yours."

He handed me a small box-like lamp molded from somber rippling brass. Silver bracings extended into a curving spout on one end and a sturdy handle on the other. The pinnacle of the slender handle rippled before cascading into a full curve terminating at a sharp angle. A few jewels studded all sides of the contraption's hull with accompanying etched grooves. The edges and corners were smooth and rounded. I had never appreciated such a peculiar lamp. If not for such beauty, it would almost resemble a beaten tea kettle.

I would have denied owning such a prize, but because of its attractive texture, I decided to keep it. "Thank you."

"Flower Juna spotted Ding trying to steal it from you and stopped Ding. Be careful."

When Ding and Juna arrived, we sat around the campfire eating meals from metal plates Kute brought. The main dish consisted of a nice vegetable stew made with tiny chunks of meat. An engraving with a vine exploiting a variety of fruits and vegetables encircled the rim. I thought Juna looked charming sipping from her miniature bowl. Kute's underbite did not seem to get in the way.

The lamp would not leave my thoughts. For me to crawl toward the mountains out of that foray did not sound possible with this strange lamp. Weightless, despite the metals forming it.

Ding's ruddy face glared at me, sizing me up; examining every aspect of my physique. I found myself doing the same. Our interests became locked, as if the stare down signified the beginning of a battle of wills. This made me sick, but I dared not keep my sights off his. I had hoped Kute would tell us to stop this nonsense, but the Plant's famish took precedence.

"I am the leader," Ding stated with a disquieting tone.

Kute glanced from his munching.

Ding and I stayed locked in our battle of stares. I felt very uncomfortable. A strain struck me. I wanted to discontinue this ridiculous affair so bad, but I could not. The Dwarven thief seemed angrier by my act of resistance.

"I am the leader." He was sterner.

Juna flew to my protection. "Leave him alone, Ding. If anyone is going to head this party, in my opinion, which supersedes everyone's, I choose the Elf."

"Ygl."

"Eagle? Is that your name? What a cute name. You see, even his cute name makes him a leader. He is named after a majestic bird, and your name reminds me of an idiot."

"I would not mind the general being our leader, Flower."

"I said I am the leader!" In great anger, Ding grabbed his ax lying next to him and leapt at me.

I rolled away from the onslaught leaving Ding crashing to my side, pulling Welbern out of my scabbard.

"Ding!!" Juna screamed.

"Let them be, Flower. I have always wanted to see our stalwart companion get taught a lesson."

My right leg's pain made me limp. With both hands grasping Welbern's hilt I waited for Ding's next assault. We circled each other searching for an opening. Ding struck first, swinging his ax downward with all his might. I dodged his offense, but my hesitance failed to block the ax from nicking above my left side's other wound. Warm blood oozed out of the fresh opening.

Fierce Welbern slashed out looking for a place on my opponent's body to eat. Ding moved back and attacked with a more robust assault. I parried and reengaged with a firm grip. This serious thief combatting a persevering general. I retained a defensive position against his attacks. My wounds became more fatiguing with each round. Unfortunate luck would not be long before Ding overtook me.

Slashing Welbern resumed with renewed strength. Each clean stroke, closer and closer to a desperate target. This thief would not attain the benefit of defeating me after all.

"Damn you, Elf! How much can you take?"

Enough to neutralize you... I delivered quicker strokes, sparks glinted from each contact, forcing him to leave his chest open to a forward assault.

"*What is that behind you?*"

He tried to glance, but his mishap allowed Welbern to lunge. Ding withdrew acknowledging he held no defense against my deliberate offense. In an attempt to escape, he tripped over the boulder behind him.

My plan worked. I took his blunder to my advantage, knocking his ax from his grip with Welbern's fuller, and pinning his arm down with my left leg. My leg scabbard produced my readied dagger.

A growl and bared teeth rushed at me. The wolf's jaws targeted my throat. I could not retain him.

Kute ran to my aid. "Off him, Redfang, before I tear you asunder!"

Juna fluttered forward. "Come, Eagle, let me help you bandage your wounds. You have won the battle. You are now the leader."

CHAPTER 6: Swen

The party rested under the woodland trees' welcoming shade. I needed the breather, but with Los and Num's light becoming more prevalent, we needed to move on to Khun as soon as possible.

Kute packed stuff on the large mounts' saddles. The first horse's name was Crater; the other horse brandished mighty gray wings—a pegasus named Stonecrusher, my mount. Majestic, Stonecrusher may have been, but nothing compared to my Steadfast whose larger spine was a joy for me to straddle... I missed my unipegon.

Ding sat opposite of Kute cleaning his diamond headed axe he named Gore—interesting name. The wolf, Redfang, lay next to him.

Juna stayed at my side no matter how I protested. Of course, she would not stop talking. At least, I was able to tell her the correct spelling of my name. She told me about everything so far. To her, my wounds needed a lot of attention. A new bandage wrapped around my right leg's injury replacing my headband. I squinted at the pain as she pulled upward tightening it. Another bandage wrapped around my abdomen.

"If you only hold still, I will probably be able to fix this bandage," she advised.

"Juna, do you know that if we do not get to the Forest of Khun fast, they will also fall victim of the mist?"

"Of course, I do, but that will not stop me from trying to fix you up for the journey." She was acting like a second bloodmother to me. How humoring...

I glanced back at Ding gathering his supplies for the journey. I felt a tinge of regret. Maybe we should talk to each other and make up for the past misunderstanding... No, he would get mad at me again.

"Tell me, Juna—"

"What the Interim!!"

"Sorry, I am a telepath."

"Oh, you read minds. How wonderful! Is that your royal gift?"

"Yes. I do not think Ding is very happy about it—me defeating him."

"At first, it seemed like he was going to win then, all the sudden, you just catch him by surprise. Things like that do not usually happen in every **cloudnoon**'s **growths**, you know. I was simply amazed and I really should commend—"

"'Cloudnoon'?"

"Okay, now is the cloudnoon. I see this is going to be long trip."

"I am going to talk to him." I started to rise.

Juna pulled at my belt. "Do not go, you idiot. Can you not see, if you go over there, he will probably start fighting you all over again and you are already in a bad enough shape. Speak to him during the journey. By then, he will probably sober down. He is a pretty toxic person, anyway. I only tolerate him because he is Kute's friend. He is so toxic."

"The only power anyone has over you is the power you give them. That is what Advisor Sylvia used to say."

"That is why I keep away from toxic **roots**."

I muffled a chuckle. She seemed so juvenile, yet wise. "All I want to do is befriend him, Juna. He came all this way with you."

"Then, do it in a precise manner. Remember the old prejudices between Dwarves and Elves alike."

I slumped against the tree to soak in her stunning advice. The duel did symbolize a sort of hatred between Ding and I, but I did not start the fight. Ding did. Somehow he had a dislike of me, and I did not know why. Many tales have stated Dwarves did make merry companions, though callous at the core.

Something against the tree jabbed at me from behind. I searched and found the lamp still in good condition considering I must have dropped it when Ding charged at me. Upon closer scrutiny, I noticed the lamp's etched grooves adjacent to a different glistening gem on the hull. A set of grooves intertwined throughout the curvy spout that reared back as if flexing a sinewy musculature ready to strike a potential victim. A couple of other grooves meshed with the handle's uppermost point while the rest of the grooves meshed or evaded about the lower end.

"Pretty lamp, is it not?" Juna fluttered about the strange box like it was her first toy. "Kute must have told you about me trying to stop Ding from stealing it."

A strange feeling emitting from the lamp's depths dissuaded my answer. Somebody, or something, tried to communicate with me by placing a mental hold on my psychic powers. I tried to fight the communication off for I feared my assailant had evil intent.

The mental hold eased as if the assailant sensed my feeling. Their humbleness allowed my mind to ease its resistance.

"Save me…" the telepathic sending felt effeminate, soft.

"What?"

Nothing more was said.

I turned to a mystified Juna. "Quick, Juna! Since you are Flower of the Fairies you must have the power to shrink yourself to any size you feel? Am I right?"

"Well, yes, but that is hereditary. Mine is the power of the white light, a divine right granted to me by my god, Ethnel. My **seed**, Ood—"

"Then, please hurry and shrink because I sense someone within this lamp. You are the only one of us who can tell us what or who it is."

She shrunk herself tinier than a fly to fit the outlet, unnerved by my reaction. With dagger in one hand, she opened her other hand—a blinding splatter of colorless power emitted growing wilder. With her pure white light ablaze, she ventured into the aperture.

I marveled at her power. My bloodfamily's individual gifts, our divine rights, were all psionic, therefore, psychic. Moreover, I anticipated Juna did not need to use her gift. I felt sorry for what I asked of her, but I just had to find something out. If this something turned out true, then maybe, just maybe, old legends did not meet the end-of-seasons so easy.

Puzzled Kute glanced at an unsettled Ding.

Juna's tiny form popped out. "Remarkable! I just cannot believe it!" she flitted about the air in a fit of joy. "I just cannot believe it!"

"What is wrong, Flower? What did you see in the lamp?" Kute asked.

"Oh, I am sorry. I forget to tell you. Ygl, rub the jewels on the lamp."

As I did, through the spout's opening a couple of enigmatic runes floated out in unison with a black twinkling gas that began to fume and form. This proactive gas, unlike the milky mist, billowed compared to being slow and insubstantial.

The shady gas reshaped. A transparent female's figure crackled within the cloud. The upper part of her body was one that would attract any creature to her side exploiting a pair of small supple breasts. Her eyelets, a twinkling cosmos. The alluring tresses of her silvery hair flowed like silky swirling fibers throughout a billowing elaborate dress within the nebulous gases. She did not seem to possess a neck and arms, though everyone could perceive the transparent contour of hands through the nebulae. Her dress discontinued its form at defined slender hips. From this point, her remaining figure continued within the same gases that produced her, "Spirit rises to the surface; integrity is born. Courage be thy shield. Truth be thy sword. The one who rubbed the jewels is the one who rules."

Breathtaking, yet she shouldered certain sadness that drew me to her.

Kute edged closer with a titillated Juna following. "Why, it is a genie."

"I am he who rubbed the jewels, great genie. What is your name and can you help us get to the Forest of Khun sooner?"

"I am of the world of men; my name is Swen. I am truly sorry, Master. At this place I cannot help thee travel faster but once thee reaches the forest, it is the beginning of the test." Her dress' vacuous bodice displayed the initial runes fluxed within accompanied by more runes, lacking in luster.

"Genie... Swen, you are giving me riddles. I do not understand what you mean about a test."

"As thee goes along thy journey, thee will find what I say to be true, but as thy troubles get deeper, thou are going to wish that it was through. I do not want to make thee slow. Please master, let me go."

Without further word, the nebulous gases enveloped her making her delicate figure fade. The nebula swirled around the lamp, in a few moments funneling within.

I did not order her return. Instead, I faced toward the others gaping behind me. "When do we start moving?"

"Right now, if everybody else is well and able, General."

We set off upon the dirt road to Khun after packing. I rode the gray pegasus, Stonecrusher. Kute helped me mount Stonecrusher because of my wounds. The lamp was deposited inside the pocket of my cloak—the handle's lengthy stem poked out a bit for an easy grab. Prince Kute pulled Crater's reins. An interest to note, the hooves the equine mounts sported were forged into razor sharp claws, horseshoes maybe. Ding rode Redfang, his wolf.

I surveyed the jagged grasses on the plain to the left of us wondering what really happened to my kin and my bloodfamily. Some of the weeds spilled upon the road's edges.

What was the mysterious mist's purpose? I wished that you, my beautiful Thalla, my mate, was more with the seasons than with the end. Maybe you would provide better answers for me.

CHAPTER 7: Royal Welcome

A solemn throne room.

Emperor Rondo brooded upon his throne awaiting Werkle's arrival with more news. Demonguards posted at the doorway as well as both sides of his throne, melding along with the noiselessness.

Footsteps approached outside... The doors unlocked allowing Advisor Werkle, cool air, and possibilities yet to come.

A frantic mouse scurried across the polished floor. A Demonic tongue, slathering with purplish goop, lashed out from a cryptic oral cavity procuring the mouse within for a nice meal. The sound of crunching bones did not disconcert Rondo or his advisor.

"Rondo, Spenz has returned from Lorel."

"Quit your jabbering, Werkle, and tell me what news he brought."

"It is one that will both anger and delight you. First, The Forest of Lorel has been captured along with the enslavement of the Elves."

"Marvelous, now I don't have to worry about the eavesdropping of those meddlesome creatures in my personal plans. What else is there for me to know?"

The unsettled Werkle did not speak, permitting his meandering to express volumes.

"Well..." Rondo didn't like these odd games his adviser played with him in past. Quirmeans who enacted conduct like this before the emperor would be punished, but Advisor Werkle was a higher authority. A person whom Rondo himself could trust—his brother.

"Please, Sire," Werkle begged, "do not get angry over what I am going to tell you."

"Just get on with it."

Werkle turned red. "The Elvin general, Ygl, was unfortunately the only one to escape and we have... I believe... lost the lamp of Swen."

"You... lost..."

"Well, I really didn't want to tell you, Rondo, in the first place."

"That doesn't matter. What does matter is that I want both found before any problems arise. Go tell Spenz that I want a thorough search throughout all of Lorel. Go. And don't return until Spenz gives you an answer."

"Yes, Sire." Werkle turned and started toward the open doorways. He halted. "By the way, the three prisoners that you requested for are now here."

"Splendid. I can at least enjoy myself for the moment. Bring them in."

Werkle motioned the guards. A male Elf in his late forties and a younger one in his mid-twenties with a young female of equal age accompanied them. The younger Elves surveyed the room with a calm bewilderment. The senior Elf kept his attention affixed onto Rondo.

Anyone could have misconstrued the trio for Quirmean dignitaries from a major city. They wore rich garbs with draping capes to match, except for the younger male who donned no cape. The slight point of their ears, youthful complexion, and modest ethereal flair revealed the truth.

Rondo smirked. "Welcome to Gablen, King Methelo, Prince Rolando, and Advisor Sylvia."

CHAPTER 8: The Road

The twin suns' hotness stroked my face. We had ridden what seemed like a long period for such a short road, Khun should be near by now. We should reach the shady forest soon.

Juna relaxed on my shoulder. Her flimsy wings tickled my cheek, reminding me of her presence.

Aloof, Ding saddled upon Redfang seeming resistible to Los and Num's rays. Sweat formed all over his roughened face, but he did not bother to wipe off the beads. Instead, he stared ahead waiting to acknowledge an early glimpse. His ax, Gore, straddled a very special sheath upon his back.

Stonecrusher trotted at a normal gait. How the noble steed kept himself alert signified there must be belief within him invoking his purpose for this journey.

Kute's restrained eagerness piqued my curiosity. While trudging along pulling Crater's reins, he refused to relax, epitomizing his solemn fortitude. The annoying heat could not penetrate him neither, though, I must admit spring did provide a bit of a cool breeze. Much like his compatriot, his club was stored in a leather back sack.

"Kute, why are you not riding Crater? I mean, I am sure your legs must be a bit weary after traveling this far."

"I am sorry, General, if this may give an unnatural impression to you about the way my **roots** are, but to me this is a tradition. For **growths** my **trunk**'s Treedom has always been warlike. My roots were forever working hard, waiting every cloudnoon for The Coming of the Unknown Land. We work so hard that we do not have any leisure to ride our mounts. Most moments we do ride them is during tourneys. Occasionally, my roots will ride the mounts for either emergencies or pleasure, other than that, it can be strictly for battle... a battle we have yet to have. Tourneys are good practice for battle.

I love Crater as much as I would love my roots. If my roots did not care for our mounts, then there would be no loyalty between rider and mount."

Steadfast, how much I cared for you. I knew you always appreciated my adoration. Now you were gone from my side like Thalla and Limbus. I would never forget any of you.

"Roots? Do your kin come from the ground?"

Kute bawled. "Oh, General, you are too funny! Not anymore than your roots come from there!"

"I am glad to make you laugh—"

"Believe me, it does not take much," Juna murmured.

Of course, I already knew this difference in our races' dialects. I found our talks interesting, learning a different culture despite our situation. "You said something about an Unknown Land, Kute. My kin have never been taught of any such thing."

"The Unknown Land is real. I do not know anything about its origin. All roots should have been aware of it. I do not know why the Elves did not."

Or, maybe Scall, my bloodfather, never enlightened Methelo and me.

"There is really not much known about the Unknown Land to any of the royalties, except that my roots were told to always guard against it, by our patron god, Lolung-Cor."

"You have gods too?"

"And, who would not?"

I turned to our Dwarven companion. "Ding, I can see you have hate for me, but it does not tell me why you came all the way from your estate to attempt saving my bloodbrother's kingdom from the mist."

The Dwarven thief grumbled. He knew he had to talk sooner or later.

"All right, Elf. I will tell you this and this alone: the Dwarf **Grand Diamond**om has been captured by the mist."

Juna sprung from her nap, her wing providing my cheek a final tickle. "What? You are crazy!"

Kute remained calm. "You are a fool, Ding, for not asking my trunk to come aid your grand diamondom, but do not worry. We will succeed where you have failed."

"Even Ood would have come to your aid," Juna added.

Ding just stared ahead. "This is not the first something as strange as this has occurred. When your forces would have arrived, it would have been too late."

First, the Dwarves were attacked, and now Lorel. Who would be next? "How did you escape?"

"I told you—"

Juna curled back on my shoulder. "Oh, quit being stubborn, Ding. We are all as curious as Ygl. I swear!"

"... I was to be hung that **great light,**" he grunted, "for stealing. At that moment, some Dwarven **ore** began to panic about a mist rapidly approaching Zak, our capital. Zak was where I was being hung because I was loathed by many of the royalty. In all the commotion, the Grand Diamond's guards did not notice my escape. I leaped upon Redfang and raced for the mist. When I entered it, I was being attacked by creatures that I have never seen before. They swung at me with their weapons. Since I could not see anything in that blasted mist, I started to swing my Gore around me. We were even attacked by giant spiders—"

"Spiders?"

"...Yes, spiders. Redfang bit at one before we got away and come out with a leg in his mouth. As I fought to escape, I heard one Demon say the Forest of Lorel was next."

"You are a fool, little friend," Kute padded Ding on the shoulder, "but I can understand your motives."

Ding felt ingratiated. "If you are sick of me, Kute, then let us fight to end it." He wielded Gore; Redfang turned growling.

"Oh, Ding..." Kute chuckled. He leapt upon Crater's saddle and shook his head in disbelief with open arms mocking Ding.

"Oh, Interim..." Juna muttered near my ear, annoyed.

I rode between them. "You are fools fighting over things that have happened in the past. Think about the present and the future. You can always make up for past problems in the future, but as for the present, always take it as the season itself." I felt pretty smart. I guess I did pay attention to Advisor Sylvia ever so often.

"Ding and I have been friends for long, General. I know how to handle Ding."

"Look, everyone!" Juna shrilled like a whispering wind. "Down the road."

A large expansion of dense trees with deep emerald leaves lined the border. Leaves that accumulated much shadier hues than Lorel ones, and trees much thicker and healthier than normal: regal redwoods, majestic oaks, haunting sycamores... a very dappled woodland sheltering blossoms much greater and loftier than Lorel's.

"Khun!"

All at once, everyone raced for the forest. Khun at last!! Now, the Khunians, the Protectors, would be prepared for the mist. The shady thick trees grew larger and larger as we sped closer and closer.

I charged ahead of everyone except for Flower Juna, who zipped into the shadowy woodland. When Stonecrusher neared entrance, a rustling in the underbrush arose. I directed Stonecrusher into the sound's path.

Skinny hairy legs swung out toward us. Stonecrusher steered away from the assault, knocking me upon the dirt road. Fangs dripping with venom advanced.

Ding and Kute had arrived to confront two more assailants. The party was under attack by three massive spiders.

CHAPTER 9: Oreol & Mitral

The sudden downfall forced my wounds to rupture. I dragged myself up and presented Welbern. Ding and Kute had already charged the other two spiders—subjects of a Dwarven accidental premonition. My eight-legged opponent tried to take a bite out of me. Welbern blocked eager poisonous fangs and slashed at its face. Clear green blood spurted from the incision. The spider hissed and retreated, sizing me.

I took a chance to sever the monster's anterior legs, but the alert spider sped around me trying to attack from my right. My body twisted—a sharp pain seethed from the wounds on my left side allowing Welbern to slash out again. The monster shrieked as it bled from the nearest of front legs.

The monster's eight bulging orbs scrutinized my blade with rampant curiosity upon a hairy face. The bulging octet further examined my blade as if they recognized Demonslayer. The spider swung an able leg at my sword arm attempting to disarm me. I dodged the leg, but fell from the force of the spider's next blow to my bloodied cheek.

The spider took my fall to a voracious advantage and leapt upon my disoriented frame. In this weakened state, I became helpless. Poisonous venom flowed into me via my shoulder.

A warlike "neigh" accompanying lengthy gray wings revealed a stalwart Stonecrusher pouncing upon my arachnid assailant's posterior, razor hooves digging in deep. The spider shrieked and jumped off me to confront a retreating Stonecrusher.

"General!" Kute ran to my aid after granting a smashing blow upon his spider's head with his bulbous club.

Ding slashed the abdomen of the other arachnid assailant. I expected him to come to my aid as well, but he did not. His sullen face appeared to have a look of shock.

A perfume permeated the air—sweet apricots in a summer breeze. "No! Leave Ygl alone! Creature of the wicked pits, this is the end of it! Mine is the power to diminish, and thou, creature, is finished!" the tender voice echoed from all sides.

Innocuous murky gases spilled about me rising toward the heavens. Within, I could perceive Swen's silhouetted form. She chanted indescribable incantations below her breath, her abdominal runes shimmering with each. Her cosmic eyelets became contoured furrows presenting an inconceivable anger.

The obsidian cloud headed straight to the spider—a luminous thundercloud with no thunder and numerous spindly legs. The spider, whose pair of vertical fangs clanked like swishing knives, spun to challenge an eager opponent. The massive arachnid geared up, bounded within Swen's sentient domain, and there remained in the billowy pockets. A soft brilliance exploded from her gases' interior reminiscent of a newborn star's beginning. An understated clap replaced absent shrieks.

Ding's spider rose to attack the Dwarf again. Kute rode to Ding's defense. Stonecrusher followed close behind. I surmised our arachnid attackers did not expect such a defense.

I trembled, the venom circulating in my blood. My wounds bled more, my end-of-seasons neared… Welbern came to my side.

"Do not strike thyself, brave Ygl. For thy injuries were not caused by thee. Come, master, let my slender fingers feel. For I have the power to heal."

Streaking comets swelled from Swen's eyelets, tears. I did not reject the pressure of her delicate digits. "At my fingers' touch the wounds that were thine will come to me, its destiny, and shall forever be mine."

Her voice—melodious. When her amorphous membrane connected to my body, a strange sensation coursed throughout my veins extracting the venom from my figure into hers. She withdrew the end-of-seasons out of me. After that, she healed the other injuries starting with my cheek, tracing

36

each tendon—attaching, knitting each one together. Her soft fingertips stroked over the incision leaving behind skin anew.

Pity struck me when I witnessed her chant become true. The wound abating from my cheek reappeared upon hers as contoured patterns. The pain must have been... immense to experience her own membrane being torn asunder, but she showed no signs of grief. Her persistent face maintained a calmness. She did not acknowledge the pain she inflicted upon herself. Her cosmic eyelets, a void I could fall into.

"You are so beautiful..." I whispered. I could not believe myself making such a statement, but I did with little regret. Why?

The thought of my left side's large wound transferring to hers, it could not escape my mind. I was glad that my leg wound would not appear on her leg since the bottom of her bodice was billowing nebulae.

Kute and Ding killed the last of the spiders. The friends dripped of all sorts of arachnid goop. They turned to witness Swen mending me.

"I need a bath. General, can you get your genie to give me a bath?" the Plant joked. I cocked my brow at him. "Okay, how about she create a bath for me with a nice cotton sponge?"

The branches above rustled, down landed another spider's gigantic shape. My two companions were too far away to confront the arachnid. Swen, too busy concentrating, failed to notice our vulnerable opening. The spider raced at my healer and me.

A blasting pair of tiny colorless light struck the spider's thorax. Shrieking, the arachnid spun around to meet the assailant who shot it. To my relief, our savior, Juna, swooped in and not alone. Indigenous creatures of Khun, forest animals, swarmed upon the creeping catastrophe: foxes, wolves, deer, and the like. Gnomes, miniature Dwarves, accompanied them riding various birds and rodents. The Gnomes rained poisonous wooden arrows upon the arachnid's hairy hide.

Sprites, celestial relatives of the Fairies, swooped along in interweaving threads spearheaded by their very handsome **Leader**, Oreol. Their elegant clothing, an abundance of draping fabrics reflective of their home's colors; not trendy, like Juna's outfit. Their wings, quadrupled and birdlike, harbored deep chromatic greens to browns resembling their somber home's trees. Their hair, like the oncoming of spring, flaunted verdant highlights replacing the russet shades.

In all the excitement, I did not notice Swen leave my side remitting to me remnants of her service. I stood to assess my right leg… no pain. What a miracle to acquire this genie.

My Khunian rescuers' intrepid onslaught dispatched the final spider, a decisive marking for such transgression.

After a little swiping upon the grasses, Welbern was sheathed. I slipped the lamp out of my cloak's inner pocket replacing the handy gift into a package on Stonecrusher's saddle. I made sure to tuck the handle's longer stem within. The flattering present induced me to remember Steadfast. My lost unipegon would never tolerate a saddle—such an impediment would be too intolerable for such a wild beast. Our trust was our constant bond for his strong soft spine.

Many of the bestial rescuers returned to Khun to seek out more enemies, but a grouping stayed behind with the Gnomes and Sprites to bury the four corpses into the road. Badgers, moles, panthers, and bears did much of the digging. Gnomes riding rodents tied the spiders' legs together with the other small animals while other Gnomes riding birds supervised everything. A fascinating teamwork to keep the foul monstrosities out of a woodland they considered so dear.

"Well, well, Ygl," Juna flew overhead with Oreol, "it looks like your **growth** was saved twice in almost two cloudnoons. The other two and you better be glad I looked back or else there would have been another body to bury along with those four spiders."

"I cannot help it, Flower Juna, if I was so useless at the moment, and besides, this was more than enough rescuers to bring along just to kill one big bug."

"Oh, my Ethnel, look at those outfits! You will need to excuse me." Ecstatic, she flitted into her buoyant bazar.

Oreol was a bit peeved. "Actually, General Ygl, this is only a small contingency of the Protectors excluding the Khunian Elves who are within safeguarding the forest itself. If we would have known that three spiders had already met the end-of-seasons, Mitral and I would have certainly not assembled a force as large as this to aid you.

Now, follow me."

"Please calm down, Oreol. No need being upset over nothing. You should be as happy as I am to see young Ygl now a grown general of the Lorel army. Do you remember me, Ygl? I am Mitral, Leader of the Gnomes, and this is Jinx, my steed." A middle-aged plump Gnome riding on a bird as rare as a unipegon spoke. A prominent steely beard and hair popped out of an acorn shell he wore as a helmet. His hair draped upon a brown tunic. A quiver of wooden arrows slung across his shoulders along with the bow he sported. His bird exhibited a slight red coloring with a blue underbelly—and had four legs.

Our inattentiveness to Oreol's order did not placate the Sprite's annoyance. "How did those spiders make it all the way through our forest?"

"I do not know. They certainly have the audacity to travel through here from the Dark Plains," Mitral answered.

"They are not creatures from those plains."

I interceded, "Pleased to meet you, Mitral and Oreol. I remember Oreol, but not you so much Mitral.

I understand you said something about taking us somewhere, Oreol?"

"Okay, I am here," Juna interrupted with much glee, "and, oh, I cannot wait to see the rest!"

Her behavior annoyed Oreol more, he darted back into Khun. "Yes, if anyone was listening. Let us go!"

"Juna, did you not see the Sprites' outfits when you first entered the forest?"

"Oh, I did, but then I heard all the commotion behind me and I had to set my priorities straight."

I straddled upon Stonecrusher. "Is anyone else coming along?"

"No, Ding and I will stay to help refill the pit; Kute might go along." Juna answered. "I cannot believe these **roots** are messing up such nice outfits with all this dirt." Juna rushed to perform her idea of humanitarian aid. "Hey, do you not see how long that sleeve is? Why are you getting it dirty?!"

Kute laughed "Oh, Flower! Yes, I will go, General. I have never seen these

Elvin warriors. The rumors say that they are very excellent in battle; even the females are excellent."

"Whoever started those rumors, Kute, speaks the truth. The Elvin warriors of Khun have always been the indispensable standard of the Protectors. They have—"

"Hurry up, General Ygl." Anxious Mitral rode off on Jinx into the wholesome foliage. "I do not want to get into an argument with Oreol. Come one, Jinx."

Jinx chirped.

"Jinx? General, did that Gnome call his bird creature 'Jinx'?"

"Yes."

"Why give it such an absurd name?"

"I do not know, Kute."

"What type of creature is it?"

"It is called an archeornyx. Very rare like my Steadfast. That is all I know."

Jinx flew past a Gnome lounging on a branch scooping a meal out of an acorn shell. The Gnome wobbled a bit and fell off.

"We follow carefully?" Kute inquired.

"Very."

Khun's three armies, the Protectors, fascinated Kute. Everywhere I spied, two different races observed Kute and me with more interest on Kute. Sprites fluttered and whirred from treetop to treetop, a mesmerizing display of agitated green and brown quadrupled wings on tanned bodies, a floating jumbling of mythic leaves. Gnomes either tended to their steeds or loitered on tree branches gossiping with each other, or played with passing animals.

Oreol and Mitral flew ahead to lead us through the semi crowded forest. They wanted to take me to Blasmle and Rungna-Olivia.

Compared to Lorel, the more robust and denser Khun foliage always amazed me. Not a single tree diseased or any signs of decay. Of course, spring was amongst us, but even the colder periods had little effect on Khun. Many of the trees, twofold the size and thickness. They exuded certain peacefulness. The intense greenery seemed to impede us from our goal with the oversized blooms, but still we trudged on.

"The air smells good here, General. We do not have these strong scents at the Cory Mountains."

"Or such big flowers and trees?"

"Yes. Yes, this is fascinating. I like it. I really like it."

At last, we came to a clearing crowded with more animals. Plant Kute would witness the first sign of Khunian housing here. Scarce in this area, a couple of huge trees had been fashioned into homes. As a collective, the Sprites had the knack to shape the trees' interiors and exteriors into makeshift dwellings for the Protectors to reside in. Manipulated branch awnings safeguarded shrewd outlets representing doors and windows. As we peered farther upward, more windows and doors became apparent on the thickened trunks—sentry outposts.

In Lorel, we did not have the luxury of such housing. The Sprites would never depart their sacred forest. Lorellian treehouses were constructed out of countless big branches and weeds crafted together with effortless skill. Both our forests did share interests in makeshift tents, but not in nature. Lorel was more preoccupied with meditations—an item I had little concern with. Some Lorellians even learned carpentry from Man before our estates' relationship went sour, focusing their experience upon the Majestic Treehouse's renovations. How funny, I could not remember why our relationship ended with Man, or even how we learned carpentry.

Diminutive sallow warriors stood posted at certain parts of the clearing. They sported skimpy metal armor contoured to their small frames. Unlike Quirmean steel, a pliable blackened shell molded their special armor with the vambrace and greaves strapped on with leather or some other hide. Both males and females exhibited flowy murky knickers and sleeves created from the same material like the Sprites' garb, appearing like flimsy tree trunks with shades of dark green. Unlike Lorellians, they did not believe in footwear and believed their clothing should be as stark as their attitude. The majority maintained long hair braided in vines while others had crude short haircuts.

"Are these the vaunted Elvin warriors?" Kute inquired.

"Yes, they are the third part of Khun's Protectors." His confusion tickled me.

41

"Why, they are so small and paler than the moons, and skinny, and their ears and eyes are much bigger and pointier than yours."

"Do not mistake their small size, Kute. The battle is a part of their seasons, for, Khun is very hallowed to them. They will protect Khun and its residents to the end of their seasons."

"And, their armor… it is fascinating—almost Dwarven. It looks like a titanium chain mail, but it is so murky."

"I do not know, but it is not chain mail. Their paraphernalia is meant to be murky to conceal them in the shadows." Interesting enough, Methelo never allowed us to wear armor. A nice breastplate would have been enough, but I guess he did not want to alarm Emperor Rondo since we would have been acquiring Quirmean armor. Khunian armor would have been too few and unsuitable. Too bad such protection would not have been enough against the mist, anyway.

In the clearing's center a great number of **bloodchildren** congregated. But, Khunian Elves have never had bloodchildren.

By Achal!! These were Lorellian bloodchildren! When many of them spotted me they smiled, but with weary elation. Many cats resided next to their youthful master. There was no playing around like bloodchildren should, no gallivanting. They still wore their festival clothing.

Some knelt in reassuring meditative postures—customary amongst my kin. In contrast, I felt like such a hypocrite. Mine was the divine right of telepathy, a gift of the goddess, yet I rarely meditated. The Khunian Elves' art of battle became a higher priority for me. This warrior privilege became my joyful onus while Methelo, my calmer bloodbrother, attempted a failed diplomacy with Quirm. Nonetheless, these bloodchildren had put me to shame. I smiled in return and hoped my response would be reassuring considering our circumstance.

The crowd parted offering a bloodchild in deep meditation with his faithful feline lying beside him. The cat, furry with a beige coloring, bulging eyes and a dark brown face, got up and wagged a very elated tail acknowledging my presence.

A familiar hooded tunic… I noticed the leglet.

In response, the bloodchild glanced up at me from within the hood's shade. Silent for a moment, we tried comprehending each other's position.

A drizzling occurred; yet there was none.

Tears welled in his inquisitive eyes as well.

The bloodchild sprinted to me; I vaulted off Stonecrusher to greet Limbus, my bloodson.

"They must be yours, General Ygl," Mitral stated.

CHAPTER 10: Meeting of the Minds

"**W**here did we go wrong?" King Methelo asked Rondo, believing the relationship with Man had been equitable. When Emperor Rondo made angered overtures to his kingdom, Methelo made sure to visit once during a set period. He never went unaccompanied, always bringing Advisor Sylvia with him and a band of escorts. On occasion, Rolando or Ygl tagged along for the tours. The public affairs was important for the sudden change in character of a realm thought so loyal and amicable.

The emperor sneered down at the trio. He had ordered all his Demonguards out of the throne room and had the doors locked after departure, accepting Werkle as the "just one" to prevail next to him as he conferred with his recidivists.

A table with refreshments set not far from where the Elvin king and his two companions positioned to the emperor's far right.

Rondo motioned to the table. "Go ahead. Refresh yourselves while I recite to you what Werkle and I have done and are going to do when it behooves us."

The mandatory guests walked to the table to dispense themselves a drink. Designer cups and plates blanketed the table's anterior. Behind the cups and plates, glass goblets lined in front of bottles of beverages. The sugary whiffs of pastries nestled in their sinuses.

Prince Rolando tried not to slide a glance at Methelo as they poured, *"I do not like this, Bloodfather. The way he just sits upon his throne as if we were his bloodchildren almost makes me sad. Have you seen his face closely, Bloodfather? He is not the Rondo we used to know."*

"He has changed, Rolando, however, our relationship has rarely been easy. He has some explaining to do about that mist attacking our kingdom. If I am right, he may have some connection to it."

Advisor Sylvia scolded them, "Excuse me, Methelo, but, you are both fools to believe Rondo has no connection with that atrocity. Holding us hostage is proof enough for me. I warn you. Did you see the size of those guards? They are not the normal size we are accustomed to encounter. We better watch our step from here on."

"Methelo, I'm sure you've learned of the Jode. After all, the royal families should at least know about its existence in Zaendara."

The curious king of Elves remained affixed upon the emperor while startled Sylvia placed her drink down.

"I have heard of the Jode, Emperor. Legend has entailed that it has potent mystical powers rivaling even yours."

"And, indeed, it has. You see my advisor, Werkle, and I have planned to find it and rule all of Zaendara with it. In order for the plan to go into effect I must slowly strike down one kingdom after another until it is found. When the Jode is found, all of Zaendara will bow to me."

"You have gone insane, Rondo." Prince Rolando was beside himself, but remained calm. "For sure, you will fail in this."

"I've captured your father's kingdom if you call that failing, Rolando. And, along with it, the Dwarf Diamondom has been captured. The advantage appears to be mine."

Ardent Sylvia refuted, "This cannot be. The estates have been on peaceful terms for ages. You cannot invade sovereign estates for no reason at all. War is what you are heading this continent into, Emperor Rondo, when the others catch word—"

"Who said the others would know, Advisor? I said the estates will fall one by one, not all at once."

Methelo motioned Sylvia to silence. "Rondo, you have no right invading other sovereign estates. What matters more than anything is that your gods will severely punish you for such transgressions."

Rondo snickered a laugh resounding about the room enough to make any uncomfortable. "I see that I'm the only one who knows the real past of

Zaendara. My gods! My gods! Let me tell you, Methelo, Istratos and Welna are no longer my people's deities. Xurchon, the All Powerful, is the one being worshipped."

The Elvin royalty remained calm. Methelo felt a psychic tug in his mind. He relented on his psychic block, recognizing the telepathic signature,

Sylvia spoke to him. "*His treacherous plan and he must be stopped. If ever he ruled Zaendara with the Jode, then all of the continent will be in total chaos.*"

"I know, Sylvia. I will try to distract him for Rolando and you. Rolando?"

"*I hear, Bloodfather, and I know what I must do.*"

Methelo proceeded coolly to Rondo, "First you have your people worship the shameful god of evil, and now you plan to possess the Jode by dominating all of Zaendara? You have truly gone mad."

"Mad is all you can call me, eh, Methelo?" The livid emperor asked. "Mad has many forms to it. When one is murdered before others we call this act mad. When one loves another whom is of lower class we call that lover mad. When one tries to do the impossible we call him mad. But, no, I am not mad. I am just... clever... clever and clear enough in my convictions to have a god who is more powerful than all the gods on anyone's side. I'm sly enough to have Xurchon aid me on my conquest for the Jode."

"You speak in dreams, Rondo. The fabled Jode has never been found anywhere in Zaendara. Let us keep it that way."

"Do not change my mind by lying to me, Methelo. The Jode is real and through Xurchon, I will find it."

While the two argued, the busy Prince Rolando and Advisor Sylvia snuck their hands across the table to a set of nearby knives, gripping the handles.

"*Now!!*" Rolando threw his utensil first followed by Sylvia's.

Knives darted across the room toward the Quirmean emperor and his brother, interrupting the argument. Before the knives arrived within proximity of their destination, the air itself became an invisible barrier impeding the sharp projectiles from delving any farther. The knives fell to the floor with a disappointing clatter.

A restive Werkle stumbled.

"You forget, Methelo. I practice magic. I'm the top practitioner of my kind." Rondo's smugness would not deter the Elvin royalty.

"You are very resourceful, Rondo, but we will not lose so easily.

Quickly, the goblets!!" Methelo commanded.

"THOU WILL BE DESTROYED, METHELO." From nowhere the portent revealed itself via an abysmal, paradoxical voice ricocheting from the walls. Methelo could not place the hollowed sound, but he feared the declaration's effect. A primordial gloom so despairing shredded through the Elvin king like a smoldering hurricane with no wind, but he persevered. Somehow, the power augmenting the voice was being restrained.

A senseless discomfort sliced through and around Methelo's left upper torso. The Lorellian king relinquished.

Several glass goblets dashed past him casted by Rolando's telekinesis as Sylvia hurried past wielding two splintered ones.

"*Rolando, before Werkle acts...*" Sylvia, a precognitive, warned.

Werkle took a stubby step forward as she predicted.

With a wave of hand, Prince Rolando's telekinetic vibration casted the wobbly advisor against a wall incapacitating Werkle.

Emperor Rondo had already gone into action himself. A bluish-yellow glow sputtered from his rested palms. The flying goblets crashed upon each other in midflight, transforming into a storm of broken glass amongst the selfsame sputtering. A strange glow emanated about the Emperor's hands as he erected from his throne upon the expansive dais. An identical glow radiated about the lucent storm—butterflies appeared in place of the glass.

The three vacant thrones faded away.

With a telekinetic swoop above the fray, the tenacious Prince Rolando charged in with splintered goblets in both hands.

"*Rolando, do not!*" Sylvia endeavored to presage.

Too late. The emperor had vanished into a mist the prince flew through. Rolando crashed into the gilded throne, a telekinetic skin shield buffered his plunge. The Lorellian prince jumped up unfazed upon the dais ready to strike with one of the goblets when he felt slimy scales writhing upon his arm. The goblet had transmuted into a viper!

Rolando tried to agitate the creature off. He could not. He swung his other arm over to stab at the elapid's head, but instead he beheld another slithering catastrophe. "He transformed my weapons into serpents! I cannot shake them off!"

Methelo floated to the air. "*Sylvia, go help Rolando. I will handle the emperor.*" Being the monarch of his people, Methelo possessed all the gifts his gods bestowed upon his family, their divine right: telepathy, telekinesis, and clairvoyance.

"*You have it within yourself, Methelo,*" his advisor answered.

The Elvin king had no idea what her reassurance meant as he hovered toward their enemy, preparing for a long-awaited battle.

When she reached Rolando, the Elvin prince's telekinesis strained to retain both vivacious vipers.

"What damned evil...? These are not normal." An eager elapid's fangs attempted to sink into his bicep, unwelcomed ichor dripped from the curvilinear bone.

Sylvia threw one of her goblets at the venomous endangerment. When the goblet hit the serpent, fangs wheeled around to face a new adversary with lashing thrusts. Sylvia sliced off the snake's head with her other jagged goblet.

With his free arm, Rolando gripped the remaining viper around the neck before the relentless reptile could overcome his telekinesis.

While prince and advisor wrestled with the viper, the two rulers combatted each other. Methelo flung the entire banquet table at Rondo. Emperor Rondo obstructed the table in midair with a simple shot of the mysterious bluish-yellow magic and pitched some of the items on the table back at Methelo.

The Lorellian king's telekinetic swipe repelled the obstacles, his curiosity unfolding about Man's strange new magic. Rondo sidestepped the items allowing them to shatter behind him.

In turn, King Methelo dodged the emperor's insidious blasts. A prompt telekinetic link to a looming statue thrusted the marble mass downward at Rondo.

The Quirmean emperor transformed the statue into a mist.

Methelo avoided divulging a solicitous response. He recognized this newfound power was beyond Rondo's mystic gifts. Man's magic required a vehicle of sorts the emperor did not exploit. Methelo garnered all his psionics into a ball of impenetrable energy; he casted the ball.

Rondo blocked the psychic blast with a unique static radiation, though some of the blast almost landed him. He laughed. "Even psychic energy has to pass through the metaphysical, King Methelo."

"This is not you, Rondo. This power…" King Methelo felt more confident with his assault acknowledging the breach. He pressed forward blocking the mystic momentum assaulting him from side angles while returning psionic fire.

"*The door!!*" Precognitive Sylvia warned.

Unnoticed by all, except her clairvoyance, Werkle had crawled to the ebony double doors, seizing the knobs, twisting them. "Spenz!"

The loyal general, his brother, rushed in followed by half a dozen soldiers.

With a telekinetic wave, Prince Rolando thrusted the reinforcements out before anyone could act.

Methelo worked toward leveling the field, however, a minute bluish-yellow fallout glittering about his right hand caught the Lorellian monarch off-guard… he keeled forward from his upper torso's rekindled pain.

The Quirmean emperor took advantage of Methelo's mishap. Rolando and Advisor Sylvia twisted about to witness their king succumb to an uprush of Rondo's newfound power.

"No!" Sylvia's heart descended witnessing Methelo's tumble upon the polished floor, fortune delayed.

Before Rolando and she could react, a glittering bubble encased them. The bubble receded upward until transforming into a helmet encapsulating their heads.

Gruff Spenz and more soldiers reentered encircling the Lorellian royalty with swords unsheathed. "What would you have me do with them, Emperor?" A flute hung on his leather belt.

The satisfied emperor leaned victorious upon his modest throne. "Take them to the dungeons—their execution will be in three days."

"Murderer…" Prince Rolando mumbled. The heightened mystic barrier thwarted his telekinesis, bouncing the divine gift onto the stunned Lorellian. He writhed against the unexpected.

"Silence," the triumphant Quirmean emperor ordered. "Take them away, Spenz. And, please don't struggle, my little Elves, or else I will have your beloved Methelo killed on the spot."

They were traipsed out the entryway with the humiliated Elvin king lagging last, hampered with the same helmet.

"Oh, Methelo, I will find Ygl."

When General Spenz's squad dispatched, the Demonguards retained their former positions.

"Werkle."

"Yes, sire?" He shut the doors.

"I appreciate you helping me out, but I assure you I can take care of myself against such buffoons."

"I am sorry."

"Apology accepted. Now what we should be planning is how we are going to capture the Elvin general before he knows what we are doing and tries to warn Zaendaran estates."

"That, my liege, I have already thought of."

The pair of scheming brothers convened toward the remaining refreshment table on the far side.

CHAPTER 11: Behavior

How happy I felt when I, at last, found the bloodson thought lost to me forever. Limbus and I would not let each other go. Our constant tears a testament to our love. Limbus kept blubbering so fast about "the terrible mystic mist".

A crowd surrounded us. A familiar athletic silhouette emerged over me— a very satisfied Plant Kute observing.

"There, there, Limbus, you have nothing here that will harm you. Remember, you are amongst friends in Khun. How did you escape?"

He directed his head toward a yipping Snip, our jubilant melody.

I laughed. "Of course, it was the asegafian cats that helped you get away from it. Who could have thought of such an idea?"

I already knew. Snip and his pack were teleporters loyal to Lorellians because of a psionic bond specific to the bloodchildren. Asegafian cats could travel from place to place in moderate distances, disappearing from one to reappear in another. No one could understand such a talent, an inarguable welcoming feat of nature indeed.

"It was me, Bloodfather," Limbus struggled to beam with confidence under such circumstances, "but it was really out of pure fright. I will not lie. I was so scared by that invasion of Demons—" A murmur stirred throughout the crowd, "—that I just did not want to see all the Elves get captured. So, I just rode around with Snip to all the bloodchildren and told them quickly what to do. I got help from Ploone, too."

My bloodson pointed into the crowd. Another bloodchild of slight heaviness stepped forward with his asegafian beside him. He wore a small leather vest with light slacks and small boots.

"Ploone."

Limbus' best friend hurried to me. They shared similar enthusiasm in learning the arts of combat. I messed his hair around a bit and give him a big hug.

"Ygl," Oreol hovered overhead, "I and Mitral would like to speak to you inside the tent alone."

I consented, and Kute followed. The crowd diminished leaving the bloodchildren to mingle amongst themselves. Jinx's wings had just passed over the low branches to the right of me with Mitral aboard making me a bit nervous. Stonecrusher swaggered behind Mitral and Oreol's lead.

Los and Num's sunlight poured through the vivacious leaves flaunting Khun in all the wonderful forest's serenity, exposing the immense flora. Cherry racajaandoos, brown sugar lilies, poisonous fervorflowers, medicinal willowberry roses... no matter what, these fascinating creations flourished here and provided a nice vegetarian existence. Female Gnomes and Sprites milled about searching for rations for the mid**sunday** meals. A group of Protectors gathered to discuss the upcoming dance in the next two sundays in honor of their god, Ethnel. Some Gnomes and Sprites rested upon the supportive petals or snuggled within the flower tops during this grouping. The forest had not changed since I first arrived as a bloodchild twenty seasons ago.

The animals behaved quite indifferent to each other here, also. A tan wolf trotted past my steed and headed in a small herd of deer's direction. The wolf's intrusion did not alarm the grazing stag looking up. The wolf glanced also and reciprocated a nod to the stag, even nuzzling one of the fawns before trotting away. In Khun, the creatures were always benevolent; that was an imperative.

Memories of what I had been taught about the Khunian animals entered my thoughts. The carnivorous beasts were allowed to eat meat only when another beast had met the end-of-seasons. Other than that, the Sprites and Gnomes fed them or they retrieved their food in the Dark Plains. The herbal eaters stayed to help out in the camps. Nonetheless, all animals thrived in Khun for two reasons: to protect the sacred forest and to stay sheltered from the Dark Plains' monsters. Once any animal broke these edicts, banishment became their penance. Asegafians fitted very well here being consumers of anything.

The invisible path terminated at another clearing where tents abounded. The encampment had warrior Elves all over the place performing different chores. The males crafted new weapons, bathed their hippogriffs with water from nearby creeks connected to Lake Ban, or assisted other neighbors. Hippogriffs, undomesticated noble mounts, were winged creatures whose feathered anterior resembled a bird of prey meshing into a horse's barrel and hindquarters. The Elvin maidens prepared the meals and even participated in combat training via swordplay and archery upon round wooden targets. Equal to the males, the maidens bested some who conceded defeat with grace.

"I must applaud these Elves in their war play, General. Their skill is definitely one to take into consideration for such diminutive **roots**. One cloudnoon I may visit to challenge them."

"The Khunian Elves thrive for this, Plant Kute. They taught me."

"Well, maybe I shall challenge you one cloudnoon, General."

"And I may just take you up on that offer."

"But, let us do it in a more open field like what I am accustomed to."

"Where do you reside again?"

"The Cory Mountains."

"And there are no trees there?"

"No, General. We are farmers. We have fields upon fields of grain. On other parts of the mountainous region we train."

"Okay, let us make a deal."

"Ho-ho-ho, a deal?"

"Yes, if it ever comes down to it. I will battle you in your mountains and you in my kingdom. A deal?" I put my hand out.

A twinkle shimmered in his eye as he shook my hand. "Oh, you have more than a deal, little warrior. By the way, those mounts they were cleaning, I have never seen them before."

"Hippogriffs. They are very wild. Only the Khun Elves can ride them, though three were granted to my royal bloodfamily. They were intended as gifts, but I think there was another attempt behind the gifts."

"Another attempt?"

The Plant and I passed a grouping of six Elvin men locked up in stockades—an unusual sight even for me. Their dangling pale heads, pointy ears, and hands resembled peculiar fruit indeed. Their limp bodies, a fatigued vine within the shifting shafts of sunlight allowed through the leafy canopies.

Mitral arrived on Jinx.

"Mitral, how long have they been there?" I asked.

"Who?"

"Those Khunians at the stockades."

He was reticent. "A couple of sundays."

"Are they not being fed?"

"No."

"Why?"

"That is a part of their punishment."

"General, the Khun Elves have a right to deal out punishment as they see fit," Kute participated.

Another Khunian warrior walked up to them with a long whip ready to flog them.

"What are they being punished for, Mitral?"

Uncomfortable, the Gnome Leader answered, "… Same-sex behavior."

The whip cracked; the flogging began.

"Same-sex behavior? What is that?" Kute found himself interested.

"They were lovers, Plant Kute."

The whip cracked steadily.

"Lovers?" Kute was beside himself. "Lovers? You are punishing them for love?"

The offenders moaned slight.

CraCk!

"I am not punishing them, Plant. They are—their Elvin Leaders, Blasmle and Rungna-Olivia. Gnomes do not prescribe to such laws. Khunian Elves follow a strict edict of celibacy at all costs. They feel sex weakens the fighting spirit."

craCk!

"Is that true, General?"

"Yes."

"Why, that is outrageous. My roots and I are a testament to that. Love is love. Love is grand and war is glorious. We are not a weakened, but strengthened by love. This is insanity."

CrACk!

I did not want to address Kute's hypocrisy. "In Lorel, we are very moderate on matters of sexual orientation, Kute. The seasons are too short to worry about such minutiae. Same-sex couples are few, though, from what I could tell."

"I can... and have courage that one cloudnoon these Khunians will see past their ignorance. The lovers will survive this. They are love."

CracK!

Mitral added, "We are not permitted to kill our own here. Eventually, they will be set loose and we will tend to them."

I did not know Kute, but for one who seemed so happy-go-lucky, he was serious about this matter, and correct. I never thought about orientation. My army had some same-sex soldiers. Their relationships never bothered me and should not. Most Lorel Elves, I would say, focused more on matters of the mind, of thought. Sexual orientation was just so trivial to us. We bore our bloodchildren while the Khunians, who did thrive much longer than us, maintained dwindling numbers.

crAck!

With every flogging, I must admit, I understood the Khunians' attempt at this point—guilt. For the first instance, I felt sorry for these male warriors. I mean, an individual spent all their seasons being a Protector, enacting more profuse prayers to Miredo than Lorellians did to Achal... I just could not comprehend how all that love could not be spread to another.

"Mitral, even opposite sex couples are punished, right?"

"Not that I have seen, Ygl. It is usually same-sex ones."

Well, that did not sit right with me, either. I never knew of this bias amongst my trusted neighbors. How could one set of kin not be punished for the same act? This policy sounded very strange and biased. Your guilt worked, my Khunian bloodbrothers and bloodsisters, but not in the way intended.

The whip's eerie cracking relented.

I could never survive like that. Without intimacy? Without love? Maybe our two kingdoms worshipped opposite gods. But, their god was the god of nature. Nature—was that not what we were discussing here? Why would the Khunians not accept nature? Moreover, I must admit again, Plant Kute did maintain a sense of positivity for this. I guess I may be a bit cynical and confused.

In an expanded tract, a prominent tent of integrated animal hide situated with few residents around the camp. This must be our last stop. Kute and I pulled the tent's flaps, a stoic Oreol squatting on a rough wooden table greeted us; Mitral presided next to him. Blossoming foliage and constant fertile earth permeated most from this spot overpowering the unclean hide's odor.

"What is this about a mystic mist, General Ygl, your bloodson keeps repeating about? Does it have anything to do with Khun?" Oreol never pulled any punches.

"There is not much that I know of it. I only know that it attacked Lorel and the Dwarf Grand Diamondom, and now both realms are under enslavement. My comrades and I figured it would attack Khun next."

"Khun? I would dare them to. Khun has always been sacred even to the gods themselves. Who would want to do such an evil deed?"

"I agree with you, old friend." Mitral stated, "But I am sure the answer to that question will remain a mystery to us as well, as to Ygl. Besides, we are to have the Dance of the Vernal in two sundays."

"We are not friends, Mitral," Oreol responded, "simply partners in the protection of a forest we hold dear."

Mitral rolled his eyes.

"Your celebration will not stop this mist from attacking your clan. I suggest you have some of the animals and Protectors stand guard for it while the Dance goes on." I suggested knowing such a defense did not work for me.

"For sure, we will do that," Mitral agreed.

"I still do not believe something like this will happen to our sacred woods."

I bent toward adamant Oreol. "It will happen, great Sprite, or else I, who is of good heart, would have not come all the way to warn you."

A disturbance erupted from outside, an argument arose. A crowd had already surrounded the opponents.

"If you dislike accompanying the party, Ding, then maybe you should leave," Flower Juna advised.

"I do not listen to the petty counsel of a small no-good Fairy, including one that is as conceited as you," Ding retorted.

"How dare you say that to me, you... you lowly Dwarf! I do not need to brag. I just go by the consensus. I should strike you down where you stand." Brightness, blinding, flickered about her teeny hands. Juna prepared to shoot one of her beams of white light. She must have not known about Khun's inviolable laws.

Kind Kute stepped in with his hand upraised before I could interrupt the bitter dispute. "You will not do such thing, Juna, and neither will our Dwarven companion do the same."

"Do not tell me what to do, Giant oaf! Remember I am a Flower you are speaking to!"

"I know who you are—"

"Then, let us keep it real."

Oreol intervened, "Also, Flower Juna, you need to remember that it is not you who rules Khun. This means if, in any way, any of you start brewing up a disturbance in our sacred forest, I guarantee you; the both of you will suffer consequences. I, Blasmle, Rungna, and Mitral do not care what class position you represent in your estate. The moment you enter our forest, you are no higher than those that are lower. Khun is a forest of safety and solitude, not of such disturbances."

Juna's head drooped, unabashed embarrassment took over for a moment. "You are right, Oreol. I am sorry. I did not know." She tried to look at him, but could not. Her pretty eyes tried to hide her shame as she fluttered away. Not a speck of dirt stained her person... very impressive.

Ding sauntered toward some bushes. No one could see the expression on his ruddy face. Not that he would care.

CHAPTER 12: The Trio

The dungeons of Quirm were never hygienic, but on the other hand, they never retained Elves within them either, including Elves of such prestige. Unbearable to most, the heavy stench of sweaty bodies coalescing with the stygian dreariness did not inconvenience three wearied detainees aided by infravision.

Infravision: an innate Elvin ability to perceive things well in light's absence. Warm blooded animals and heated objects were perceived in red tints while cold-blooded animals and items in blue tints.

The bed of hay scattered on the floor would not be slept upon any longer, yet no escape from this place of gloom could be realized except through the locked steel door. Guards could be heard walking up the hall.

Prince Rolando's reddened outline crawled up to Methelo. "*What can we do now, Bloodfather?*"

Methelo paused for a moment. "*There is nothing we can do, Rolando. Lorel has been captured and pretty soon Khun will be. If the Jode is found, then all the estates will fall under the rule of an insane emperor... that is something I do not want to witness. To me, the end has come at last. An illness has befallen me.*"

"*Wrong, my liege,*" Sylvia disagreed, "*the end has not come at all. Remember the legendary custom of your kin: if a king must meet the end-of-seasons, he will do it bravely but must never give up hope. These were the very words of the goddess, Achal. So, please Methelo, respect and obey this ethos as you would any other. You are one of the bravest and just I know.*"

"*You mean well, Sylvia, but there is no hope for the Lorel Elves. Oh, why did I ever become king*?" Methelo started to whimper.

Rolando caressed his king. "*Do not worry, bloodfather. It was not your fault. It was your bloodfather who chose you for this position, instead of Ygl.*"

"*Ygl is too erratic. King Scall made the correct decision when it needed to be made. That is it!*" Sylvia had something up her sleeve. "*Only one of us in the royal lineage was not captured by Rondo's mist. If all three of us focus our telepathy through Methelo to reach Ygl, wherever he may be, we shall tell him to bring out our allied army in Khun and head toward Quirm with it.*"

"*The Protectors are strong, but the Khunian Elves are much smaller in number than we.*"

"*Methelo, the plan may be risky, but at least it will give the other estates enough preparation to stop Quirm themselves,*" Sylvia insisted.

"*I already tried sending.*"

"*You did, but now it will be with three, instead of one. Believe me, I know you have it in you.*"

Methelo smiled, almost ashamed. "*Sylvia, I do not know what I would have done without you. Let us begin, then.*"

Together they convened in the tenebrous cell disregarding past memories that thrilled or wounded their fortitudes. Places appreciated by them became waned images, feathery reminiscences. Internal thoughts and feelings diminished. With this ritual completed, Rolando and Sylvia's psionic powers dispensed into the aperture within King Methelo's mind.

The threesome's psychic union broadcasted throughout northern Zaendara trying to locate the one place Ygl absconded to. At last, an image of the Elvin general's face registered in their minds. A short struggle occurred from the receiver's end; the transmitting trio eased their sending. Ygl relinquished his mental block for a telepathic call primed to transmit.

A sudden metaphysical blast hindered the call. The blast was immense, so insidious, slicing through Methelo, Rolando and Sylvia's mental defenses. Sylvia cried aloud and collapsed upon the soiled ground. Rolando sprinted to her aid, leaving the Elvin king alone to wrangle with a resounding headache; soon, Methelo succumbed as well.

The locked door disappeared. The dungeon's wall parted. Emperor Rondo glowered at them. Hulking Demonguards positioned around him joined with General Spenz possessing a flute at hand.

As the Elvin royalty clambered up, Prince Rolando assisted a beleaguered Sylvia huffing and puffing with a mixture of embarrassment and resolve.

"I guess two days without food doesn't seem to bother you Elves. But do not worry about hunger any longer because tomorrow is your execution. I'm sure it will put away your miseries with much efficacy," Rondo joked.

"You are just as evil as Xurchon will ever be, monster." Rolando remained calm. "And we feel sorry for you."

"And I thank you for the compliment, young prince, for I have been practicing much. My god will be especially pleased when he sees that I have sacrificed to him the race that he has despised the most."

"Why you..." Rolando sprinted toward the emperor with extended hands intended for the Quirmean neck. When Rolando's hands made contact, the Elvin prince yelped holding his head.

Sylvia and Methelo ran to his side. Sylvia whimpered as she rocked Rolando's scarred head back to consciousness.

"I am sorry, bloodfather. Emperor, I apologize for my outrage."

"I'm amazed, Methelo, your son's anger is quite controlled. Meditation suits your race well. I seriously doubt Ygl fairs better? I mean, for him to be your general. Does he meditate as much as you do?"

"You will not get away with this, Rondo. The estates will stop you and if they do not, then I am proud to embrace the end-of-seasons for mine," Methelo asserted.

"You surprise me with your bravado, Methelo, though I fear it will not sway me from having you executed. I'll meet you at the pit." Rondo strolled out, allotting the Demonguards to secure his resolute hostages to their deaths.

The Lorellian Kingdom would soon lose a trio of very valuable persons from their race—a threesome that strove to acquire valuable happiness and peace between Man and Elves alike. A threesome whom had rendered efforts for many Lorellians to disbelieve such words as hate and anger. Now this trio would forever be wrought from their race, and their names would be nothing but a legend to those being enslaved by Man.

But, an individual related to them, the last royalty, still roamed somewhere in Zaendara preserving the regal family's existence.

CHAPTER 13: Disbelief

Two moondays elapsed since I waited in Khun and nothing happened. Like I, Oreol posted sentries about the forest to safeguard the traditional Dance of the Vernal's arrival. I knew this defensive maneuver would not be enough. He relied too much upon Ethnel and Miredo's aid. If Achal came to Lorel's aid... how could I believe as the Khunians did, Achal? I, we, needed you...

The Sprites danced around in circles singing lofty songs in praise of Ethnel. They soared, spiraling upward into the moonday air, until they dove into counter spirals to perform the dance over again.

Gnomes galloped about on small beasts thrusting hearty wood into the dynamic bonfires. The flames stretched higher toward the sky providing an unnatural licking to the frolicking Sprites' soles. Brightness from the fire disseminated wide revealing another mass of Gnomes frolicking hand-in-hand around the bonfires. The Lorellian bloodchildren created a larger circle in the opposite direction.

Asegafian cats ran amok everywhere adding more fun to the celebration challenging the bloodchildren to chase after them for a ride. The felines almost caught teleported away.

The tree I slumped against was not the most comfortable padding on Inner Earth. The celebrators' enchanting singing aided my posterior to overlook my awkward position as I shifted a little. Their songs of homage eased my nerves as well. As a matter of fact, animals from all over Khun streamed to the Dance of the Vernal just to enjoy the enrapturing Sprites' harmonies.

Proud Flower Juna debuted soaring from another end of the cavorting. Her colorless light, sparkling and trailing from both hands, matched the sparkle upon her countenance. A band of warrior Elves followed her, a pale cloud of welcoming strength additional to an already mesmerizing event. An event that made Lorel's spring celebration amateur by comparison, but who was comparing? Each enthusiastic warrior joined into the games with everyone else reminiscent of little bloodchildren with much pointier ears, virtual albino skin and skimpy body armor. Some ate the food displayed on the tables provided at the dance area's farther end. Some staged symbolic combat before an enthusiastic audience.

And still many Khunian Elves supplicated in upright prayer before one of two makeshift statues sculpted of mulberry bushes, the Sprites handiwork. The amassed clamor overpowered their boisterous holy rites, though. I found the Protector's resourcefulness interesting. They applied certain berries for significant items like eyes and, per se, embroidery. The first effigy represented a male Elf standing tall and true raising a fancy bow higher in the air than his pointed ears, daring the very skies to an affront— Miredo. The other, a somber robed and hooded being. A being flaunting immense quadrupled wings, insect-like and feathered—Ethnel, god of all faerie. Some Sprites relaxed upon the Ethnel effigy, feasting on the available fruit display, but none dared to rest upon the Miredo image.

A joyful scent could be detected permeating the atmosphere. The scent pulled me off from my resting place against the tree... Oh, I could use a little exercise.

Dizziness overtook my mind. A throbbing, like piercing sunlight, seethed through my thoughts consuming them into nothingness. Someone wanted direct contact with me via telepathy, but the way this stranger caught me by surprise did not present the sending as welcoming.

I played on the defensive and put up a mental block. Just like I thought, my assailant struggled with the psionics, but struggling harder made the telepathic sending worse. Was there more than one assailant?

The sender stopped its assault and returned with a more humble exchange. This sender wanted to communicate with urgency, I sensed.

My mental block dissipated, a soft glow occupied my mind's vacancy. Three figures commenced to form, though a bit blurry. Fragmented bodies, by increments, appeared in my psychic view. The first, a female; the other two, male. The ragged sparse clothes they wore were of certain rich material. The last stage of metamorphosis had ended. I could not imagine my surprise acknowledging my senders' presence: Methelo, Rolando, and Sylvia!

The environment was more appalling than I imagined, a bleak room, windowless. A door was on one side with heavy locks and dry grass covered the floor. The mystic mist must be holding them prisoner somewhere unknown to me, but where? And, how could the royal bloodfamily send from there? From so far?

Methelo commenced to send... static entered the link... no sort of telepathy could be felt.

I tried to catch the psychic link again, but the static kept holding me back... Another obscure link regained the hold. Rolando? Sylvia?

I awaited an answer... No one did. Instead, this newcomer probed me through the haze. My careful bloodbrother would not do things without a reason... In other words, this could not be Methelo or the other two!

"Who are you?"

No answer.

I broke contact. Buds of sweat cascaded down my forehead. This shocking event baffled me. Whoever held them captive must be connected with the capturing of my estate, and of the Dwarven Grand Diamondom also.

Thalla, my mate, wherever you may be, please do not be the mist's hostage. Our love had brought us so close together that nothing as terrible as this would break us apart. If I knew your whereabouts, I would be at your side sharing your burden with you.

How embarrassing. Kin who thrived too much within dreams spoke such petty words—dreams that both initiated and ended at an instant. When the delusion terminated, the dreamer would lie back and try to figure where they left off in the reverie... and would be happy when they did stumble upon the spot. For to the marvel, this was the season.

I strode with a mission toward my tent. My lids knew they needed to have rest. They would soon get that wish.

A rustling came from the underbrush. Out stepped Limbus, Ploone, and Snip. Limbus' face presented much concern.

"Bloodfather, we want to ask you why you have not joined in the celebration along with the rest of us. If it is a problem please tell me what it is. I am your bloodson, you know."

Typical Limbus, he cared for me whether I wanted his sympathy or not. He always had a strong will for everything, except for love. Nobody could defeat the emotion named love. Not even the strongest warrior, who had never been defeated in anything, could defy love. Not even hate could deny this most tender of emotions, but somehow my Limbus could. No, my loyal bloodson, above all else could not be devoted to love. Well, to romantic love. He loved Thalla and me.

If I told them Lorel was captured they would be frightened because of inexperience. "Why do you not go have fun with your cats? Ploone, where is yours?"

Ploone would not have any of my avoidance. "You treat us as if we are really bloodchildren, kind general. Limbus and me are not bloodchildren anymore. We have always been learning the arts of being like those older, and we have passed all of them. Is this enough to tell you that anything you tell us we can take?"

"No. There is a lot more to being older than being protective, and that includes proper grammar." I tried to wink.

"Lorel was captured, was it not?" Limbus asserted.

"No, it was not." A terrible feeling erupted within me. Never have I lied to anyone dear to me; now that I did, my surprised bloodson and his best friend...

Ploone whistled. His asegafian cat, Winky, appeared. Winky derived from the same litter as Snip, but not as hairy, and had a squinty eye.

"In that case," Limbus continued, "we better gather all the other bloodchildren to come back to Lorel." They climbed onto their respective mounts.

"Wait!" I demanded. They halted. Clever Limbus used his words well, he did. "It is true. Lorel has been taken over. It hurts me to tell you this."

Limbus ran and hugged my leg. "Oh, bloodfather, you do not know how happy it makes me just to see you at last, look at me as your bloodson. Sometimes I think you never know I am there. Now, I see I am wrong."

I bent over holding him close. "And, I see you have become a better Elf. Do me a favor, remember I will never regard you as less than me and never have. My Achal, I gave you that leglet. Can you remember that, Limbus?"

"Yes. How are you going to save the kingdom?"

"I... I do not know. Right at this moment, I believe, Khun is being guarded from the mystic mist. It will be quite a while before we can attempt to take ownership of our land from what attacked it.

Go have your fun at the dance. Having fun there will make up for the one we missed. I need some rest and to think."

Limbus ran and hopped back onto Snip; Ploone followed right behind him.

"Oh, do not tell anyone about this unless I think they should know."

"We will not," they chimed.

"Do you promise me by Achal's psionic sword?"

"Yes." They laughed. Youthful hands tapped asegafian napes. Without a trace or sound the foursome vanished in a wisp.

How could you fight a mist? Again, my promenade through Khun continued. The outing felt a bit nippy the farther away I walked. I wrapped my dense cloak about me. The lamp, tucked within the pocket, snuggled against my waist.

A pang of guilt crossed me. Limbus did not know the whole truth yet. How bad would the news be for me to tell my bloodson his bloodmother met the end-of-seasons? One of these sundays, I may need to break it to him, but not now.

The twin moons' beams permeated through the branches blanketing the dew covered grass. A camp could be detected not very far away harboring a large tent amongst a small cluster—my tent. Two big logs situated around a smoldering tenacious campfire in front of the tent. The first log was long and somewhat bulky; the other, smaller and much stockier. Both logs did not appear so ordinary because they seemed to taper at their ends.

The bigger log moved. My infravision inspected further, I could perceive tiny inlets of red aura not quite as rich as the fire, but enough for me. "Kute?"

He lay admiring his stony club. "Yes, General?"

"Is that Ding next to you?"

"Yes."

"That is a fighting flame there."

"Strong wood."

"I have something to tell Ding and you."

"Go ahead. Ding and I are listening."

"Just a moment ago I had a telepathic call sent to me by Methelo, Rolando, and Sylvia of my bloodfamily—"

"Really?"

"Yes. It was from somewhere not known to me. They are being held prisoner."

"There must be optimism."

"...They tried to send to me, to, uh, reach me by telepathy, but we were blocked by someone... or something."

"More than likely whoever is holding them hostage? Another Elf?"

"I seriously doubt it."

"Who else has this telepathy?"

"I do not know. Only Elves have this divine right, I believe. I guess... I do not know. Achal, that would be awful if there is an unknown royalty doing this, but that mist..."

"So, somebody wants to take over Zaendara. First the Dwarves, and now the Elves. I wonder if Xurchon is behind this."

A surge of anger riled my nerves. I feared the name just as much as I feared Demons. Xurchon, the ultimate God of Evil, the Father of Demons, and the Maker of Lies was a name I did not want to acknowledge.

Ding moved a little in his slumber giving us a confounded look. "Who is Xurchon? Is he a friend?"

Kute let out a booming laugh. "Watch your tongue, friend Dwarf. A god, like Xurchon, is not well liked by any of the royalties. Of course, Xurchon is a companion—a companion to all that embrace every hue of malevolence.

I warn, not only you, but all who worship this god of such foul incarnation: you, who follow and obey this despairing deity's inclinations, will only fulfill your **end-of-growth**. And, not by those who come to defy Xurchon, but by Xurchon's hand alone. By Pyty's sickle of sustenance, Xurchon does not growth to have one rule for him. Xurchon growths to obtain power selfishly. When Xurchon has that power, Xurchon will strike and dominate everything. Zaendara will fall. All Inner Earth will fall afterward. Mark my words."

Ding stared at the campfire, stoic. "I do not believe in gods. There is no truth behind them."

Kute placed his hand on Ding's shoulder. "That is all right, friend. You have your beliefs; I have mine.

It is... it is not unthinkable to me how estates are being seized and nobody, except us, is aware of it. The estates comprise sovereign existences. We relate very little with each other. This is the first I ... we, have ever met an Elf, Ding. I think that is very sad, but there is always tomorrow.

General, you are the head of this group. I suggest we warn Khun about this mist. After all, this is why we have come here for. What do you say?"

"I intend to do so. By the way, how do you think Xurchon is doing this? He has been nothing but a legend ever since the beginning of any estate's foundation. I mean, I am not an atheist, but..."

"Everything is a mystery. I have my hunches."

With that I headed into our dim tent. Hunches could not be plausible when related to a god, even one of malicious nature. Maybe, since the Demons were real, the likelihood would not be impossible if Xurchon was too. Elves have been taught Xurchon as being mythos. A simple thought, a fearful story for everyone. Of course, what did these teachings say about my belief in Achal?

I squatted upon the makeshift bed of bundled thick leaves and animal hide to ponder a bit, preparing myself for the next sunday. Another campfire within would have been a nice luxury, however, what luminance could be afforded from the exterior would suffice. Fireflies always provided some Khunians such luminance without falter. I wondered how the Khunians compelled those special insects to do that.

CHAPTER 14: Skavir

The city of Skavir held an exquisite appearance at dawn. Unlike Gablen and Rondoville, the prompt populace commenced attending to their jobs before anything. The streets engaged with people performing different chores with the help of their newfound Elvin slaves. Much artwork abounded within and without the numerous art shops—statues, paintings, metal works, glass works, etcetera. The children still slumbered, but soon they would have chores to do as well.

Every major city in Quirm harbored its own governmental establishment as the urban heart. Gablen had, of course, the emperor's citadel with surrounding structures where all politics derived. Rondoville had the head worshiping temple, Rykon Tower. The Quirmean forces stationed and trained at Fumi with a central headquarters at Morro Ascension. Entertaining Wyp discovered much talent at the Grand Theatron. Hethomes College of Academics was a mainstay in Vante, a collegial town advocating much sports. Chrot, by inverse, became the current warden of slave auctions merging with the usual food consortium. The consortium located itself in the slave piazza's outskirts while Chrot accommodated disseminated agencies along the piazza's internal periphery.

And, Skavir interned or executed many criminals. Following the numerous art shops, behind iron gates, an arrangement of regal court houses set punishment for indicted criminals with potential persecution.

The slighter Torture House, an answer to such realized persecutions, was more menacing and bolder at the epicenter. The house secreted an execution chamber entrenched underground, a very damp room with large rhomboid columns bracing the ceiling. Exquisite decorations set upon the walls to balance such horridness. A brazen semblance of the outside environment. Dust drifted in the musky air.

Emperor Rondo snickered down at the three helpless hostages that paraded into the room. Each of them did not attain a fearful guise despite their cheated existences as prior internees had.

The bold trio positioned before the emperor awaiting for him to announce his next move.

King Methelo would have none of the emperor's theatrics. "Get on with it, Rondo. We are not here to be mocked. If you want to execute us, then proceed while you have the chance, but I surmise you will not win in the end."

"Xurchon aids me, Elf King. I disagree with you. Your abilities are hampered here, so don't try using them."

"You have everything anyone would ever ask for in your empire," Methelo proceeded. "Your empire is stable. Your kin really has nothing to worry about... you have so much self-hatred you cannot see it. The more you dislike yourself, the more arrogant you become because you need to be better than somebody.

I have faith you will find it within you to end this insanity before it becomes your undoing. We may not be bloodfamily, but I still care for you as if you were. I will always care for you, Emperor."

Rondo hesitated absorbing Methelo's final message. He signaled the executioner to pull a hidden switch. The floor released beneath the trio plummeting them into an abyss.

Forever became an unreachable ornament as they tumbled deeper into the stygian, smacking upon sandy ground. Another dungeon... different. A terrible aroma invaded their senses—blood, old and new... pungent. They could never be accustomed to this fetid truth, having thrived in peace for so long.

Methelo pondered briefly how he endeavored so hard to maintain peace, however, immediate action became the highest importance. *"Quickly, use your infravision. We must see where our slayer will be."*

They skimmed their surroundings. Scarlet smidgens plastered the walls; on the ground.

"*Do you see anything, Sylvia*?" Rolando asked. Some of the smidgens were a cool azure and better shaped in contour. Some contours were oval heads with slanted optical craters "*All I see are bones… Elvin.*"

Advisor Sylvia gripped his hand tight. "*The same here. Such a shame for these occurrences, but—*"

…a shuffling sound…

"*—wait… I see something deeper in the murkiness… Oh, great Achal!!*" Sylvia let out a horrific gasp.

In response to her gasp, the huge creature precipitated closer to them from a hill of stacked bones' peak. A red aura depicted its scorpion tail elevated high, but attached to the appendage was no scorpion. Instead, a snarling lion skulked. Varying reddish hues depicted a thick muscled body.

A bluish-yellow glow outlined the room. A barrier to psychic sendings, the glowing outline exposed the voracious beast, further relieving auxiliary use of infravision. Within a frazzled mane's shifting framework, a very inhuman face glared in their direction.

Prince Rolando recognized the creature, "*A manticora…*"

The manticora's leonine physique hunched forward ready to leap at more intended prey.

"*Remember, no matter what moves you make, never stop focusing your psychic energies onto me,*" King Methelo cautioned.

"*It is our only chance,*" Advisor Sylvia agreed.

And so, they did. Nothing else mattered at this point in this ossuary of the damned. All diplomatic prospects had terminated. Rondo took everything away from them: their land, their homes, their families, but, not their dignity—and their gifts. Their gifts, their divine right, could never be stripped by him or anyone. Their dignity, a choice they would never deny. They were Lorellians, after all. Their expectations could never be too much or too trifling. Or at least they aspired to such beliefs.

A soft bluish-yellow gleam sputtered from the Elvin king's corneas. He gasped, "*What is happening?*"

The manticora whom thought more of hunger than anything bounded at the trinity.

The Elves tried to scatter from the manticora's path. Sylvia, not quick enough, got slashed by one of the huge front paws, slumping to the ground.

"Sylvia!!" Rolando charged the manticora. A rapacious roar greeted the prince of Lorel who dodged the King of Kills' next attack and, without warning, he snatched the frazzled mane. Rolando slugged the manticora on its face.

The King of Kills emitted a terrible pungent howl. The scent of endless meals wafted throughout the pit. The Elves never experienced such rot and had never accustomed themselves to such a repugnant atmosphere. Unspeakable prizes for the Quirmean emperor's apparent pet.

Meanwhile, a half delirious Methelo, wrestling with the eerie effects of his strange optic discharge, dragged Advisor Sylvia's helpless body from the battle. *"Sylvia. Sylvia."*

"Do not worry, my king," she answered, *"though the seasons are slowly leaving me, I will not stop pouring my psychic energies into you. By Achal, I will not stop."*

Methelo's side started hurting again; he held tight to the soreness.

A scream erupted from behind them—Rolando! Like a flag, the manticora's scorpion tail, with a flexible point, brandished the Lorellian prince about with a puncture wound piercing through his abdomen. The skewering knob locked him in until, upon satisfaction, Rolando was cast across the room near his family. His red hued blood splattered everywhere securing a new scent.

Sylvia cried out in grief, *"Rolando..."*

Methelo, aching, acknowledged their slayer as the superior opponent. His pain worsening, he staggered rearward, waving, to lure the creature away from Sylvia. The manticora, a little intimidated by Methelo's glowing optics, followed in defiance, snarling; its scorpion tail a swaying menace.

Sylvia, whimpering, crawled her injured form to the Elvin prince, *"Rolando..."*

He tried to do the same, lying on his dorsum facing the ceiling. *"It is over, Sylvia. I may lie here, but the end-of-seasons will not force me to hesitate in telling you what I have always—"*

"Oh, Rolando," she crawled faster, sobbing, *"you do not need to tell me what I have always known… we are just the same and I should have never been mad at you. There are just certain things I could never tell you. Our end-of-seasons may have opened our eyes before they could ever close."*

"I love you!"

"And, I, you. By Achal, Rolando… Come… Reach your hand toward mine… I am almost there… May our bond never break."

Despite his position and agony, the Lorellian prince clenched his paramour's outstretched hands. She placed her head upon them sobbing.

Methelo alerted them, *"Sylvia and Rolando, I cannot withhold the manticora any longer. We will need to focus all psionic energy onto me before I fall. Ygl must be warned about Rondo's plans."*

King Methelo dodged the patient manticora's next pounce and sprinted toward the expiring lovers, grasping his thorax. The bluish-yellow emission flickered stormier about his eyes. *"Now, while we still have a chance! Our combined energy is at its greatest. Warn Ygl. I do not know why, but I think we can do it."*

"What is he—?"

"Our last hope, Rolando. Just focus…" Sylvia clenched her love's hand tighter as the lovers embraced a fate she could not avoid. Psychic energies decanted into the central regal mind combined with telepathic alarms.

****

Above ground and out of sight, Emperor Rondo sensed their calls for help. He laughed. "Again, they use their telepathy to reach out to Ygl. What fools you Elves are to think you can get past me with another one. The slightest portion of my new power can block these ridiculous telepathic sendings."

Rondo did not know the Elvin royalty was being assisted by another—a surreptitious power that could surpass his duped static block in order to attain the psionic sending's intended objective.

****

73

Below, Rolando and Sylvia's eyelids never opened again. Their clenched hands released a little. Methelo, adjacent to them, pressed on sapping the duo's psionic vigor's final remnants... getting feebler, yet stauncher in his mind... the unusual agony on his upper thorax more unbearable... heat... heat... the pain... unbearable heat.

"Bloodbrother, this is beyond urgent. Please listen and understand what we have learned. Rondo plans to attack and rule all of Zaendara. His intention for this is to find the Jode... you must protect... by Achal, Sylvia was right... it has always been—"

Fate had already tallied a calamitous cost onto the valiant Lorellian king, for the manticora's leonine leap granted his irrevocable oblivion.

CHAPTER 15: Blasmle & Rungna-Olivia

shrieked a most horrendous scream. A scream that tore me from my sleep and drove me from my rest. Out I ran from our tent past the small camp's shocked residents toward the Great Wall of Quirm's direction.

"You will pay!" My vengeance verged onto madness. "Do you hear me? I, Ygl of Lorel, will kill you!"

A perfume… a brew beyond mesmerizing… a thin cloud of nebulous gases besieged me. Delicate Swen, my genie, touched my shoulder with her detached hand providing a warmth I had never experienced. I forgot the clunky lamp was in my cloak's inner pouch… I defied her with Welbern upraised.

"Please, Ygl, my master, thou leads thyself into a terrible disaster. Come. Turn around. Embrace my sounds. Thy heart and head will ease from the deaths of loved ones near thee." Her voice… so enchanting…

My tear-stricken face met her cosmic eyelets. This was a genie, a spirit who cared, but in what ways I could not comprehend. Her beckoning, so hard to resist. I complied, but not with Welbern sheathed. She seemed of Man and would meet the end-of-seasons for that reason.

When Swen realized my intent, she sidled out of Welbern's path. The genie knew my sword—the only weapon invulnerable to anything of magical nature. Stories had been related that even the gods and goddesses feared my Welbern, the Demonslayer.

A reckless mess, I charged into her churning mystic embracement, her mystic runes shimmering about me. A relaxing surge gushed throughout my delirious form as a captivating harmony lulled me from generating any further damage… I plopped upon the ground. Welbern fell by my side, Swen's gases whisked away from me.

Kute, Juna, and Ding came hustling to the scene with some of Khun's Protectors.

"What the Interim is wrong, Ygl? Pick your head up. What happened?" I knew Flower Juna was being a caring person despite her delivery. I did not say a word. I could not say another word.

Snip teleported Limbus in front of me. My bloodson knelt, trying to read my face. "Bloodfather, it is true, is it not? King Methelo, Prince Rolando, and Advisor Sylvia have met the end-of-seasons? Only you would know this."

The crowd stayed silent, waiting for my answer. How would he take my reply? Our race was being wiped out. Our royalty, gone. We remained.

Swen floated closer trying to keep away from Welbern's sting. "Master, I would tell him if I were thee. It would show thy true inner bravery. Though, it fills thee with great woe, at least the people will hear what all should know."

A murmur went throughout the crowd. Did our supernatural visitor jar their wits?

Limbus leaned forward; his forehead touched mine. *"Bloodfather…"* he knew the answer.

At first, I grabbed his shoulders, then held him tight attempting not to cry. "Yes, it is true."

"How terrible." Juna jetted backward and up as if trying to keep away from a ghastly leper. Her white light surged about her hands.

The listeners became restless, yelling vows of retaliation for the Lorellian royalty's end-of-seasons. Never had the Protectors been so enraged in all their seasons. The Protectors of Khun loved and respected Lorel's royalty even when we did not acknowledge everything in the same perspective. Quirm would pay for their emperor's heinous act.

"Who dares do such a thing?" some exclaimed.

"The bloodfamily royal will be avenged," others promised.

Plant Kute was solemn. His peculiar face set; his limbs—immovable amongst all the protests. He found the urge to kneel to me, assisting me up. "I had never thought our enemy would be this bold... this dangerous. I promise you, General, my **roots** will not take these end-of-growths lightly. To decimate an entire royal lineage would mean to destroy a belief system that race holds dear. It shows defiance to that race's gods and goddesses, denying the very gifts provided by the Divinity to shelter that race. They defy our divine rights. This is an act of war."

Juna, beside herself, buzzed about like a frenzied dragonfly. "This is insane!"

Our Dwarven friend sulked off dragging his ax, Gore, behind him. Not a wild cry came from his lips as brutish Gore chopped at the thick trees nearby. Merciless blows from the diamond double-head splintered the trunks midway with only three swings. Without pause, pristine wood replaced the trunks' damage, stopping Ding short.

Quadrupled fluffy wings harnessed Oreol before Ding. "That was a minor distraction of my power, Dwarf, to hinder you from accidentally destroying the forest. You will understand Khun will come to your estate's aid only if we have the capability. At this point, protecting our forest is of utmost concern. We are not even organized for battle, yet."

Ding grumbled within his hood.

"I can fix that for you, Oreol." Mitral rode Jinx, his four-legged archeornyx, above the hesitant crowd. How could everyone acknowledge such a small being?

"Listen, my friends and clan," his voice echoed everywhere to my surprise, "stop the useless exchange of words and start banding together. If we are to do what we have vowed, then let us begin now. Where is Blasmle? Where is Rungna-Olivia? Gather all the Protectors of Khun toward the main camp. Gather them. The Lorellian general has something to say."

"Humph. That is all his divine right is good for." Oreol, still aloft, hovered close to me with his arms crossed upon his chest.

Sprites, Gnomes, and available Khunian Elves spread to disseminate the dreadful news to others, though I doubt anyone could not concede to the Gnome Leader. A booming voice like that could do some probable damage, putting Oreol's disapproval to shame.

Limbus' crying replaced the deserted area's stillness. Kute knelt to hold my bloodson. "Now, you have a chance to tell all of Khun about the mystic mist, General, if it was not for the Gnome Leader and his loud mouth. I mean, where does all that voice come from in such a little form?

Aside from that, since we six are left here alone for a while, I would like to know how, in Lolung-Cor's name, you knew about your royalties' end-of-growth?"

I did my best to adjust myself. "To me, my friend it was a dream, I think, that evolved in my thoughts as I slept. But I realized it was more than that. It was somewhat an admonition being sent to me by my relatives begging me for help. They told me who was behind this before their seasons ended."

"Who?"

"It is Emperor Rondo of Quirm."

"How dare him!" Juna interrupted.

Ding grumbled, "My **ore** never liked Man. At least we have a reason why."

"Uhm, Ding, your ore never cared for anyone," Juna replied. Oreol and she may be related.

"The Giants will stop him before other estates fall." Kute insisted almost relishing the thought of battle.

"But, we cannot!" Juna objected, "If it is obvious he has this mysterious mist on his side, then there is nothing we can do but retain our services to guard Khun against it, and have someone else warn the estates."

"Spoken like a true Protector, Flower Juna." Oreol beamed.

"Preferably, by someone with flight—like me."

"Oh-Ho-Ho, Flower Juna, are you afraid to fight?" Kute joked.

Juna, flustered, zoomed up to his face, her power blazing, finger pointing. "You stupid Giant, I am a Flower with a divine right like you. Just because your race is of warriors does not mean my roots will settle and allow Zaendara to fall."

Impressive. "You demonstrate your wisdom quite well, Juna, though a bit immature. We shall be the group going on this lengthy journey to the estates through the Dark Plains. But I am sure our heraldry will not end there, my friends. King Methelo told me, still yet, one more hint of knowledge before I felt his season end. Emperor Rondo seems to hunt for something he plans to rule all of Zaendara with. It is called a Jode. We are to track it down before he does or else everyone will bow beneath his reign. I have no idea what it is. Does anyone else?"

Kute scratched his beard. "The Jode?" He turned to look upward for an answer. "I have been related of such a name when I was just a **sprout**. It appears as if it has been erased from the very depths of our memory."

Oreol agreed. "We at Khun have known of such a name ourselves, but never took the occasion to solve its meaning."

"Maybe Swen knows some information about this Jode," Juna added, "after all, it may be as legendary as her."

Inquiring eyes shifted to where our resident genie resided. Billowy gases had already swirled behind me into my cloak's hidden pocket. I did not dare halt her misty shape from evading into her boxy lamp with an aspiring whimper.

"It may be a good idea to order this spirit back," Oreol stated.

Kute intervened. "Let her be. If she must grieve, then let her."

Limbus unburied his face from my shoulder. "But, bloodfather, since when do genies grieve? Do they?"

His question stunned me. "To tell you the truth, Limbus, I do not know. I simply do not know."

"Hurry to your tent, Ygl," Oreol interrupted, "the Protectors are already gathering."

"Okay. Kute and Ding, could you please get the mounts ready while I get myself washed?"

"General, I have been thinking about this mystic mist. Ding and you have both said it was inhabited by Demons. My roots will not have to worry about any attack set upon the Giant Treedom by Man's devious emperor because, in our myths, the Demons have always feared the Cory Mountains."

"I am sure he will find a way, Kute. I am sure he will."

I ran inside my tent to clean myself. Soon my group would venture throughout Zaendara against a mighty emperor with an empire as strong as all the estates combined... or maybe even stronger. Already, two seized estates had reduced the strength of our endangered continent.

The cool water from the basin refreshed me for a short while. The painful cries for help kept returning concluding with Methelo's marked scream.

I shivered. Man would regret they performed such acts to my kin; to my lineage. The insolence ... I did not understand.

Vacillating voices seeped from outside. A gathering audience awaited me to deliver the message. Every Protector overcrowded the whole campsite. Sprites and Gnomes crammed upon each other within the trees' branches ascending toward the top or nestled within the blossoms' carpels. Some of the celestial Sprites wheeled over the patient contingency's heads anticipating my arrival upon the wicker table centered amongst the populace. Even the bloodchildren awaited for what they already knew or would learn. Animals meandered between the different fixtures. A show of natural wonderment, the gathering almost put Lorel to shame.

Cautious, I made my way through the packed crowd. Kute followed along behind me with Juna scouting upon his broad shoulder.

Situating myself upon the table, I prepared to address the motley group surrounding me. "Fellow clan and Protectors of Khun, it behooves me to convey to you that the sacred forest is in danger of attack. To my dismay both Lorel and the Dwarven estate were under attack and enslaved in the previous sundays by a mysterious milky mist somehow being controlled by Emperor Rondo of Quirm." A sense of betrayal did not go unnoticed amongst the bystanders. "I know how you must feel about Man's treachery toward the peace our races have cherished since the beginning of uncharted ages. Twice I have received telepathic admonitions sent by my royal bloodfamily. On the second one, their seasons ended. This is why my companions and I are here. Because we must put an end to what Emperor Rondo has started. If he dares capture another estate then our remaining combined forces will be no match for the Quirmeans."

A male warrior and maiden stepped forth from the gathering. Unlike other Khunian Elves, a thin covering of greater forgery clad each personage. They garnered a fantastic set of bow and arrows, and displayed a more sinewy musculature. The male's intricate armor was embellished with small oval dimples flowing in a slant and crooked engraved streaks spanning. The maiden's armor exploited a variety of animals: a lion and a tiger descended from opposite shoulders; a strident hippogriff belted her waist; a rabbit here and a bird there. Their skintight vambrace and greave displayed the same etchings with steel daggers attached. Of course, proud bare feet would never entertain boots. Fellow Protectors yielded this duo much regard whom were no doubt regal in nature.

The male, pretty big for such short stature and paler than most, imparted a stern look on his face with permanence. His bald head overshadowed a tempest within deep set pupils. His voice, a rumbling, "Please excuse us for the interruption, Ygl General. I am Blasmle and this is mate my, Rungna-Olivia. I am sure you know us as the Leaders of the Protectors Elvin who guard Khun. We have taught you some skills combat when you were a bloodchild and handed the reins to the warriors other when you got older. Your bloodfather, Scall, and I were close quite. You come to us and relay such plight great you have experienced, I am sorry to say, that is not proof enough for us to believe."

Rungna-Olivia exhibited her untamed hair and shaggy arms. "We have never trusted Man, but forces our will not be permitted to do anything until we do know evil has havocked Zaendara." Wild animals in a scuffle, the root of her natural voice.

"I do not understand, Rungna-Olivia."

"Please, call me Rungna. You see, Ygl, Quirm has always been nonintrusive with the races here at Khun despite reservations our. It would be nonsense to say Rondo Emperor is behind these attacks so-called. These attacks seem unreal so."

"General, I... I do not mean to be rude, but what are they saying?"

"Not now, Kute." Kute caught me a little off guard. Juna must have told him about my telepathy.

Juna was not as polite. "What the Interim are you saying?!"

"What they are saying, my Fairy Flower," Mitral echoed, "is they will not help until they see proof. I knew they would say this."

"What?" Kute was baffled.

I proceeded, "Blasmle and Rungna, are bloodchildren Lorellian not proof enough?"

"No," feral Rungna snarled.

"How about the presence of this Giant, this Fairy, and this Dwarf?"

Bald headed Blasmle took the lead. "Creatures interesting, but, no, this is not proof enough. They come in faith good and friends yours strange, so allowable. You must remember, we may protect Khun with fiber every, but there has never been a war in Zaendara. This means it is impossible for one to launch unless he who starts one has a reason insane why."

My confoundment knew no bounds. "But Rondo Emperor does have a reason insane why he is doing this. He plots to find something native to Zaendara called the Jode."

"The Jode?" Rungna asked.

"Aye, mate my, it has long been since we heard of name such. Since the Jode is nothing but a legend to clan our, it leads us to believe that what you say is not true."

"Then, tell me, Blasmle, how you can explain the existence of Demons?" I insisted.

"Demons?" Rungna echoed. The confounded crowd chattered amongst themselves.

Oreol spoke up. "You see, General Ygl, the Elvin warriors, though mighty in their skills, will not protect Khun from outside intrusions without good reason, in some cases, including a perfect reason for something as outrageous as war. Zaendara never had skirmishes before for something as mythical as this Jode."

"But, they are true, Oreol, whatever the Jode may be."

Alas, perfumed wisps curled above us from behind me. "Do not speak anymore words, master Ygl, for to their minds thy message falls feeble. Let me show them in my own way. Perhaps their thoughts to us will sway."

Ambivalent awe struck the gathering. They had never witnessed a real genie in all their diligent seasons—no one had, though there was no doubt word spread of her earlier appearance.

"I take my chances with these dances," Swen affirmed. Her unexpected arrival to the forum would, with confidence, change everyone's decision to stop doubting the legends. To partake of such an idea, her cunning shown. Had my leg rubbed the lamp by accident? Nonetheless, with the crowd believing in the youthful stories related to them, her presence would dictate a belief in my message.

With a telepathic sweep, I could sense some dissent. *"Swen, some still will not consider this truth. Use another tactic."*

Swen drifted high above the assembly. "I ascertain that thee do not understand the danger at hand. Thou have had me moved for the want of more proof. Proof thee will get when my power melds with the mind of the child whom within his memory has kept filed the dreadful attack that had come and caused the capture of the Elvin Kingdom.

Come forth, young boy, for thy mind I employ to surface a memorial from the Forest of Lorel."

Limbus, nervous, stepped forward one step and stepped no farther. Motionless, Swen's magic paralyzed him. His eyes shut allowing his remembrances to project from his opened mind... Swen's archaic symbols shimmered... Colorful bands swirled about the small breathing statue of my bloodson. Tiny glittering bursts of light danced throughout the memorial vapors. The vapors glided over Limbus's head so everyone could observe the fantastic spectacle and parted away exhibiting the solid figure of an elder Elvin male screaming in terror.

"Demons! Demons!" the elder repeated as I, once again, witnessed his poor head lop off his neck.

More images appeared of the milky mist flowing across the forest toward the fleeing Elvin kin huddled together in the dancing area. Shifting scenes of the mist shrouding the reticent and retaliating Lorellians kept flashing in and out.

In one scene, Limbus searched for someone in the chaos—Ploone. "Limbus, what can we do?" There was no denying the evidence of tears streaming down Ploone's cheeks. "We are... we are surrounded!"

Limbus' best friend stopped to pay attention to what we could not comprehend. "Do you think it will work?"

An answer. Ploone gave a wry smile. "Let us do it!"

Subtle Swen chanted another spell triggering the escapees' faces to interchange within the magical memorial. Each at first hesitated, but felt elated with Limbus' extraordinary plan. After that, the faces disappeared and a mass of bloodchildren grouped burdened upon their asegafian cats' spines. Corralled, the arching cats snarled yips and hissed with bared fangs defending their masters—their tongues, much like a butterfly's mouthpiece, whisked aloft in the air.

The mystic mist had reached the dance area's rim. Elves scrambled about looking for someplace to get away from the mist while others, to my satisfaction, stood in defiance.

On magnificent Steadfast, I appeared calling my guards to my side.

A primeval growl reverberated... The mist crept, rising within an instance before Snip, wrapping steamy entrails around my bloodson and his mount. Monstrous deformed claws reached out.

Blackness...

A change of scenery: the moonday remained the same, but Limbus and Snip relocated to the Forest of Khun. Lorellian bloodchildren sprawled upon the ground. Grieving cries curdled from between shivering lips.

The shimmering vapors began to dominate the picture, initializing the vision to become blurry. Once completed, Swen's shimmering enchantment lowered itself encompassing Limbus... the memorial vapors dissipated. The spectators, amazed.

Swen whisked away to her lamp. "Now that thou has seen thy proof. I admonish thee—accept the truth. Master Ygl, if it will put thy mind at ease, I will smile for thee." She vanished within.

A short moment of silence pervaded. The Khunians had thrived by themselves in solitude for a many seasons with no contact with anyone but my kin, however, they could not deny this occurrence.

Blasmle turned toward me. "I apologize, Ygl, for not believing you." He unsheathed his sword and turned facing the great multitude with point uplifted. "We are the Protectors righteous of Khun and forest our sacred shall be protected!"

An uproar of cheers saturated the air. He continued, "We have never given up in the past; we will not stop now. For ages we have wondered little why we defend such ground hallow. Reason our has at last come. Forces Quirmean may show aggression, but instead they will discover opponents who will be ready. They will discover an army unlike any other ready to meet the end-of-seasons for Khun our blessed."

More great cheers arose from the growing multitude mixed with tributes in honor of Khun.

"Khun! Khun! Till the end-of-seasons! All praise Miredo! Praise to Ethnel!"

Rungna stepped forth to address the eager crowd. "I, as Leader second, say we still need to bolster strength our in opposition to Quirm. We need the bloodchildren Lorellian by side our in battle. They will be trained quickly and harshly for battle by us. Will you, Ygl General, accept this decision?"

I did not know what to say. The bloodchildren themselves seemed to agree with the adventure, but their innocence bothered me. I instructed Limbus from my Khunian training; maybe Ploone learned from Limbus. This offer could be very hard on them because of their youth. I just wanted to take my bloodson and coddle him from all this insanity. Was there really a choice? Khunian Elves, a dwindling race, did not have bloodchildren. They would not understand.

Limbus stepped in front of the bloodchildren, earnest. "*Bloodfather, what you taught me, I taught many of them. We can shoot bow and arrows really well. Please, let us. For bloodmother...*"

"*Are you willing to follow Limbus? Can you follow him?*" I asked the bloodchildren.

In unison they arose, earnest as well—a willing respect toward a general's bloodson. What brave souls.

I knelt to my Limbus, kissing his forehead. "*I love you.*"

He touched my arm, stoic. "*You will be back. You are my bloodfather. A brave general of Lorel.*"

Emboldened, I answered the Protectors' royalty. "I accept, yes. Even moreso, the bloodchildren accept. You have made a decision righteous, Blasmle and Rungna. I am thankful of it, but we must begin fast before Rondo Emperor launches assault his. Part every of Khun encompassing from the Road to the Quirm Great Wall must be guarded. Meanwhile, companions my and I will try to warn Zaendara ourselves. Before you leave, please remember you do this to protect Khun, but also in memoriam to Lorel."

"Ygl, the end-of-seasons of lineage your will not be in vain." Blasmle reached out his hand to shake mine.

I returned the favor. "Thank you. Please protect bloodchildren our as you teach them. They are legacy our only."

"Worry not; we will. With aid of Miredo, we will." Blasmle gave me his bow and a quiver full of arrows, the fletching made from a trophy kill's reddish feathers from the Dark Plains. "Here, you will need this."

"Thanks."

The crowd disengaged. I stepped off the table and headed for Stonecrusher as Kute and Ding mounted their steeds awaiting me.

Oreol fluttered by. "I wish you luck, Ygl."

"Thanks, Oreol!"

"General, these Elves have a strange way of talking."

"They just place much of their descriptions after their words, Kute."

"Descriptions after their words?"

"Yeah, something like that. Possessive words follow their words, too. When you have been around them enough, you kind of get used to their language. You know, like engaging with you."

"Oh... heh-heh..."

"Juna, are you prepared to lead us out?"

"Whenever you ask me." Her insect-like filaments more silent than the Sprite's feathery flurry. "Where to?"

"The Ogre Treedom."

"Are you sure it is a treedom?"

"I guess we will find out when we get there."

She giggled. "That is very true." Juna's tiny form zipped ahead into the shady forest's southeastern end.

Limbus impressed me with his admirable initiative. I hesitated to admit the truth, but my bloodbrother, Methelo, and I never wanted to lead. To us, governance was a debt, a duty. We wanted a normal existence: Methelo with his constant meditations; me with my antics... My antics attracted Thalla to me.

When our bloodparents, Scall and Rarle, met their end-of-seasons, they left Methelo and me no choice in the matter. Our kin needed sustained governance. I loved fighting and had anger issues, therefore, being granted my status became logic with infrequent interferences by Methelo and Advisor Sylvia. Not that I cared for my status, but the prestige was nice with the favors given, Steadfast and Welbern. My kin needed me, especially my bloodson. Well, we could see how much help I had been so far…

I never even asked to head of our little group, but somehow that duty fell on my lap. Who knew the seasons would produce such change. I had no idea what kin perceived in me.

As Kute, Ding and I followed Juna, I glanced up. A movement in the branches caught my interest. Mitral, the Gnomes' Leader, stood next to Jinx, his archeornyx. To the plump Leader's other side accompanied another Gnome, a slender male—holding Mitral's hand. Both Gnomes nodded their heads to me in calm assurance. I could perceive a sadness imparting from Mitral.

Was that Mitral's mate? I never clasped any male's hand. How sad Mitral had to shroud his relationship from others, a member of the Protectors' royalty.

Were the conditions this bad for same-sex relationships in Khun? What a shame. Why did Methelo or the others not tell me anything about this? Maybe they thought I knew, since I had been familiar with the Khunian clan. On the contrary, I trained in a designated area learning combat when I visited, and Khunian Elves maintained such a rigid fortitude denying much of anything to anyone. The Gnomes and the Sprites were of little consequence for me to notice.

In Lorel, we never had an issue like this. Our ambivalence about same-sex relationships governed, moreover, such relationships seemed uncommon. And maybe most kin thrived in their heads so much they never paid much attention? I did not know. No one really discussed anyone's romance.

Deeper and deeper my brave little group dashed to Khun's perimeter onto the Dark Plains, and from there, toward the Ty Desert. A number of scarce camps were passed. The sound of galloping hooves overtook the sound of voices being left behind. Some branches swiped at us as we bounded over the advanced undergrowth and tree roots. Incremental sunlight sliced through the emerald green canopies.

Grassy terrain rolled where the lush forest terminated. The grassy terrain carpeted toward a region of varying grassy stalks as large as Kute himself. The stalks concealed the inhabitants of this spotted rustic region from the wanderers' sight.

Our steeds halted before our advance.

Juna buzzed around. "Well, here we are—the Dark Plains. The most infamous area in all of Zaendara. By the way, Ygl, why are we going to the Ogre Treedom? The incredible heat of the Ty is not very inviting by itself. Why not go to the Giant Treedom since it is much closer?"

"The answer to that, my Fairy friend, is quite obvious. You remind me of my bloodfather's parable. If you had your own pouch of gold and had nowhere to put it, you would probably give it to a trustworthy friend of yours, would you not?"

"Yes."

"All right. Now let us say you were not planning to let your friend hold that gold forever so you built a chest with a lock to put the gold away in. This is exactly what we are going to try and accomplish, Juna. With the estates of northern Zaendara warned, Rondo will have problems fighting to get past them so he can attack the unprepared estates of the lower region."

"Huh? I do not know what you are feeling, but it is not happiness! I did not get that. Did you understand him, Kute? I guess I understand what you are trying to say, Ygl, I think. I just believe we should not need to go through this crazy terrain. We should go through another way?"

Kute enjoined. "The way through the Dark Plains is the shortest and, therefore, quickest route, Flower, for the group to get to the Ty. I know this region is evil, but we are forced to journey through it."

"Okay. Whatever."

"I am actually amazed, Flower, that you would ask such a question with your great sense of direction."

"I am just trying to make roots see reality compared to your unhampered maddening idealism."

"Maybe if you fools can quit moving your mouths we can probably get somewhere." Curt Ding hid his face within his hood.

I laughed. "You know, Ding, on this occasion, you are right. Shall we go?"

The steeds galloped into the thick province of extended grasses and unwanted weeds. While we picked up speed, Stonecrusher and Crater left a clear path for Redfang to race upon in the rearguard, taking distances up.

The plain's grasses, innumerable hues of green and brown, were a dense package. A compacted land striving for a sense of balance compared to the adjacent forest. A jutting field populated with copses of tree-sized grasses. A challenge for any traveler. Nonetheless, Kute informed us about a few spacious clearings where travelers could uncover resting places.

We sought a resting area hoping the respite would make everyone's trip a little easier. Little creatures scampered in distress while larger ones paused to glare at our ongoing band through splitting silhouettes. The smaller ones were harder to distinguish—slinking shades melting into the stalky variety. The larger beasts, fewer at this juncture, kept their distance. I guess they believed a Khunian party trailed us.

We still had a long way to go. Another clearing, but not a beneficial break area. I unraveled my cloak and crammed it into my saddle's satchel.

As we careered through a scanty tract of browning land struggling to survive amongst indifferent taller neighbors, an insidious halo of bluish-yellow brilliance exploded roundabouts us. A flapping of giant wings descended from behind—their outline grew ever larger.

A brilliant bolt of gray energy streaked past and almost hit Stonecrusher in the head.

"Look!" Twisting Juna ordered while returning a blast of her divine right at the intruder.

A fat Quirmean male shot the powerful discharge. He danced with such elegance upon his mount, a giant bat—a creature not native to our continent at all. He seemed tribal in his gestures as he raised an arm, elbow prominent, from a quasi-squatting position. The monstrosity's grin resembled his.

In their background, a huge spherical void vibrated whose circumference exuded the same bluish-yellow brilliance. They teleported? Quirm was indeed behind this! I could not bring myself to remember this Quirmean's name. On occasion, I went to Quirm with Methelo but did not remember this male. From his chubby hand sprouted a sinister grayish emanation.

We circled our mounts and attempted a resistance. Kute raised his bulbous club to throw, but his success faltered.

"Kute!"

We became more alarmed with the Giant prince's downfall. Redfang dodged a magic blast while his master pulled out Gore equipping for battle. Juna veered onward to distract our invader.

I pulled out an arrow from my new quiver. My notched arrow prepared its release when I witnessed, seething from the portal's borders, the same mist that attacked Lorel! The marauding mist assaulted our quartet transgressing its amorphous shape upon our determined selves with a quickness.

This mist was different. An enchanting spell's hint I could not resist replaced the Demonic inhabitants, hampering my telepathy within another psychic sludge. I could not send out to anyone.

Colors flowed in my mind causing me to get drowsy... my vision, too blurry... the enchantment... too powerful... could... not be... resisted...
I tumbled to the ground...

"*Not... again.*"

Ding grumbled a growl; a yelp aroused from his devoted Redfang. Juna's pure beams sparkled bright within, but the nothingness soon engulfed them.

Quirm had prevailed and we... I... had failed.

CHAPTER 16: The Empire

The windowless dungeon's shade was not inviting to me at all. Twice I witnessed Quirm's milky mist's attacks, and have now become incarcerated. My two companions, glowing red, had not awakened from their unconsciousness. Iron shackles fastened to our wrists and ankles, the only belongings we bore.

I saw no small red hues. Juna must have escaped our opponent's terrible power. She may have shrunk her size so she would be undetectable, but what can a Fairy queen do in a continent as expansive as Zaendara?

"The lamp..." I muttered. My surprising treasure must have been lost in the fray. I could imagine Juna having a favorable stumble upon it. Alas, again, with her petite frame she would not be able to carry the vessel by herself; not for that distance.

I searched for my blade like a fool. If the Quirmeans should realize the cache that settled on their laps... If Emperor Rondo found out about Demonslayer...

My burly companions stirred. They dragged their sluggish selves against the nearest brick wall.

"Where are we?" Kute moaned. His constrained wrists rattled his chains when he tried to stretch. "Why am I manacled?"

"I believe we are captives in the hands of Emperor Rondo, my friends. I am truly sorry."

Ding fumed, "Sorry will not get us out of here, Elf."

Ding attempted to assault me. I rolled out of his path. My feet swung up and struck his abdomen, forcing the Dwarven thief into his original position squirming on the ground from the pain. "We (cough-cough)... should have not... saved you (cough-cough)... or else (cough)... this would have not happened... (cough). I knew I was right (cough)—"

"Ding, be careful. There may be a lot of dust in here."

"You think a little bit of dust means anything to me. I am a Dwarven miner of the Endoworld. This is nothing. I knew I was right when I objected you being leader (cough-cough)."

"Even if you did not save me, our estates would still be in danger."

"The general is right, Dwarf," solemn Kute intervened, "Calm down before you become a liability. Fate may have decreed this to happen to our growths even if this whole continent depended on us. I do sympathize with you that the party could have proceeded with our mission leaving the general behind to contend with the assailant, but considering the fact he is our leader I could not turn away like you would have. I do not leave anyone behind—even you, my little friend. Especially you.

General, can you use your mind powers?"

"No. They have been cancelled somehow."

"Well, that is not good."

"How about your gifts, Kute? Can you use yours?"

"No, I am sorry to say. It appears we are both cancelled."

Strange bracelets, molded from a mixture of metal and another material, manacled Kute and my wrists. I rubbed my fingers over the material and squinted from the pain. The material was my skin! How were these bracelets burned onto my wrists without my feeling any pain?

Odd enough, Ding did not brandish any bracelets. My belief would be these bracelets hampered Kute and my divine rights.

clickity-clack... clickity-clack

Keys wrestled unhinging the lock on our cell door. The lock's mechanics gave away allowing the door the undeniable privilege.

In the dim corridor stood an armored Quirmean accompanied by five guards. He carried himself with much prestige. A flute dangled from his belt's side. "Greeting, visitors, I am General Spenz. Welcome to Quirm. I fancy you enjoyed your stay here because you are heading somewhere else where you are likely going to not feel very comfortable. I have been ordered to bring you there by my liege, and so I will.

Do I not know your name, Giant? I am sure we have met before."

"I have never met you, General."

"Spenz, that is none of your concern."

Spenz laughed. "And, pray tell, how you are going to stop me, General Ygl? You're the last of your royalty, an extinct creature. That does not matter now. There is business that needs to be taken care of.

Maybe the emperor will recognize you, Giant.

Guards, unshackled their ankles."

Four rugged guards performed as commanded. Three bent over liberating our ankles while the fourth gave us stalwart scrutiny. After the unshackling, they led us out and down the passageway. Their constant prodding, a thorough act they relished, headed us down another corridor going to where? We did not know. Everything had happened with such immediacy. I had no idea what we could do at this moment. As Rondo's captives, there would be no logical way the other estates could be warned.

Could the truth be the seasons were filled with ironies? Ironies used to default what other seasons attempt to accomplish? But these ironic events seemed to have a peculiar force behind them. As if the gods and goddesses enacted these ironies as an assistance and I ruined their plans by falling for a trap.

This could be my fault if I went according to Ding's disapproval. I did not know, but an adjustment was of utmost importance.

The passageway terminated. We straggled up a long flight of stairs. Seasons must have elapsed since these stairs initial stone molding. Dust particles upon the aged stairwell whipped up revealing a track of prior footsteps entrusting their mark; marks not thick enough for Man and too big for a bloodchild. These prints were Lorellian adults indeed. Methelo? Rolando? Sylvia... Thalla? I struggled to keep my tears from forming.

Another locked door presented itself ahead, a mocking ready to ensure. Spenz rapped upon the door permitting the respective guard to concede. A couple of dim lanterns provided some illumination, inviting our group to observe a miniaturized version of a torture chamber constructed to operate for the emperor's purposes. Interesting enough, the chamber was empty. In one corner situated a menacing bed of nails—the bed's sharp interior boxed in a bulky no-nonsense frame. The hungry bed anticipated the next victim to plummet from four sturdy ropes dangling from the ceiling's rafters. Dried blood caked the bed's unsatisfied teeth. Sporadic reddish slivers indicated recent slayings.

My kin…

Across the bed of nails was a wooden stretcher—a different kind of haunting cot. Taut leather straps hung from the four corners. The top and bottom platforms separated revealing a paired brace beneath holding the frame together. The braces extended outside the platforms' ends. The pool of blood beneath the separation unsettled me.

A guillotine erected from the other side above everything, the room's eerie lord. The lengthy blade gleamed a bit in the dim light. The catching barrel was too far away keeping its hideous hoard hidden to my relief.

Whips laid about on the ground aside several uninhabited stockades like leathery snakes maintaining constant vigilance for their next victim.

From this room of horrors, General Spenz led us upward through a couple of cleaner stairs and other halls, some carpeted, past various rooms. The mood became more energetic and unassuming. Paintings and eclectic curtains adorned the walls. Many doors were secured as a gift of privacy while others left ajar.

A bustling room produced a hurrying Quirmean female and her Elvin servant getting her dressed for an apparent meeting.

"Elf!" The Quirmean shrieked.

The alarmed Lorellian bowed away. "Yes, Madame?"

"You fool of a servant! Don't you know how to put powder on? It's too thick on my right cheek. Now, get over here and clean it off. Oh, I don't know why…" and so, the conversation went on…

Musical sounds swelled from within another room. What were these instruments, these weapons of abundant creativity? I had never experienced such sweet strange sounds. I wanted to peek in to witness the unabashed beauty that I could compare to the sweetest songbirds or a grouping of reeds creating euphoria with the attending breezes. How could such beauty emerge from such a horrid empire?

More rooms were passed, more luster crept in on our trek: the clanking of pots and pans as the royal cooks prepared the meal for the sunday... the splashing of water as the royal laundress washed clothes... a ball room... a royal banquet hall... a tearoom...

At last, we arrived to heavily armored sentinels safeguarding a pair of hefty black doors. The sentinels moved aside when they saw Spenz approaching; the oaken doors swung open.

We entered a well decorated room with an adjacent balcony welcoming in the sunday. Looming statues almost touched the ceiling with fanciful tapestry.

More sentinels, larger ones, guarded this room. Their regalia could disguise their bodies, but not their faces. Some exposed jagged teeth. Some had scaly bits and fur peeking out of the array. Their hollowed eyes bared the mark of sinister depth. These were Xurchon's bloodchildren. These were Demons.

A comfortable male rested upon the gold-laced throne at the room's end: about fifty-eight seasons of age, a little older than Methelo maybe, although more fit but not as youthful. His short black beard with gray whiskers and leering demeanor pronounced from a modest tunic, cotton slacks, and slippers completing Emperor Rondo. Interesting enough, four other thrones populated the chamber unoccupied.

He initiated, "It has been long since I have gazed upon the likes of you, Giant prince and little Dwarf. I am sorry you were found along with these imbeciles, Prince Kute, but like them you must be interrogated."

"You speak in untruth, Emperor." Calm Kute asserted. "I have never met you. You do not wish to interrogate anyone. I know of your treacherous plan to rule Zaendara in want of a Jode. I, unfortunately, believe you would rather kill to have knowledge of it. You killed the Elvin king, prince, and their advisor—"

Rondo, surprised, arose from his throne. The pedestal the throne rested upon placed him near Kute's height. "And it strikes me to ask you how you know about this?"

I answered, "Let us say it is a bit of secret relations on my part."

"I see. This must mean you know something of the loss of the lamp of Swen… especially you, Elvin general—Ygl? That is your name? It was the Forest of Lorel where it was lost, I'm sure you know."

No doubt, Kute and Ding became mystified by this remark. Swen and her lamp were thought to belong to me since the attack. Now, someone else boasted the lamp's ownership and demanded its whereabouts.

I remained unfazed. I knew the lamp did not belong to me, but this would not force me to tell a person of such power what we knew about it. What connections did a genie have with an emperor's scheme to rule an entire continent? The lamp could have something to do with the mysterious Jode. If correct, then he must not find out.

"When Lorel was seized by your fiendish mist, I was too occupied to know anything about a lamp or a Swen." I never stated a falsehood. I just admitted what occurred at the moment.

"He lies, my liege. As I have reported to you: Lorel was already scanned by my search party and my magic. Not a trace of the lamp was found." Spenz brandished a vindictive smug.

Kute stepped up. "Then take the word of a Plant who is true at his oath."

"A plant? What plant?"

"A Plant. I am a Plant."

"You are a Giant."

"I am a Giantic Plant."

Rondo became more perplexed. "Spenz, have you given them any drugs?"

"No, sire."

"Did you find any on them?"

"No."

"Okay, clearly, Prince Kute, you are not a plant."

Kute laughed. "That is what I am."

"A plant?"

"Yes, I am Plant Kute of the Giants."

"'Plant' means the same a prince," I interjected blandly.

"Oh…" Rondo tried to mask embarrassment.

Kute continued, "On my oath, the general was not marked with any evidence of a lamp being in his possession when I first saw him."

Well, he did not see Swen's lamp on me. Juna did.

The emperor snorted. "Spenz, is there any way the lamp could have disappeared when we assaulted the Dwarf kingdom? I'm quite sure a low level thief could have stolen it."

Ding struggled in his anger.

"Leave him out of it, Rondo," I interfered.

"Silence him." Rondo ordered, focused. A Demonguard knocked me down with its spear's staff.

"You…!" Kute stepped forward to strike the Demonguard with of his shackled fists' combined might but three other Demonguards subdued him.

Our Dwarven companion let out a roar, breaking free from his chains. A furious Dwarf would be difficult to hinder. I knew. I had firsthand knowledge.

Ding rushed toward the surprised emperor before the Demonguards could prevent him. Unfortunate for Ding, Rondo had erected a magical barrier… Ding's senseless form was picked off the ground. Okay, magic could stop him.

Rondo continued, "I don't see how you received message about my plans, but under no certain circumstances will you be allowed to live, especially you, General Ygl. Oh, especially you. The three of you will be executed on the following three days one after the other starting with Ygl. My plans will commence.

Oh, if you feel that burning on your wrists, that's my mystic bracelets hampering your gifts leaving you impotent."

"I think that was pretty evident from the start, Emperor. Why is it that you feel so much antipathy toward me? Toward us?" I asked. "You barely know me."

Rondo chuckled. "I do trust you are not upset about your brother's death because you are the next to go. Please do not struggle, for I know your strength is not equal to the Dwarf's."

"You're evil deeds shall be stopped, dear emperor. You will not be so lucky," Kute warned.

"Luck is not the key to my ambition, prince or Plant, or whatever you want to call yourself. It is the power of Xurchon that has led me toward the rightful path my empire, as well as Zaendara, shall take. He has shown me the evil you Elves have done in the past to Quirm, all of Quirm, and for that the Elves will suffer. Tomorrow, I will be pleased about the long-awaited day of reckoning my people have looked forward to. The Elvin royal line will, at last, come to an end. Xurchon will forever rule."

Kute fell silent. His guess had been proven correct and he seemed uncomfortable. With this belief in Xurchon being genuine, the danger Zaendara faced had become worse. Could a Giant feel fear? I mean they thrived for war. They trusted in war. Maybe he was more concerned than anything.

"Rondo I do not understand." I pleaded, "What did we do to you? Is your choice infallible? Do you not see the terror that will occur if you begin to worship him?"

"I do not see anything except the fact that, with their heavenly wisdom, Istratos and Welna would have thrown my entire empire into total despair."

"What despair?"

"I grow tired of your questions. Take them to Skavir, Spenz. I will be there by morning to see the execution."

Kute persisted. "Please understand there is simply no way you can escape with this, Emperor. Remember, a Plant is present before you. If my blood is ever spilt by another, then you have the Giantic Treedom to contend with."

"'Treedom. Diamondom.' I think the first thing I'll do when I conquer Zaendara is have everyone speak the same language.

Do not worry, Prince Plant Kute. I'll probably have that taken care of ahead of schedule. What if I contacted King whatever-his-name-is and informed him that you have come for a small meeting and will arrive back after a few days, or sundays, or whatever you may call it? You just won't be back for a while?"

"You dare..."

"I have already formulated a plan that will totally obliterate the Giant Kingdom-Treedom from attacking my empire as we go along our business."

Like a boulder dropping into a small puddle, I would have expected the tension between them to build, but Kute espoused calmness. "Glory to war."

"Interesting." A stunned Rondo scrutinized him.

I added, "You forget the Giant gods. They will not tolerate the spilling of blood of one who highly worships them."

"Did Miredo or your Achal, ever come to your brother's rescue, General Ygl? I see they did not which means they were never true deities to believe in. The deities of your races are just statuettes waiting to be thrown their annual sacrificial dish. Xurchon is the one true god."

"...You have seen him?"

"Oh, yes."

I would not concede. "And what if our deities were real? What if they arrived to my companions and my rescue? I am certain your Xurchon could not overcome the might of two gods, or four, or six."

"You, like the rest, have a lot to learn."

I noticed one of the enormous statues to his right. The royal icon was a resolute female's unique, bronze sculpting poised with her hands to her hips, evoking an air of dominance within her short dress and strapped sandals. Unlike Rondo, she possessed a kinky bushel of hair with a pair of vertical braids traversing; she had wide nostrils, a Fumian. "Why are your thrones empty, Emperor? Where is your mate? Where is your Empress?"

Without pause, Rondo continued, "Take them away, General Spenz. I will expect to see the young general, my greatest treasure, at Skavir tomorrow morning. The other two I want incarcerated at Chrot with the other slaves that haven't been sold until their turn comes."

"Yes, my liege," obeyed Spenz. With the Quirmean general's waved hand, the Demonguards redirected us to an adjacent set of double doors.

"Emperor, you need a hug." Resolute Kute echoed.

Kute's final response stunned me. A prince true to his word. His unselfishness amazed me as a Lorellian who remained moderate in many matters.

Rondo's prolonged silence spoke volumes to me. Where was Empress Maxis? Where were his bloodchildren? A Demonguard blocked my view.

The doors unfastened before anyone could touch the brass handles. In waltzed the little chubby capturer we encountered in the Dark Plains. A member of the royal bloodfamily? His name skulked somewhere in my mind's depths, somewhere on my tongue's tip, and, somehow, I could not remember him.

"That was a job well done, Werkle." Rondo gave me my answer. How could I forget such a name? I met this male. I knew I did.

"It was a job well done with your assistance."

"Oh, yes, my assistance." Rondo pulled on a long necklace suspending an item hidden in his tunic's bowels. Small, multifaceted and colorful, the object hung with pride from his hand, harbored within a triangular encasement's walls. The enigmatic item, hard to distinguish from our angle in the case's interior, could almost be distinguished as a gem of sort. The multicolored facets on the item became very attractive to me. The soft colors held a certain appeal; even the shadows exuded appeal.

The small gem of pure elegance dangling so unabashed from the chain even mesmerized the Demonguards.

After Werkle's intrusion, our band continued the distressing march out of the throne room, along the emperor's private hall: Ding a little in front of me, then Kute behind me. Though the hall was rather tight, a Demonguard secured every corner, however few. When we arrived to the door at the endpoint, a squad of Quirmean soldiers replaced the Demonic sentries on the opposite side equipped to escort us to our designated areas.

I attempted to communicate to Kute and Ding via telepathy. The strain felt unbearable—the unison screech of a thousand hungry bats—my wrists warmed from the mystic bracelets. "*Kute? Ding? Can you feel my thoughts…? Can you feel my sending?*"

"*General? Yes, yes, I can hear you.*"

"*Ding?*"

He did not respond.

"*Let us quickly communicate this way,*" I proceeded.

"*It… it is a bit difficult to hear you, General, but I understand.*"

"These bracelets..."

"I understand. I feel sorry for that emperor.

General, you do not think Xurchon has truly gained growth? The emperor could not have had that experience."

"If by 'growth' you mean 'seasons', I fear he has." The bracelets warmed hotter.

"Yes, yes, that. I mean his... his existence."

"We saw Demons, my friend... there can only be one possibility."

"But, it cannot be happening—"

"Face it, Kute. You are intelligent. You have no need to fear anything that is evil—that includes Xurchon. If Xurchon is powerful enough to scare the wits out of a fierce Giant, like you, then you have got me as an ally. Quirm will perish when the estates combine to help each other. Remember we are friends here even if one of us faces the end."

"You speak encouraging words, General. Giants do not have fear. We raise concerns. The glory of battle is what we thrive for. My will adheres to your wisdom."

My instincts proved correct about Kute. I could tolerate the burning bracelets no more, *"Thank you... Let us end this for the moment. I feel a headache coming."*

Our trip through the palace completed, we entered a courtyard filled with the high household's Quirmean elite. The ladies convened gossiping beneath the trees either with themselves or with the nobles. Farther out in the courtyard, some nobles played different sports, and the bloodchildren ran around chasing each other or other things. A number of young females relaxed along a small pond singing a song of praise to Xurchon. Unbelievable. To have such a quick turnaround from believing in their gods, Istratos and Welna, boggled my mind.

The noisiness concluded when everyone spotted our little group parading down the path toward the large iron gates at the end. Most peered at us with pure disdain while some were puzzled.

Our Dwarven companion returned the favor with an unfettered turn of his head and a flipped upper lip. His shirt's hood and his unruly curly hair hid most of his face, but I could still sense Dwarven abhorrence seething out.

He scanned their faces with a similar appeal. "I hate Man," he muttered loud enough within my earshot.

I felt my Dwarven friend may have some anger management issues, but let us face the facts, I epitomized no perfection. I got pretty angry at particular moments. My bloodfather, Scall, picked Methelo to lead our kin for that reason, I guess. Methelo, the calmer of us two, abided to meditation's practices. I had a tendency of being a little hot-headed in my younger sundays which prompted my bloodfather to send me often to Khun to learn combat. I guess I needed an outlet for my issues. Funny, I never thought about how Khun treated their same-sex kin until I met Kute. I thrived too much in my own world of combat and females.

An oaken wagon's unwelcoming enclosure greeted us when we stepped out of the courtyard. The Quirmeans practiced an art form called carpentry which they used to create this boxed-in black carriage. Most of my kin was not familiar with carpentry. We constructed all of our huts, our treehomes, via simple measures.

How did we know about carpentry? I did not know. How odd...

Five guards positioned around our threesome ensuring our entrance into the blackened enclosure. We could not escape from our destined future. Nonetheless, importance laid heavy for me to believe our minds and hearts' fortitude would remain resilient in providing us the will to flout these ill intents.

Emperor Rondo, this sacrificial destiny for the peaceful continent you dared assail did not come lightly to me.

A secured lock left us alone in our new emptiness. I whispered, "Hate is a strong word, Ding."

"That makes me a strong person, Elf."

CHAPTER 17: In the weeds

A tree grass was an enduring arboreal species that camouflaged well within the Dark Plains' leafy environment. Much sturdier than a river carrizo, this wild plant disguised so well not even the trunk's stiffness relinquished anything noticeable. Nevertheless, if a breeze blustered, the tree grass would bend ever so slight to maintain an appearance, but if anyone endeavored strolling through a patch of them— that would be another story. The tree's roots dug so deep into the soil that its foundation did not interfere with the nourishment other grasses sought. An ideal refuge a copse of them made for vulnerable animals.

Queen Juna awoke within a tree grass' trunk, a sharp pain in her neck reminiscent of the past event's fading pictures. She had just flown ahead of everyone when she flinched to a searing sound hitting the ground. The moment she returned to her companions, Prince Kute was already lying unconscious while General Ygl and Ding seized their weapons. A strange male jockeyed above her on a giant bat...

On a giant bat?

Then, a colorless mist launched to envelope her. She knew she reacted too late. Every direction she evaded there would be that dratted mist, and so she resorted to the singular mean left to her: her skill to master and expend white light.

She fought with valor, but in vain. How could she strike at a nonentity? Who was the enemy? Alone, she was at a loss. "What am I going to do?" she thought.

The tree grass' deep crevice spared her life, impeding her careless elusion from the intangible threat. She must have striven to get out, but succumbed to a delayed unconsciousness at the crevice's entry she found herself at. Her body slumped onto its left side against the masquerading tree's trunk; her head rocked a bit to the right almost regarding the clouds. Her eyelids, ajar to a peek. She must have slid against the crevice's sloping interior.

A figure aligned next to her in the periphery, difficult to discern through her blurry vision. An exquisite Fairy male in a fine trendy tunic outlined with a nice embroidery of small obscure circles. The circles configured into moons and dandelions upon better viewing. He sported short chestnut hair with yellow highlights as if a dandelion plopped off the embroidery and flopped upon his head. As her vision cleared a spot healthier, she perceived her visitor showing much apprehension.

"Ood? Is that you?" she attempted to mutter in her perplexion. "Seriously? You could not wait till I returned **hollow**?"

A loud crude squeak erupted overhead, forcing the Fairy queen to deny her neck's tenderness and her peripheral image to conceive the squeak's originator.

The discomfort was too sharp, so she settled with a glance through half opened lids again, and beheld a flying squirrel's salivating jaws swooping closer to her with the lowering suns.

Closer... ever so closer, out of the graying skies.

"Oh, Interim..." she muttered squinting at the pain.

CHAPTER 18: The Art of Pain

S Kavir, major Quirmean city, locale of the infamous Torture House. The guards who led me through the streets to this proud butchery knew my feelings about the execution. Their harsh comments and goading disclosed their enthusiasm. Maybe season was ironic, but these unfair ironies' interferences with my attempt at accomplishment were inexcusable. Seriously...

A rather beautiful city, the streets bustled with busy kin buying or selling items—artwork, the predominant trade. An assemblage of paintings and weavings accompanied scores of sculptures. Some of the avenues had vendors' booths displayed before the eager shoppers, awaiting to see what golden payment the sellers could earn for the sunday. Some booths contained figurines while others jewelry. An assortment of dishware exhibited at another.

I had considered this craziness about something called money. Lorel Elves never thrived that way. Why not share the land? We understood not to share everything, but this excitement of little golden trinkets astounded me.

The buildings, tall and majestic, shaped rectangular and angular with few curved structures—carpentry and stoneware at its best. Moreover, the Majestic Treehouse inherited this trait from Man many seasons ago; no other home harbored such fashion. Everyone else resided within grass huts or homes stylized amongst trees with articles of nature, another form of a treehouse if you would. The Khunian Elves attempted to shame us into respecting our forest. Nonetheless, carpentry became a skill handed down through the generations to a select few to maintain the Majestic Treehouse's upkeep.

We were far from mundane to not have our own artwork in Lorel, though minimal the luxury may have been. Ancient royal monuments scattered throughout our forest with other fanciful projects. We also possessed our own glass dishware, in contrast to our Khunian neighbors who defied anything of Man.

The Elvin Protectors of Khun avowed to never visit, so disgusted by our perceived constant disrespect for the trees. However, Lorellians were allowed to visit Khun as long as they adhered to Khunian edicts. Lorellians made rare visits, except for mine. Khunian law, too rigid for my kin, hindered the desire to hunt, for instance. Lorellians could find better solitude anywhere in our own forest.

How did we learn of such a craft, carpentry, if not, from Quirm? We even knew sewing. Did we learn this from Quirm? How did this craftsmanship and artistry ever happen considering the awkward relationship we have had with Man for so long? What was our past? Why did I not know this information?

I realized I did not know anything about our past. Was our history erased? Achal, goddess of memory, why did we not know this—our history?

Everywhere I became aware of Lorellian slaves cleaning, carrying, or displaying items. A number of Lorellians watched after mischievous Quirmean bloodchildren; others performed chores around the stores they toiled for; and if any performed their job wrong, a good whipping came to order.

A female scream erupted not very far away from my location, jerking my head in the plea's direction. A belt thrashed an Elvin female dressed in rags outside her assigned store. Her smallest features did not escape my keen carefulness despite her bedraggled hair.

Olives... the aroma of olives... My heart sank... my beloved Thalla.

"Please, Aman, I am tired!" she cried. This final and much needed testimony tore deep into me. This slave... my Thalla so close to me.

"You shall not rest until you have finished with your work! Get in there!" Aman belted her again forcing Thalla to run in crying.

"Thalla!" A spear's endpoint struck my posterior knocking me to the ground. Two guards pulled me up.

"Come on and quit your yelling," my assailant ordered. The twisted tour continued. Thalla, my vengeance for you would be swift. Man would suffer for committing such travesty.

Deeper into the city we journeyed. Quirmeans bumped into one another in the hustle and bustle of discovering. Not far away from us, beyond a set of iron gates, the oblong Torture House loomed. This location, like I figured, was where Quirmean official buildings existed—the city's center.

The Torture House, a smaller unit than the surrounding courthouses, an awkward windowless boulder with one portal, rested atop a set of steps on a steep hill raised in the middle of a crossroads. Thick marble walls muffled tortuous sounds within from leaking out of the structure. This bland design quelled the artsy passersby's uneasiness. How odd everything was designed beautiful to mask the hidden ugly.

Once we paraded through the pretentious structure's lengthy hallway, the interior appeared different. The hollow foyer's doors and interior walls were constructed of thick oak wood. Few torches braced against the walls and the few outlines created exhibited an eerie form onto them, as well. The dust in the air caused a guard to sneeze. The wails of the tortured chilled my soul upon descension underground via a stairwell to another singular world.

Oh, Achal...

The Torture House's rooms could not compare to Rondo's private one In his palace at Gablen. The first room filled with stockades and whips, however, near the center some Lorellians' hands and ankles attached to these stockades, exposing their posteriors to the executioner's delight. A crude scent introduced us to another room containing a huge pit of boiling lava. Cool red outlines were visible from within the gases pouring out of the pit. I shuddered witnessing my kin being pushed in, trailed by terrifying screams. Against a wall in another room, shackled Lorellians presented as easy targets to the knives being hurled at them. We were Man's entertainment!

With each passing scene, my anger intensified. I tried to calm myself, but fell short because of my ignorance toward meditative practices. If my bonds were not so durable, I would break loose and kill every Man here until my season came to an end. How terrible this predicament my kin faced... my kin who always sought to enjoy love's pleasures and beauty's visions. Now, their seasons must end with something opposite from what they always believed.

But in the midst of this cruelty, I notice many of the tortured in these rooms were elders and many of them being asked the same question about a Jode's whereabouts. What was the Jode? This Jode must have special qualities unique to Rondo to make him order his men to get answers from the elder Lorellians. Not even I knew about it, so why torment so many Elves just to know?

The next corridor seemed to slope farther downward a little. Deeper the corridor progressed into the earth as if engorging the underground with a fanciful treat. An unlocked doorway became access to another hall. Cells dominated this area, each filled with many elder Elves awaiting maltreatment. Some of the lucid elders recognized me and ran to the bars crying for me to save them. Anxious hands reached out for my clothing. The hall seemed endless with their laments until a solid wall concluded the long path of sorrow.

I realized the prisoners who did not seem lucid were, in fact, lucid. They knelt with their heads down like some of the bloodchildren at Khun, these proud Lorellians in deep thought. They had accepted their fate and had found their own resolve. I did not know which side made me prouder—the lamenters or the meditators. I could not identify with the meditators, but the strength they retained for calmness under such misfortune I found noble and respectable.

I wanted to fight... I wanted to kill.

Moreover, I almost felt guilty wishing I could reflect like them in honor of our goddess, Achal. Our goddess of memory and history, yet I felt as if I dishonored her. We were not a fundamentalist race like our Khunian neighbors. We did not pray daily to our higher power like Blasmle and Rungna would. We never demeaned her, but we did not feel the need to pray on a regular basis, neither. Did she really abandon us? Did you, Achal? Could Man's emperor be right?

A lighted archway presented in a short distance. A squad of Demonguards arrived prompt with two captives before our admittance.

"Take those lowlifes back to their cells. They will be executed another day." The guards' superior shoved me to the Demonguards.

The two captives in tattered shirts and trousers, an elated elder Elf and his probable mate; but, when they noticed the candidate replacing them, they hesitated.

The elder male knelt down at the captain's feet. "Please, I beg you. Do not kill him. Take our seasons instead—"

"Yes," his mate echoed, "We will do anything, but please spare his season."

The captain kicked the elder male away, "Get away from me, filth," he snickered.

The defenseless elder careened across the hall.

In anger, I lifted my foot kicking the guard in front on his butt, knocking him onto the ground. I barreled closer to the startled captain, but the rest of the guards subdued me before I could get nearer.

The elder Elves whimpered returning to their cells at the corridor's end. They began to cry. A cry not of mercy, but of revelation. A revelation accompanying the fact the last of the royal line would be extinct.

Oh, great Achal, preserve us... how odd for me to have used my goddess's name in vain. I did believe in her. I did—just not as voracious as a Khunian believed in their god of nature... or some of my kin believed. Were we being punished?

The archway led to a damp room with rhomboid columns; the walls hung with much decoration. Grand statuettes entailed possible emperors prior and samples of Quirmean culture. Odd how a statuette representing a riding hunter in pursuit of a fox reflected a truce our estates held so long ago. Situated on a huge chair at the chamber's opposite side, Emperor Rondo. My Achal, he liked to sit a lot.

"Rondo why are you doing this? Why are you torturing the elder Elves instead of placing them in enslavement?"

109

"It is me who should be asking you questions, not you. Nonetheless, I will tell you. These old Elves are of no help in being slaves, and they will take up too much room if kept alive."

"You control all this territory for your empire, yet you will not allow the elder Elves to work upon it for you? You just want to kill them?"

"It is the word of Xurchon."

"Xurchon? Do you always listen to his wishes?"

"He is my god, and I trust him."

"You would worship the God of Evil, instead of Istratos and Welna?"

"He is not evil. He has guided and shown me that peace arrives after power. You may think this is absurd, but Xurchon told me the secret truth behind it. He has taught me to abhor you Elves for it was the Elves who lost the Jode and caused his domain to diminish. If it were not for him, my people and I would have been unaware about the turmoil our gods were leading us into."

"Istratos and Welna would never do such a thing to Quirm."

"Since when did you know the traitorous gods of Man?"

The rest of the guards entered after silencing the prisoners.

"Rondo, your thoughts are so heartless."

"Maybe I am heartless to your people, but my thoughts are always correct. Unshackle him, guards. I tire of listening to the screaming of these petty old Elves. I hunger to discover the scream of a young one, including if that young one is the last of the royal family whom I so dearly wanted to kill first."

The guards did as ordered and stood a bit away. The floor broke away beneath me. I hurtled into a new black abyss, the emperor's raucous laughter followed. The unexpected surprise alarmed me a bit. Executions were not the Lorellian custom; not even Khun executed, but I guess the Khunians would execute an enemy, if need be.

My infravision enabled me to perceive an abysmal hole with the bluish chasm's building encroachment. I braced for the landing... an unfortunate sharp pain struck my ankle. The hole seemed large and circular. The blue glow issued from the walls conveyed to me the chamber's moistness.

A shuffling sound... from behind.

In an instant, I turned to confront my adversary. From the darkness emerged a lion's red image with giant unfurled paws and a distorted human face. The creature's cavernous maw produced three rows of sharp teeth. As the creature pressed forward for the attack, a nefarious scorpion tail curled above its mass.

A shiver coursed throughout me for I knew this creature—a manticora, one of the fiercest beasts from the Dark Plains, the King of Kills.

What was the manticora? A Quirmean who had done something so heinous that accursed him or her to thrive this way? How could this monster not be?

I stepped on my sprained ankle; a whimper slipped my lips.

The manticora attacked with full force; I leapt out of the way. The ferocious manticora did not hesitate when it sensed me and attacked in my direction. Though caught by surprise, I rolled out of the way.

Somehow, the King of Kills knew my whereabouts and would not stop attacking me until I exhausted. Oh, how I wish Welbern was here at my side rather than this sprained ankle… The manticora would not stand a chance if I had any weapon at my side or my telepathy.

Bewildered, my bestial executioner seemed to search for me as if not identifying my whereabouts. This fortune encouraged me to try a direct assault. If I did not, my seasons would end. I edged in on the manticora with clenched fists, hoping my predator would not notice me.

The manticora reacted with a swiftness. The King of Kills knew! A huge right paw flung me toward the room's other side where large objects amassed.

Bones—ominous remains of those that fell victim to this gruesome demise, so many their stench began to obstruct my sense of smell.

The rapid manticora advanced upon me.

Pain, sharp, maligned the left side of my abdomen when I tried to get up. My hands clutched my side to ease the pain. My fingers slipped into a deep gore in my skin… blood. The creature wounded me and would leap upon me with another crushing blow if I did not defend myself quick.

Frantic. I felt for a weapon in the rubble as I held the manticora's muscled throat at bay. The heavy monster toyed with me with clawless paws. This act, I ventured, would be the King of Kills' hubris.

Alas, I found something. The item's texture, smooth enough to say, was another type of object but not desirable. A gnawed bone slid between my fingers—the manticora's teeth marks feeling like tiny pins.

My hand slipped upward from my spot on the manticora's throat, ending a little closer to ravenous jaws. The slippage spared me little occasion to acknowledge if the correct bone was picked amongst the choices.

Reflexes, though quick, could not stop the creature from injuring my hand with eager sharp teeth. With my bleeding hand out of the way, the beast took a chance in trying to rip my throat from a snug place. As the cavernous orifice of terrible incisors sought toward the desired destination, I dodged lower.

My spine pressed upon the ground. I struck out with all my might with my weapon: a long rib. I gored my would-be killer through a vulnerable right cheek.

The manticora retreated in anguish belting out immense roars. Bewildered, my hunter kept looking for me—the scorpion tail stabbing about in the air seeking prey to snare.

An idea came to me. Never was there a moment when a beast, like the manticora, could see in such stygian blackness. The monster may have a cat's body, but its face belonged to a Quirmean, so maybe this beast depended upon two other senses: hearing and smelling. With the wounds I placed upon my opponent, the manticora may be disoriented. Now, I could use the King of Kill's advantage to its disadvantage.

A familiar bluish-yellow effect stirred not far away from me, minute in size, reducing from its initial radiance.

My infravision skimmed throughout the bones lying about, detecting a skull's azure hue. Taking the skull at hand, I threw my globular object toward the lair's outlying wall.

The manticora turned toward the decoy's sound, attacking with a slink.

While my foolish opponent fell for an old trick pouncing upon another bone stack, I made my silent crawl to the glow. The journey, a bit sluggish.

Ugh... my hand...

Closer and closer, I secured the gap between the glow and me. The brighter the glow illuminated the closer I crawled. The light uncovered a long rib, some of the bone's meat gnawed off, sticking out like a withered twig from the rubble. The uncanny glow swathed the gnarled bone still attached to a crooked spine. Although motionless, the rib seemed to vibrate as though still reaching for the season cheated.

A burgeoning fatigue increased the closer I arrived toward the glow. I hoped the lethargy was not from blood loss. The intruding light reversed itself—diminishing.

I could sense an irresistible force beckoning to present to me what the unlucky skeleton possessed upon my arrival. On the rib's distal end an odd broad loop illuminated the eerie glow. The irresistible force seemed to exude strongest from the loop itself. The force compelled my hand to grab the loop!

The strange artifact, if I could call the crystalline object one, exhibited a striking semblance: multifaceted with multiple colors and interesting blackish shades. Could this inscrutable artifact have any connection with the attractive item Rondo held for everybody to observe? Were those shadows in the case holding that item another sinister light being emitted? How did the angular object get on this rib?

I snatched the unusual object. The bluish-yellow glow dispersed, an indistinct corona encompassed my hand. My wrists lightened as the mystic bracelets dissolved, blended, per se, as a waif gas within the haziness.

Mysterious echoing voices besieged me from all sides, their distressful commands eager to aid me. "*Put-put-put on-on-on the-the-the piece-piece-piece.*"

I turned to see if the manticora regarded the voices. The King of Kills did not, but the irregular atmosphere in the haunting lair made my hunter suspicious. When the beast noticed an actual skull as its potential prey, a change in posture acknowledged me next to my eccentric torch. With a tremendous roar, the aggravated manticora bounded straight at me.

The angular artifact slipped onto my middle finger with immediacy. The residual light dispersed. The voices became more fervent, more forceful, to help, "*Focus-focus-focus psy-psy-psy-chic-chic-chic ener-ner-ner-gies-gies-gies u-pon-pon-pon the-the-the piece-piece-piece,*" they echoed.

Telepathy? I did not know how these voices knew of my divine right or how they could bypass Rondo's mystic barricade, but if they wanted me to focus my powers upon the unusual artifact, so be the advice honored.

The moment my psionic barrage doused the fragment, I could feel an unusual zing surge into my body. The vigor initiated as a small tingle in my palms, then from there the vigor flooded through my arms all the way to the soles of my feet. This phenomenon I had never felt before exciting me in all parts, except my brain—the base of all my power.

Instead, a menthol coolness penetrated my mental faculties. An unbelievable force mingled with my thoughts and memories compressing them into my psyche's deepest niches. My mind and eyes, alas, were not mine! A presence roamed throughout the coolness.

The voices returned, "*Fight-fight-fight-back-back!! Stop-stop-stop its-its-its con-con-con-trol-trol-trol!*"

A psionic battle ensued within me. Heat coursed in my vessels causing my blood to boil. My head began to throb with pain. My eyes began to burn. The heat was overcoming the coolness, forcing the freshness to go into submission... but I wanted the coolness... needed the calmness... the coolness enthralled me with laughter and joy... drove my torments away.

Yet, the menthol coolness also wanted to own me. I could not allow such control, for my mind belonged to me; none shall own my mind...

The coolness dissipated permitting the psionic heat to reign, unhampering my vision. I shielded myself with my arms, expecting the manticora to make a decisive vault.

The King of Kills did not leap; rather, the monster's crimson hued silhouette dined where a wounded shape lay, gnawing on a partial eaten arm, ravenous smacking accentuated unending hunger.

Incredible! I found myself on the pit's opposite side, but how did I get here? Could this piece have performed this stunt?

"*Fo-fo-cus-cus-cus a-a-gain-gain-gain. Keep-keep-keep con-con-trol-trol-trol. Must-must-must e-e-scape-scape-scape.*"

Psychic energies resumed cascading into the piece. The encompassing tingle returned while I held the chilling phenomenon at bay. The bluish-yellow glow surrounded my hand, and my other hand as well. This power—concentrating in my extremities, felt so extraordinary. I pulled myself against the nearby wall.

The manticora sensed the light, glancing from a laborious gnawing and snarled. The creature raced at me with a vengeance upon hideous face, for instinct knew predator would not be tricked again. The boundless slain reached me before the manticora... such foul breath.

"Con-con-cen-cen-cen-trate-trate-trate!! Fire-fire-fire po-po-wer-wer-wer!"

The tingling became stronger; the bluish-yellow glow brightened bathing the unholy hole in beautiful uncanny ambiance.

The manticora hurdled.

"Fire-fire-fire!!"

Power I never experienced stripped forth from my glowing appendages bathing the King of Kills in midleap without sapping any of my strength.

More power emanated from my hands, striking the wounded beast in a vengeful brilliance. The erratic infrared glow licked about the helpless form, glowing redder as the beast began to flare up in more voracious flames. A whimper slithered from where a roar of hunger and delight had once produced.

"Si-si-lence-lence-lence it-it-it."

But how? I did not know—magic? That gift was not our race's divine right from the gods. Could this artifact, this piece, be magic? Could I have been conjuring magic spells all this while?

The manticora's mighty maw opened again to let out an anguished yelp. My hands gestured in a way I could not understand, a glow shimmered around the King of Kills, depleting the mighty roar; consuming the room in such total stillness. Lorellian hearing may not be as sharp as a Khunian Elf's, but I knew I could not hear anything at this moment. We could hear the slightest rustling in the bushes, but not someone tiptoeing from behind or a cockroach's skitter. Nonetheless, I knew. I knew. I absorbed everything.

How nice an irony for the hunted to turn into the hunter making the hunted justifiable in his redress. The flickering flames revealed a bestial gaping maw brewing with pain; no longer satiated with joy. My lips perked to a smile.

The tingling within my hands grew wilder like the buzzing of angry bees. Magical bolts exploded from my enchanted fingers connecting with the manticora's mane, replacing it with a radiant wreath melding with the burning.

The manticora's fearful screams could not be heeded, but another problem had aroused: smoky tufts floated toward the cracks on the false floor above. More unwarranted problems could need justifiable attention if the fumes seeped out.

The fumes began to deflect away from the uplift with another instinctive gesture from me, turning downward accumulating about the manticora's smoldering form. A force field, transparent to normal eyesight though not to my infravision, materialized trapping the King of Kill's corpse and the black smoke as a unit.

This fragment's power, so extraordinary. Never had I ever witnessed magic of this magnitude in Zaendara. Okay, maybe in the possession of mythical magical beings such as Swen... and Demons... yes, Demons as well. Oh, Achal, my goddess, the legends must be coming true.

But, are there gods or have my kin been praising apparitions? Xurchon... Rondo believed so heavily in him. Why question my beliefs? And, now, to think of it, was there such a thing as a... Jode?

I grew weary from my injuries. The pain had gotten worse. Escaping seemed fallible if I did survive. Alas, the end-of-seasons would call for me just like all the estates.

"*Do not give up hope, my bloodbrother.*" ... the voice... familiar.

My interest piqued; I looked about. "*Methelo? Is that you?*"

"*Yes, Ygl, it is I.*"

"*But, where are you? You are not within my sight?*"

Another familiar voice interrupted. "*We are within this jodepiece, Ygl.*"

I stared at the angular artifact shining on my finger. The glow's iridescence faded; the magic had dispersed. "*Rolando?*"

"Yes, it is I, and, Sylvia, as well."

"But, how? Help me. I am confused."

"We are sorry, Ygl, for having vindicated you in such a manner, but urgency is so dear at the present moment," a female voice said.

"Sylvia."

"Yes, it is I. We survived, but only for a short while in this small piece of the Jode cut to form this band you wear. Our bodies may lie shredded in this pit; nevertheless, our thoughts are preserved."

"You mean to say I have found the Jode?"

Sylvia continued, *"I see the wounds must be inflicting more pain upon you than we thought. The Jode, Ygl, is a much larger jewel with high mystical properties so immense that it could spell danger to all the estates. The piece you wear on your finger and the small artifact dangling from Emperor Rondo's neck are both small cuts from the whole. Powerful they may be in such a small size, each was passed down through generations until they came into Rondo and Methelo's possession."*

"If Rondo wanted to, do you think he would be listening to our telepathic sendings?"

Methelo answered, *"Even if he could, he would not be able to hinder your spell of silence enveloping us. Both gems have equal power. They come from the same source."*

"By whom? They were cut by whom?"

Methelo continued, *"We do not know. Fortunate for us, Rondo is oblivious to the knowledge of our ownership of this gem. Guard it well. He has better control of its power, but please understand, Ygl, my bloodbrother, that the Jode is incarnate evil within. You should have already experienced that beforehand. Along with its evil prowess is the capability of it to do many things thought impossible in service to its owner. You have barely mastered the fragment with our and your psionic powers—the Jode is a much more challenging task."*

"Emperor Rondo plans to find it and rule Zaendara's estates with it beneath Xurchon's desires," Sylvia added, *"It is up to you to find the Jode and warn everyone of Man's threat before Xurchon's evil plans can proceed*

any further. This is what our goddess, Achal has decreed and all Elves know her words to be righteous."

"Achal? You spoke to Achal?"

I felt a sudden lapse. A sharp sting passed throughout my body from where the manticora's claws gored me. Blood formed a large puddle upon the ground. A psychic call would only deliver more distress.

Holding my side, I tried to erect myself. "M-Methelo, I am drained." I gasped, stumbling forward...

My bloodbrother came to my aid. "*Quick, Ygl, leave your hold upon the wound. We will focus our thoughts through the jodepiece as we did before. The extra effort may diminish us. It is your season that is more important. Now, hold still and do not move.*"

My injured hand quivered as their spell delivered. The bluish-yellow glow embodied all over, centering a casing upon the terrible gash. The self-same coldness returned to restore health to my torn bowels. Nothing could be sensed; nothing could be felt, yet the coolness just drifted about cooling the injury, producing more blood. Granting me season as the mystic healing maintained a methodic pace. The glow became brighter, then glimmered and faded away, imparting fresh new skin replacing the former. For sure, the power of this fragment, this jodepiece, rendered so different from Swen's enchantments.

"I thank you, Methelo. I do not understand. How—"

"*That... does not... matter now... Ygl... my gracious bloodbrother... Please forgive us... If I had only known... it would have made... everything... a whole lot better.*"

"Methelo?"

Sylvia answered, "*He is only... tired from... the strain of... us healing you... like... we are. Remember... we are... nothing... but, thoughts... within... this small... fragment.*"

Rolando interceded, "*Hush, Sylvia... let me speak... while I still... have energy left... within me... Please listen to me... Ygl... Prince Kute... and the... Dwarven thief have been confined... in the slave city of... Chrot... Chrot is southwest of... Skavir. There... will find... mounts... also...*" His sending's vigor slackened.

Sylvia substituted, *"When you meet… escape… and find… the Jode."*

"I have an idea where Chrot is. I do not even know where to begin or how to escape." Chrot, a city of food vendors despite its reputation of being somewhat filthy. Since much livestock was sold and traded there, the citizenry tried to downplay the reputation despite the challenging upkeep. I guess slaves had now become the new article of trade.

Trade: an unfamiliar word to us, simple Lorellians. We did maintain a treaty with Man allowing them to hunt in our northern regions provided they compensated us with clothing and certain tools. I guess that was a form of trade, nonetheless we believed in sharing our existence with our independency. We had much of these items before our rift with Quirm.

This rift? Methelo never spoke of any dispute. And why could I not remember our relationship?

"Swen… Will guide…"

"Swen? You know the genie?"

"Cannot… explain… judge her out… yourself… Use piece to… teleport… Cannot… maintain… hold… very… long… Please… have faith… in… the … gods… They… you … last…"

"Do not worry, Sylvia, Rolando and Methelo. I will." Our linking withered away. *"I will."* I tried to search for the telepathic frequency… space— nothing but space… they were gone. A tear saturated with purpose rolled down my cheek.

My kin's knowledge of you, quite puzzling, my mysterious Swen. In view of genies being of nonexistence, Methelo, Rolando and Sylvia were the sole Elves aware of yours. How unusual. Sylvia's advice to judge you could be a hint, and judge you I should.

I must get out of here before anything happened to Plant Kute and Ding…

I remained still and focused my concentration upon the artifact, calling upon the extraordinary power to provide me an exodus out of this hellish pit. My mind expanded wider allowing boundless thoughts to roam. An awareness coursed throughout my body, but not the evil coldness' impression I experienced earlier. More like a tingle, this awareness tickled my hand again, washing over me; popping like a crackling fire.

My eyes widened to expose a spectacle. My whole body glowed with the bluish-yellow radiance! The very air became a part of me. My feet stepped into a horizon spanning a threshold through a limbo where the sunday substituted the moonday and the moonday substituted the sunday. Where love melded into hate and hate melded into love. Where the seasons came after the end-of-seasons and where the end-of-seasons came after the seasons. Where falsehoods became fact and facts became falsehood... an influx of fantasy and reality beyond sensory understandings...

A snort... a flash of waxen-feathered draconian wings... Steadfast?!

My body keeled over from the inconsistencies sifting through, an exposure insatiable. This void I inhabited, an unholy aspect between stations infamous to many as the feared Interim. A place mentioned during moments of slur or excitement, and sheltering influences beyond mighty. Ample sorcery persisted to suck a careless mage into dusky vacuums before he or she could make the transfer of stations. From those undesirable depths, an existence uninviting to anyone. I would not dare to plummet. I hoped I had nothing to worry about as long as this small powerful piece, this jodepiece, assisted me throughout.

The lingering scent of aged pine... a hazy scenario materialized... shelves, cabinets, drawers, quiet, and... weapons. Yes, this must be the shop.

I looked behind me to check the shop further. Rather than that scenario, I realized the teleportation had not yet completed. A part of me, an indistinct second self, still lingered at the pit stimulating my phase through. A charred manticora's crumbling corpse heaped upon the ground not far away, never to awaken again. A spiritual trail bridging the gap between my second self and I could not be indicated.

I, however, felt a gradual fulfillment despite my spiritual trail's absence. The sorcerous air expired from me once I solidified. The pit, by inverse, changed into a hazy picture drifting into oblivion... the irregular jodepiece's humbling glow persisted upon my finger.

An Elvin female dressed in rags swept the floors. At last, I found you, my beloved. At last together.

CHAPTER 19: The Parashad

A Fairy's lackluster wings glimmered like a shimmery rainbow the moment a source of light frolicked upon them, but the hues would wither away whenever dimness crawled.

The bleakness of the carnivorous flying squirrel's silhouette enlarged itself over the alarmed Fairy queen. As the flesh eater seized upon Juna, salivating teeth could not help, but ruminate how they should feast upon her tender flesh. Too many days had expired since prey like this had been spotted in the Dark Plains' inscrutable parts.

Delicious...

Juna, frantic, knew the discomfort in her neck would never cease, but she would have to cope with the pain in defiance to her hirsute hunter. First, she pretended a swoon. Second, she kept her wings apart. She gambled her ravenous opponent would be anxious, but not very intelligent.

Closer and closer...

the flying squirrel descended...

saliva slathering jaws produced a most rapacious screech.

Preparing to react, Juna knew the ache would deprive her of her rightful speed which could be a small disadvantage against the craven predator.

The stench of chestnut-brown animal derma, unclean from past slaughters, penetrated her septum—the creature was nigh.

Muscles tensed, her spine slightly arched upward, Juna paused for the unwelcomed advancement... another screech and up Juna darted within a strained flutter of wings. The squirrel, unable to halt a speedy trajectory, crashed headlong into the treegrass's crevice.

Juna grimaced, surveying her motionless adversary from a new vantage point. This creature with the mettle to assault a member of the royal family... This creature.

Off Juna aviated into her realm, the sky.

Another intrusion eclipsed the twin suns' rays from passing through the tall weeds to tease Juna's wings. A quartet of flying squirrels encroached upon her from all sides. The law of the small to hunt in packs was well adhered to within these evil creatures' region.

Dagger at hand, the Fairy queen awaited the first assault.

One carnivorous gnawer swooped forward trying to grab her before she could move aside—a failed plan leaving Juna to slice the offending leg. The squirrel, caught off guard by its prey's reprisal, turned to flee.

Not satisfied with the mark her blade had granted, Juna furthered her attack. Down her acute blade plunged into the squirrel's thick hide. A screech rang out in a plea for assistance while the creature plummeted to the ground. Likewise, another squirrel's terrible claws clutched the Fairy queen, commencing to sever her skin and tear her dress at struggling hems. Blood rushed to Juna's brain. The throbbing upon her nape intensified like miniature icy barbs sliding along sinew.

Another of the predators zoomed toward the entrapped queen with aspirations of garnering an initial bite of so splendid a meal.

Her eyes about to burst out of their sockets, Juna's brain felt encased in a constricted box. "No! You will not have me!"

With the remaining strength she could reap, Juna tore her arm free of the other flying squirrel's grasp and bit the offending leg. "See, I can hurt you too!"

The squirrel's claws pressed harder around Juna still, forcing her body toward an insidious climax before the accompanying squirrel could attain her. With grit and determination, Juna grasped her tormentor's leg with her delicate hand. A flurry of bright light sparked within the torrid connection. A hoariness shrouded the ankle.

Her captor released a shriek, but the immense claws squeezed tighter. Juna could feel her bones on the verge of collapsing. If not for her deific gift she would have been a heap. Her tear ducts welled with her intensifying persistence.

Juna whimpered, "I do not know what you are feeling," she acquired extra white light despite her weakening grip. Smoke rose from the creature's charring hide. Curdling blood's macabre scent accompanied burnt tegument's stench coalescing with fresh sullied tissue into the atmosphere, "But it is not happiness!"

Angry Juna continued searing her prideful divine right upon the quivering claw. "Do you hear me? I do not know what you are feeling, but it is not happiness. And you ruined my outfit."

The fourth flying squirrel participated in the frenzy catching up with the third, greeting each other with strange crackling screeches as they swooped down toward Juna. Confusion set them aback regarding the Fairy queen's achievement with their companion

Meanwhile, Juna's intimidated captor tore free and away into the tall grasses hoping to regenerate another foot another day from the smoldering fray.

Juna spread her dull tinted wings to keep her balance during the immediate blood rush coursing her body. The throbbing in her neck compounded as if Zaendara's twin suns disposed there to make matters worse.

A prickling intermingled with her thoughts. A nodding influenced Juna's head. "Come on!" she panted, "Attack me! Like you did all those other helpless animals, except I am not as helpless as you thought I was…" the dizziness began to overtake her, "I have got enough power to kill the both of you!"

Her fight had diminished—arrogance to no avail. The remaining squirrels deciphered her deficient movements while still aloft and sped for their bewildered prey.

Juna fumbled for her dagger amidst the fissures of her torn outfit but could not recover her weapon from the small belt. The dagger must have fallen when the unexpected attack occurred.

"By Ethnel!" Juna muttered to herself, "I do not know what kind of fool I have been…"

Juna knew she could not escape the flapping wings bearing down not far away. Instead of retreating, the awkward Fairy rose to meet her challenge. "Damn Giants and their influence."

With raised arms, Juna sent forth blinding rays of albescent fire from malignant fingers. Focusing more on her pain rather than her effort, she misdirected her powerful rays past the onslaught toward the culminating clouds secluded in the setting.

Though a bad aim, her opportunity turned into a perfect distraction startling the carnivorous opportunists before they acknowledged what had happened. Taking advantage of the distraction, the Fairy fled. She did not care how much of a neck ache she experienced, she needed to get away. She would have avoided her two assailants in the substantial foliage, if one had not sighted her escape into the undergrowth.

Spots of green greeted Juna with prospects of camouflaging her better.

After signaling its engrossed partner of Juna's trickery, the pilose pursuers descended. Though her enemies' revengeful squeaks encouraged Juna into neglecting her neck ache's recurrence, she felt compelled to turn her head to notice the gap between them had not changed for the better. The cool breeze brushing past her face was a welcoming factor. The skillful queen dodged many entanglements thwarting her path from her would-be killers before dizziness attempted to overtake her again.

The more trivial creatures scuttled away ahead of the pursuit into numerous natural havens dreading the thought they might be the next meal.

Another issue arose to Juna as she dived around one of the huge grasses massive trunk. Could there be a likelihood that the rest of her group lingered out there, left unconscious, vulnerable, upon the ground, probable prey for the Dark Plains' wandering denizens?

Shifting her course, Juna retraced her steps to the primary attack's scene, hoping to find the help she needed there. But, no matter how hard she tried to maneuver her speed, Juna discerned she could not outpace the flying predators any longer because of the troublesome throbbing in her nape.

One monstrous rodent spotted her and signaled the other. The space between hunter and hunted began a gradual decrease.

Flower Juna got nervous. She needed a little luck for her get to the site, "*Ethnel, help me... please... help me,*" though she respected her god, she rarely prayed to him.

No answer...

Juna searched in every direction, except behind. "Ygl! Ding! Kute! Help me! I need your help!" she trilled aloud.

She waited for a response. A sword, an axe, or even an echo would have been reassuring, but none came. Only a small breeze's whisper traipsing through the weeds' pinnacle caressed her.

Could the mysterious male riding the giant bat have captured Ygl and the rest? Why? Where to?

Quirm? She paused and wondered about the horrifying experience her companions had fallen into. If Man had interned them, then Ygl's warning would be left upon her shoulders to spread. If her body did not end up between the jaws of these carnivorous gnawers, this task, the extravagant queen acknowledged, would be most toiling.

Though precision was a difficult challenge for Juna to master during her speedy flight, her pursuers acknowledged her outdistancing them. Her flight through places and spaces they could not access aggravated the pairing very much, but Juna did not have much of a chance to hide from their keen range of vision. In an effort to raise the stakes, she zigzagged between thorny plants, propelled through compacted weeds' tight labyrinths, and retraced her flight pattern. Juna felt as if the trickery would persist in her favor, but the squirrels in some way retained enough competence to track her down.

Her blood? They distinguished her blood in the air currents!

Although set on eluding this difficult situation in order to progress onto her mission, Juna noticed a peculiar phenomenon happening beside her. Another Fairy, like her—exactly like her—mimicked her every move. Every element of the duplicate's frail form from the pinned hair's crown, to the tattered dress and to the spider webbed boots portrayed Juna's absolute semblance.

Side by side, Juna's clone and she dashed through the monotonous dreary outgrowths closer to where her comrades were captured. Both their wings flapped at a simultaneous rate; their moves mirrored each other better than well.

Juna desired to enquire the mysterious twin of its origin, but considering the consequences, Juna decided to ask later. She struggled to peer to the rear, witnessing ravenous jaws advancing upon her. The squirrels seemed to take interest on her instead of her unknown doppelgänger.

The Fairy glanced at the clone, receiving an unusual surprise she would have never expected—her clone had just flown through a clump of grasses without hesitating to see what occurred. As unusual as the occurrence may have appeared, Juna knew this phenomenon could not be the worsening strain's side effects driving her to the point of oblivion.

Her eyes felt hazy and her body began to falter, but her subconscious presented her a truth behind her copy. The Fairy queen's similar being appeared to merge with the scenery. Her reflection's immaterial form commenced to wane away?!

This being must be a figment of Juna's imagination invoked by another presence invested upon salvaging Juna from certain death. Accompanying this cleverness, an unusual sense of life exuded from this being as well. Who was doing this and what was this contradictory creature?

The answer produced itself a short while after her thought. "Juna, oh just Flower, let thy tired limbs go free. Allow my will to enter thee so thy lost filaments can direct to liberty."

The voice... very familiar. However, the transmission was not telepathy. For lack of a better word, it beared an expression—one with the very atmosphere, yet the expression did not mix with the passing breeze. Juna could not remember from her damaged psyche's depth of whom the voice belonged. She did not bother neither, for at this moment the voice was her savior.

Not resisting the power's sway, Juna watched herself lengthen the expanse between the flying squirrels and she before their claws could enact a repeat performance. Her body bustled like the rhythm of crickets' wings and a warmness flailed her. The neck ache subsided; nonetheless, Juna knew the throbbing prepared to inflame when given the chance.

The secretive illusion materialized the same manner it had wilted away. Juna shivered at the sight of this unknown spirit's return. Could this spirit of illusion, this apparition, be an inhabitant of the Dark Plains and was its existence, its purpose, to lead an innocent stranger toward death?

"WH-what are you?"

"Please do not let the parashad frighten thee, oh fair Juna, for within is the strength of thy freedom. Thou are correct if thee consider it a spirit of illusion, but these creatures of evil will never acknowledge the delusion that will guide them away from thee far into the forest of weeds. So, allow thy wings the warrant of many glides so that thou shall attain a place prepared to hide."

"Swen, is that you?"

"True. It is me. I speak with thee. I sense sorrow within thy regal core for answers yet untold, but wait till the danger is passed, then together the fragmented events we shall mold."

The Fairy queen did not say another word. Instead, she permitted Swen's mystic yank to heave her away to the supposed refuge that would camouflage them from the disastrous flying rodents. The squirrels tried tracking her every move, but weariness faced them now while Juna experienced new strength flowing.

Juna squinted at a sharp pain in her nape, a reminder.

The parashad aligned with her calm and true, ready to enact its part when Juna attained her destination. As the artifice's body maintained a perpendicular posture tracing the mystic pull, nothing hindered its path. Then, twisting its head, the apparition gazed at Juna. Not a hint of emotional oddness could be perceived upon the stone-like face. The lips, unmoving. The eyelids never blinked.

A soft reverberant voice wafted out of nowhere. "Good luck, fair Flower."

Juna, scrutinizing closer at the parashad, expected to catch any change in countenance. But there was none. The parashad merely stared back with the same stone-like expression, then gazed ahead again and pressed onward with abruptness.

Juna and her newfound partner curved around a grassy bend and weaved with accuracy between the huge stems—such impractical synchronicity.

127

The squirrels, caught off guard by Juna's abrupt change in tactic, sped after her straining not to lose trajectory of a meal so exquisite.

With a swift wave of wings, Juna hid behind a bunch of weeds. Before her, stacked high one upon the other, a large mass of slender leaves loomed greeting her from the perilous chase.

Juna dove in... peeking from within the stack, she spied the parashad observing her for a short moment before the spirit zipped out to continue on an erroneous path.

Juna slipped with recession into the cover witnessing the squirrels' popping reemergence, evoking their horrible screeches of hunger. Deeper within the absurd leafy home she retreated impeded by something solid. Juna flinched and noticed nothing...

She could still distinguish the squirrels' screeches overhead hounding the deceptive parashad. The dauntless sounds became weaker and weaker as the threesome disappeared within the Dark Plains' austere patchwork.

A conspicuous voice arose from the horrible racket, a soft resonating timbre that spoke to her just a moment ago when she flew with the parashad. "Fair well." The resonance dwindled away.

"Thank you," Juna whispered.

The leaves rippled. Swen spoke, "And now my mirage shall dissolve. One thou can absolve from being a pile of arranged leaves, but the enchanted lamp that shelters me."

The leaves shimmered and shrugged, and pulsated a macabre glow causing the mirage to sway with a lenient rippling, a cool breeze blowing upon a wet picture. The withering arrangement initiated a splitting that melted away bequeathing diminutive fragments of the beautiful crumpled lamp Juna had become accustomed to. A gem here... a groove there... until the illusion's last remnants had evaporated.

The Fairy queen admired the giant metallic structure quiescent before her half weary being. She fluttered up and peered inside the spout's aperture accommodating her head alone.

A cool breeze's resonance rushed up from within the lamp's anguine tube, but with an enigmatic variance, and Juna had no idea what the change could be.

"Come, Juna, enter my lamp so we may speak, per chance. This peril the estates are endangered to face must be stopped before it can take place. We may be the only ones to carry the distressful call. Please, Juna, reduce your size and enter so we may devise a proposal," chanted Swen.

"I will." Exhausted Juna complied.

Staring at the lamp's tiny vent, Juna concentrated upon the gift granted to all members of her royal lineage. She had performed the same act a mere days ago with much ease, but now she would need to concentrate harder because of the tricky neck ache. Her nape commenced to inflame with an immense fervor disseminating past her skull's base. The fervor permitted her skull's anterior to throb with the heartbeat of burning pain. Nonetheless, Juna's weight became wispier. Her body mass reduced as if the atmosphere ingested upon her physique's every visible feature.

The Fairy knew the reason why she must fight the annoying pain. She knew the dire risks at hand. What of this Jode? Would this Jode halt Emperor Rondo's schemes or would the enigma just endanger the Zaendaran estates more?

She wondered if Ood, her husband, would acknowledge the menace that had been aroused. If he did not, she would be alone in her belief. Nevertheless, the Fairies, though quite larger in numbers compared to the Giants, were miniscule in stature.

What was the purpose of that earlier vision of Ood? Was she feeling guilt for absconding without telling him of her intents? Would the Fairies be powerful enough to hinder an emperor and his Demonic allies from acquiring the Jode?

"Oh, what a fool I am," Juna thought to herself. "Of course, Rondo will obtain the Jode before they do, as a matter of a fact, he will obtain it before we all do. For only he knows what the Jode looks like and only he knows what the purpose of finding it means."

She attained the suitable size required to enter the lamp's aperture. The infinite depth beckoned her to submit within an ethereal tunnel.

While her worried thoughts drifted elsewhere, the pain's burning throb caught her off guard. Still fluttering, she restrained her head on both sides fighting to repress the pain from depriving her of the much needed information Swen needed to narrate.

Soon she confronted a new battle: power. The pain's power to deny the potent distress; and, her power to maintain her position aloft as she continued her struggle or else succumb to her internal enemy's might and descend to the ground farther away. Weakness seemed so rewarding; her attempt was too late to errand toward. Her sluggish wings proceeded levitating her tired form aloft.

Her skull inflamed akin to the Interim's deepest pits' torrid incalescence. Focusing too much on the inflammation, she would have plummeted toward a grassy grave if not for a sudden gusty wind and nebulous gas jutting from the lamp's aperture. The mixture enveloped her—a billowy deliverance from uncertain death. Supernatural tendrils, culminating with her anxiety, commenced to encircle her, obscuring Juna from the outside world.

Juna shivered at what might happen next. A comforting coolness initiated her aggravating pain's cleansing. The pain subsided toward her nape and, with a sharp pinch, the mystic soothing terminated the agonizing debacle.

In turn, the cloud of healing gases swirled around Juna faster and faster in larger masses. The tendrils parted and dissipated with a haste situating the Fairy queen within the aperture, leaving her surveying the Dark Plains' huge grasses. Her mind and appendages felt free to move about as gaily as she desired them. Juna skipped a bit happy through her fatigue until she remembered to hasten along the crepuscular tunnel. She would have flown in a cautious course if not for the strange signal Swen emitted from so sonorous a depth.

The Fairy continued her familiar precise journey into the tube's rigid channel. No matter how abysmal, the smooth grooves sliced throughout reminiscent of Khun's arboreal thick roots or the obstacle course she survived. The passageway provided a continuity beholden to semidarkness—not darkness, nor pitch blackness—just semidarkness. A twilight very pure in nature preventing any penumbra from forming upon the passageway's spherical walls. No torches were evident within the tunnel, but a miniscule amount of light sliced throughout the passage providing Juna a glistening pathway to her destination. The light brightened as she neared. Inaudible vocals evolved into more distinct incantations.

When she arrived, the scene had changed from what she had awaited. At the Forest of Lorel, when Juna had entered the lamp, she beheld Swen interned within the selfsame mystical gases lamenting for release from the bondage. The genie's imprisonment thrived at the center of a beautiful, yet barren, room with cushions sprawled everywhere. Now, the nebulous gas' slender, meandering elements whisked about the hull's access. The communal twilight thrived here as well. A certain luminance appeared to shimmer through the fog, a shining substance for the murkiness itself. There was no doubt this hull of obsidian blackness granted extensive light to the spout's crepuscular passageway.

Juna proceeded into the foggy abode. A sudden flow of exhilarating verve seethed all about her body as if compelling her to romp about in her childhood's joys, a part of the gas' defensive technique for the ensnared genie. Juna remembered this trap and trudged on to the warmth of another unusual light source radiating farther within.

"Come, come, and come here. The direction thou walks. I am near," soothed Swen.

Bright aberrant rays speared through the domicile toward Juna resembling the tunnel's shimmering path, a silent symphony of peace and sweetness. The obsidian nightfall shimmered brighter as the internal light speared through, pass the queen, and toward the channel's outlet.

Flimsy layers rolled away as Juna followed the dancing gleam up the new path terminating at a thick frothy entry. Juna treaded through the frothy ingress and noticed the area where this brilliance generated. At the epicenter erected a column of violet gases containing a female's figure positioned within. The hem of the being's dress could not be detectible.

"Swen?"

Endless amounts of nebulae jutted upward, creating a ceiling above Juna's bobbed head almost discernable from the twilight environment.

Radiant energy pulsated from the apparition's bosom enveloping their meeting arena in a hemisphere of sheltering luminance. Residue from the violet gases' column jutted forward embracing the luminance, surrounding the inhabitants at the circle's perimeter, housing the two beings.

Mysterious Swen hovered before Juna, both the same size. The marvelous genie's tresses of hapless strands remained lost in her cosmic folds.

Jealousy tinged Juna, "You have such pretty hair…"

Swen's twinkling eyelets could never obscure the appreciative sweetness hidden within. Her personal nebulous gases remained amongst her contours. The violet gases' column persisted in the backdrop.

"Swen," Juna's lips pursed, "why do you request me to talk with you inside your lamp? We have a continent to save."

"If I may converse with thee in privacy. For there are secrets I must relay to help thee along thy way."

"You mean to say I am the last survivor to the group?"

"As sorrowful as it may seem, I fear it is thee. My master has been captured along with the rest, so it leaves thee to take the test."

"A test! A test? You speak in the same riddles again. You are just as mysterious as that parashad."

"It should be no mystery to thee, my vivacious friend. Thou should know it is more than thy illusion, but also thy spirit of death and thy apparition of destiny. If thou does not believe in thyself, then condemnation becomes thy well."

"Death? What is death?"

"The end-of-growth let not be sown."

"The end-of-growth… I give you a thousand apologies for my error, but shall we now get along with what I came here to speak about?"

"Yes. Let us not speak here. Enter my chamber no magic will pierce. I must tell thee what I know of the terrible thing that will guide Zaendara's woes." Swen melted into the column.

"And magic will pierce all this mess?" Juna muttered to herself, surveying her surroundings.

Juna proceeded farther into the lighted circle speculating whether or not Swen related about the Jode or something else. The genie's vocal tone did sound a bit distressing, as if… as if abiding away from even a genie's reach another enigmatic danger lurked.

The former gases trundled along Juna's keen cornea without a sting whatsoever. Upon her foot's transit, the column of ever rising fumes brushed passed and away.

Juna arrived in an opulent room of substantial size. Shaped cushions strewn about on the apparent excavated floor. Bizarre designs, sigils maybe, drifted on vaporized walls.

The genie sat, or hovered, upon a comfy couch of flushed color with a florid design. The selfsame fumes caressed her, smelling like licorice's deep roots. "Welcome, fair Juna," she sounded so normal—no subtle echoes in the wind; no slivers in the air, "for entering my beloved abode so we may speak in secret about the infamous Jode."

Was Swen weary? She held her composure well.

"What is the Jode, Swen? Is it a curse? Is it a Demon? A... a long-forgotten member of Zaendara who has returned for revenge among the **roots** that dared place him on exile?"

Juna plopped upon the couch; unnatural floral perfumes circulated reminding her of joyous days with her husband, King Ood, at the Cory Mountains...

"Whoa!" Juna collected herself. "Please tell me what it is? Without you this whole search would be senseless."

"Thou will see the Jode since thee is the only survivor of our only hope," her lucent fingers caressed the scarlet material, "when my fingers touch my Couch of Omniscience, the fibers shall turn to show thee the answer."

The genie's slender digits pressed into the velvety fabric allowing a sweet floral essence to exude forth thru the intervals between. Faster and faster the dismembered fabric cycled. The remaining material's color receded within the depression's range.

Engaged Juna stared at the spectacle's focus, expecting to observe what she had craved she had not witnessed: the center of this synthesized spiral, with a likeness to an air-eater's interior, peeled away into... nothingness. Would the disembodied fabric tear away from the couch?

The nothingness developed into a semi-crimson pigment, initiating a mixing and a turning, and a swaying. A deep scarlet epicenter energized, ready to perform as ordained. Girders of orange light flashed like spikes from the developing outer rim, slicing through the swirl with intermittent recession. The mystical model's secondary girders extended farther toward what developed into an innermost spiraling rim of scarlet. The secondary girders, comparable to the twilight beyond Swen's chamber, deflected off that scarlet rim, instead of slicing through like all light rays should. These bouncing girders plucked back the inner spiral, meshing the spiral with the circulating encasement. All magic performed between these boundaries could not escape nor be harmed.

Now a perimeter, the scarlet axis continued its gyrating orbit, larger in its abandonment, exhibiting a promising commencement to etch onto the omniscient screen... a little swirl there... a line here and there...

Though hard to discern, the picture took structure and appearance. A little glisten presented the figure...

"What is that?" Impatient Juna blurted. "The Jode?"

"Thee will see," Swen focused her chant, "Let the contour be done; let the image follow. Let the Jode come..." her fingers waved before the screen in a consecutive sort of way—pinky first. After looping around, her palms released as if supplicant for food, then they clenched into tight fists, "Let it not be hollow."

After her chant, the genie's tightened fists unclenched allowing a soft twinkle to abscond from the mystic cavities secluded somewhere between her palms and space. The twinkling blended with the screen.

Swen's magic assisted in accelerating the solidifying of the figure. An unwieldy jeweled lattice pronounced into view. A multifaceted orbicular honeycomb exhibiting a variety of bright colors, including stimulating tinges of interspersed shadows and protective wrangling thorns. Power, unusual power, emanated forth within the bleak void's environment.

"By the gods and goddesses!" Juna's bewilderment retained more interest than surprise. "You mean to say that beautiful jewel is the one thing causing all his strife?"

"That is the Jode causing all this woe."

Juna jumped up, arms crossed behind her posterior staring at the gaseous shifting walls' bizarre designs. "Just think, Rondo arousing war between all the estates for that—for a gem."

"Do not be foolish, Juna. There is more to this than thou knows of."

"What do you mean?"

"The Jode has power unlike those that a god would endower. Magic dwells within its womb, enough to raise the dead from their tombs, enough to break down mighty mountains, enough make oceans into fountains, enough to make a king a peasant, enough to tame a mob of Demons rampant, enough to deny life its wood, enough to perform wondrous things for all that is good, but if ever it fell into the wrong hands, evil, much evil, will touch the land."

"Dead?"

"The end-of-growths I do not boast."

"Life?"

"Life is growth. The best of the sown."

"Oh… then why do we wait here? Let us just pluck it away from your magic screen out of wherever it is at." Juna slanted closer.

"Because it appears to be here, the Jode is not near residing far away where only a seeker's perception may lay."

"Then there is nothing to worry about. All we have to do is reach through and the Jode will be in our possession." Juna extended her hand.

Swen, alarmed, stopped Juna. "No! Stop! Do not let thy hand enter in unless thee wants to embrace the Interim." Her detached hand appropriated the startled Fairy's wrist. With an abrupt wave of her other hand, the sweet genie dispersed the screen from her Couch of Omniscience.

Juna gawked at Swen and at her captive wrist in a contoured grip that felt so mortal, yet divine. She gasped. With a sweep of chill, the queen's intrinsic life imploded, then exploded at once. Her gulps and sighs melded into one.

Juna snatched her wrist away…

Regaining her composure, her shoulders drooped. "You are right, Swen, and I thank you for stopping me from doing such a foolish thing. It is just that I want to end all this before all of the other estates can be harmed. You are an empath, right? Well, somewhat… Do you not feel how I care for

135

everyone, including Ygl and the rest? Did you not feel how I felt the moment you stopped me from grabbing the Jode?"

Juna slumped upon the couch gazing at the vaporous walls. "How I wish I could have the Jode within my grasp then—then maybe everything would end and no one would be hurt.

Oh, Swen! Why would Rondo do such an evil deed?"

"Juna, it is not the work of the Quirmean. Have thee ever heard of the name 'Xurchon'?"

"I abhor it as much as I do the Interim."

"Then, thou knows he is the god of everything evil. Now, does thou believe in the sayings of Ygl?"

"Why, of course, I do. If it was not for him and you, I do not think the Forest of Khun would have been persuaded to defend itself, but now since he and the rest were captured by Quirm, this makes the expedition and the heralding worse than I thought.

Oh, how could Emperor Rondo do such a thing after all the peace Zaendara has had for who knows how long... let us turn away from this, Swen, and try to save Ygl and the rest. How terrible their predicament is up there being a hostage of Quirm. If we can save them, maybe Ygl knows something more about the Jode since you seem to hold everything a secret."

The genie tilted her head down with a slow swing, side to side. "Thou cannot greatly comprehend when my master spoke about the birth of the old legends."

"Of course, I understand what Ygl said about the legends of the past evolving into unbelievable reality. You are certainly proof of that, but that..." Juna stopped in midsentence analyzing the genie square into vacuous eyelets hoping to discover some cosmic error.

Swen remained unaffected through her brumous mane of argent wisps; not a smirk crossed her tender face.

Juna gasped. "You do not mean... Xurchon?"

"Yes, the god is real. Deadly power many will feel."

Juna absorbed the thought of the word "deadly." "By Ethnel! How can this be true? I cannot imagine this happening. If he finds that rock, the danger will be worse than before. For sure, the gods and goddesses will put a stop to him before he—"

"The gods do not have the notion to overcome one as powerful as Xurchon."

The Fairy rose and pondered amongst the sea of soft pillows lying upon the floor. The soft pillows wafted aside as if fluffy feathers hid within. Juna almost envied such surroundings. "And how do you expect someone like me or even the rest to overcome the might of a being that encompasses all of evil, including since Xurchon has sided himself with the most powerful ruler of all Zaendara? I mean that is twice the magic..."

Juna twirled around and ran to her cosmic ally, stooping beside the bewildered genie without a touch. "Please, Swen. I must know where the Jode has been hidden. Can you not tell me? Oh, please tell me, or else all this land I have come to love with my roots, and all the roots I have cared for will all shatter away before my eyes. Please! I must know!"

"I am sorry, the destination I will not attest, but she did allow me a poem of my best, a helpful riddle to the test."

"She?"

"That I am not permitted to advise. If I might but allow me silence for my rhyme to recite."

"By my wings."

> "Across the sea of sand,
> In a hidden green,
> Lies the powerful Jode
> Of unusual entity.
>
> Power to rule a world.
> Maybe even more.
> Thou may possess it
> If thee only cross the shore.
>
> Some seek it for strength
> To do what they think is right.
> No matter the possessor

Many will feel its might.

Seek the danger and
Savior of the land;
Reveal the secret
Of the treachery of Man."

The genie fell tacit awaiting her aspirant augury to impress a clue in the queen's mind.

For a moment, Juna's perplexion deepened. "'Sea of sand' can only be a region here in Zaendara dominated by sand with many hills. The Ty Desert certainly fitted in that category, especially with all those sand dunes and the knowledge of the desert being here in "the land" of Zaendara.

"Swen, I do not understand about what you mean about a shore..." Another idea crossed her mind, making her giddy. "Of course! The area between the Dark Plains and the Ty Desert does appear similar to a shore. And one can say that the cactuses and other vegetation there can be said to be 'hidden' because of the small numbers. We should go find that Jode, and after that warn the Ogres about the Emperor's plan. With that done, there will, hopefully, be luck enough to hurry back and help the rest."

"I am not permitted to leave my lamp unless my master summons me, but do not worry, I will come with thee... to where thou thinks the Jode will be found. The Ogrean Mountaindom is where we are bound. Stand up and let my magic do its part if we are to hurry and depart."

The past fight-and-flight's consequences seized within Juna. "Can we wait a moment, Swen? I must rest to replenish myself."

"Then rest, Flower of the Fairies, for tomorrow we will continue the journey most extraordinary when Los and Num first peek over the horizon."

"Mountains. You said the Ty Desert has mountains."

"I made no assertion in my recollection."

"You said the 'Ogrean Mountaindom'—oh..." Juna felt a little embarrassed. "Uhm, hold on, you left the lamp before without Ygl's approval, I think—"

The Couch of Omniscience unhinged and lengthened, florae and fabric, flowing and unfurling, to form a plush unusual bed. The sweet aromas overwhelmed Juna so much she did not bother to query any further.

Some of the pillows drifted upon the welcoming cot. The violet vapors' color altered to a light blue hue. The obscure obsidian walls twinkled a little less allowing Swen's buoyant form to sorcerize more enveloped within the camouflage. Blossoms propagated amongst the ambiences. The unmitigated environment within the lamp's hull converted to accommodate the beleaguered Juna.

"This almost reminds me of the Cory Mountains." Juna allowed her grogginess to set within the efflorescent occurrence.

Swen perked, being an empath, she sensed something amongst Juna's candidness—an emotion she distinguished all too well. Courage's greatest companion, greatest balance would never go away. The greatest unspeakable testament suppressed behind the greater challenge. "Do not fear, my dear."

Juna hesitated caught upon the disclosure. She unraveled her buns from her gemstone headdress and shook her head liberating her hair of anymore tension.

The pillow felt nice; the silky blanket was as nice an accompaniment, a sentiment like home. "'Courage be thy shield and truth be thy sword'?" Juna yawned. "I do not know what you are feeling—"

"—'but it is not happiness' would be the rest."

The queen rendered her companion a shrewd lateral admonishment. "Well, look at you licking around the bowl of porridge you know nothing about. It must be pretty boring in here. Now, shut up. We have a continent to save."

CHAPTER 20: Sama

Sama glanced about the Quirmean Emperor's bed chamber. Emperor Rondo had a fetish for animal fells. He had fells on the walls, on the floors, and certain sized ones on particular oaken counters. The spacious mattress she convened upon sported some huge animal's pelt—maybe a grizzly bear, Rondo's esteemed catch.

Sama massaged her delicate webbed hands throughout the sericeous covering. The pelt did feel kind of nice tickling the webbing between her sleek digits. However, the bedding could never compare to the Forest of Lorel's supple grasses, a muddied riverbank or, better, the fleetness of the Fendor River.

The bedroom was a stark difference from Lorel. A huge domed window provided whatever available light, exploiting the constant replacement of the sky's twin celestial bodies. Sama did not bother to count the replacements. The day had relinquished to the gibbous moons' arrival and the forlorn Nixy could witness no little stars trailing as companions from her exhaustive hole…

She could not experience the animals' joyous sounds: no chirpings, no squawking, no scampering, and no rustling. What had happened to the existence here? What had Man accomplished? Where was the freedom?

A knocking at the door.

"Who is it?" Sama asked with hesitance.

"I bring more water for your bath." A meeker voice responded.

"Come in." Sama took in a breath, not acclimated to such kindness.

A sullied Lorellian maiden in a torn dress entered struggling with two replete buckets of water. She attempted to transfer the water to a wide alabaster basin adjacent to the bed.

A smooth delight to her, alabaster was an unfamiliar material to Sama. She slipped off the bed to assist the maiden.

"Do not help her, tall creature." At the doorway, Emperor Rondo heeded in a gray puberulent robe of certain intricate design. For an older individual, his exposed physique was undeniable to witness—quite chiseled and symmetrical. "Even she is beneath you. Now, come bathe. Rejuvenate yourself for the night and tell me all about your heritage. Oh wait, you call the night outside a 'great pearls,' don't you?"

"Y-Yes."

Whenever the moons emerged in the firmament, this routine continued unchanged with Man's emperor and each night, Sama, not a gregarious individual, exploited her wiles to amend his mind onto other matters. She did not know her origins and his inquiries developed into a frustration. However, survival depended upon dissuasion's importance.

She had no notion how she appeared in his bedchamber after the extraordinary mist enveloped her and her son, Ryl, who tried fending the mist off.

Ryl? Where was he? Where did he go? One day she would soothe the answer from her powerful benefactor. The Lorellian slaves' presence surrounding her in every juncture hinted for the Nixy mother to bide.

Rondo, smitten by her tall elegant appearance, aspired different services from her; and, without a husband for so long, Sama needed to take a chance with so strange an opportunity. "Has this Emperor not known of Nixies?" she thought. "There I go again. What are Nixies? Am I one? I must be."

Slipping her bare form into the warm bath water, Sama observed the Lorellian maiden secure the door upon departure as athletic Rondo stripped his robe to expose what he called his "glory." Sama did her best to conceal her approval. Noting her reflection in the water upon her hesitancy, she gave the image a pithier study than usual.

141

The vexed emperor positioned himself sideways on his bed to heed his guest bathing in his basin. A large bucket of soapy water with a floating sponge settled untouched to the side.

"Do you like it?"

"Yes, Emperor."

"Can you swim in there?"

"Yes, I can, Emperor." She waded. Her scabrous mammaries, as gibbous as the twin moons, floated with every concession upon her dorsum.

"I can swim, too."

"I do not think there is room enough for two, Emperor."

He hesitated, enchanted by her every swerve within the oversized basin knowing full well he could render the basin much bigger if he so desired. "Rondo is my name. You can call me 'Rondo.' I want to watch you swim, tall creature."

The Nixy almost likened her new owner; likened a certain sadness, a loneliness about him. She could identify with him. "Sama... Sama is name my. I am not 'Creature Tall.'"

"Well, then Sama, I want you to show me how you swim. I want to see. Then, afterward, tell me about your people, your kin. You have been here for the past couple of...... **sea blankets**...... why do I not know about them?"

"I will." Within the depths of her amorphous mind Sama beseeched an instinctive prayer to a Numr'c, the Nixy goddess of dreams and peace.

She spotted a solitary ivy reposing upon a mantle in the bed chamber, potted in sophisticated clay from Wyp. She never noticed the ivy prior— perchance—because she always kept gazing out the window. The admirable leaves were healthy with the lengthy vines drooping, dragging, and extending... much like Ryl's shrubbery shock. Such vivaciousness exuded from this evergreen. Life enough to bequeath a Nixy mother an auspicious hereafter.

CHAPTER 21: Sweat

Endless defined the Ty Desert. How much longer would Juna endure of this journey lugging the weight of Swen's cumbersome lamp through the arid region's environment? Wave after wave, the desert's torrential temperature ascended to embrace her. Wave after wave, a sea of the purest ashen sand whisked past beneath the coupling. For sure, the Jode must be here somewhere. Where was the "hidden green"?

Was that a sprightly zephyr or did her enervating wings try to insatiate her desire for rest? The heralding Fairy queen determined that her drive to progress onward a higher importance than respite.

That night she napped very well until Swen awoke her with a whiff earlier in the day. The twin suns had not yet peaked over the horizon. Swen must have surmised Juna needed the prompt boon before acquainting with the Ty's sweltering welcome... Oh, to have that resting moment restored if only for a short while in the unforgiving Ty.

At the ambivalent queen's minuscule size, she could surmise the desert had unrefined sands. The grains were a little smaller than the Cory Mountains' dirt. This did not mean the haphazard grains appeared like rocks to her, but more like rough pebbles. Translucent pebbles that intensified the overbearing effect of the twin suns' emissions. The rhombus granules sustained blinding her, making her journey a little more challenging and perturbing, "Ah Interim, it is hot..."

And, if the blinding glare was not enough, the persistent sweating facilitated in making Juna more uncomfortable. She had to shake her head ever so often to curtail the smoldering sweat from blotting her vision. No doubt, nature garnered enough sufficient defense for the Ogrean estate. If adventure did not tickle her soul, Juna would have sought to reside in her comfy home enjoying some sort of sweet nectar, but adventure beckoned the zealous queen.

Moreover, her adventurous spirit led to her to deem that if she wielded the white light, then should logic not dictate she should be able to absorb the blinding intensity? Of course! Juna fixated onto the Ty's glaring radiance reflecting upon her. Her respective white radiance commenced to flicker in response. Odd enough, the handle's protracted stem failed to convey any warmth whatsoever from the augmented energy. Feeling empowered, Juna continued her absorbing engagement with the radiance. With every level of her engagement, a brighter corona developed around her, hence, making the Fairy appear like the cutest effervescent spore transporting a bizarre lamp through the parched region.

Throughout the afternoon Juna would deposit the lamp down on the burning sands, minimize herself, and seek respite in the pipage's outlet— to Interim with ambivalence! She looked forward to the respite because, somehow, she felt much more rejuvenated than normal, as if Swen slipped a bit of spiritual verve for assistance.

"You are one strange genie, Swen."

To Juna's amazement, the high temperature from Zaendara's surface continued to not transfer throughout the lamp. Swen's crepuscular home persisted cool and comfortable.

"Maybe I should have a whole lot of these for the Fairy Treedom," she thought while comforting in the vibrant reflux within. If only to have a delightful cotton pillow to lay her head upon... And, no matter the astonishing brightness the Ty exhibited, the lamp's interior presented a defiant humbling environment with the consistent dim path and obsidian walls. The breather was momentary, nonetheless, as the heralding had to continue. This would be the ultimate lap taken.

"You will find the Mountaindom," she reassured herself.

Within the expanse ahead, the Ty's smooth horizon appeared less rigid blending with the more crooked. The closer Juna's biped wings transported her, the greater the area between the jagged line and the desert developed. A monstrous relief of asymmetrical rocks filled in the breadth between with sharpened boulders layered upon each other. The boulders spanned a great length of the region and did not seem to falter. The more proximate her progression, Juna realized the impediment as a wall of some sort evoking a strange majestic appeal accompanying the torrid ugliness.

Only one group of people could produce such a frightening beauty—The Ogrean estate, the "Mountaindom", was upon her. "By Ethnel…"

The Fairy could not believe her beleaguered eyes. Like a shimmering cloud, a throng of smaller beings swarmed from the desert's line. Their outfits appeared quite regal—skimpy trendy dresses and tunics. Their biped wings, lengthy and tapered, like hers.

At vanguard, a male Fairy flew much faster. Juna discerned his beauty equal to hers. His physique, not as slender, but much more strapping. She could almost etch out a reaction from his regal face. Was he yelling at her? A divine, black light sparkled about him.

"Ood? Is that you?"

A salty tear impaired her vision. Juna jiggled her head and struggled to maintain course. As she whipped her head, she spied a sprinkle of sweat splattering on a ruby positioned contiguous to the handle's right. The sweat traveled along the stern's grooves and propelled into oblivion.

Juna glanced up. The entourage disappeared.

"Where?" she gasped.

"It is the curse of the desert's heat," Swen lulled within the slight wind, "that has made thy vision a deformity.

Beware! I sense blood in the air of danger and war untold. When thou enters the Ogrean estate, thou must be bold."

"How do you know this?"

"Something has touched and marred one of my gems. A ruby, the symbol of blood and mayhem."

Juna did not utter another word. She comprehended war could not be forestalled with Emperor Rondo and Xurchon's threatening presence extending to all the estates, but what did the "blood" aspect of the gem mean? The salty projectile was a part of her person that excited the ruby.

Could the omen portend someone of her citizenry so dear to her would encounter their deaths? She shuddered at the thought.

To her right, a grouping of three cactuses materialized. Their angled branches, outstretched, fashioned a hospitable umbrella at their midpoint.

"The heat distortion did not fair, but I warn thee, beware of the misfortune unleashed, down will fall our sudden grief if we do not attain our destination planned to deny the conquest of Man," Swen prophesized.

Juna could not understand what Swen meant by this prophecy; she would not accept the warning.

She needed respite. Accessing the cacti's shade, Juna plopped the lamp and herself upon the eclipsed ashen sand. A wonderful coolness greeted her allowing her enervated wings rest.

Appreciative Juna knelt beside the lamp, waiting for the minimal sweat to perspire. At last she made it to the Ogrean Kingdom.

She stared with a yearning at the huge jagged walls. Any Fairy would have imagined what life would be like in the kingdom. And now, because of this desperate mission to lobby for an Ogrean alliance, she had an improbable chance.

A noise from above... a rustling? A flutter of wings?

Juna hesitated to activate her tired appendages for she discerned the fluttering's blithe had little belligerence. Glancing upward, to Juna's bewilderment she perceived no one aloft.

"Pixies...?" she whispered.

No one... maybe another illusion again, except the flapping continued in occurrence. Then, a smell aroused... a virtual whiff of something rotten.

A net plummeted upon her, ensnaring her. She struggled to extricate herself when another and another ensnared her fatigued form.

From behind the cactuses' branches a band of Pixies swooped. Each clad with a sword—a sure win against her dagger if she ever broke free. Some advanced with notched arrows directed at their malefactor, constructed from her new resting area's spines.

Except for the scantiness and dishevelment, their wardrobe reminded her of Lorellians: tunics, vests, tights, some cloaks, small pointed shoes or boots with pointed rear ends; head bands; and, short gloves. Most outfits modelled black while others' unkempt apparel sported three distinctive shades of brown, green, blue, red and yellow with leather as the dominant attribute. Some outfits exhibited a squalid pallor leading Juna to deem these inhabitants rather slothful.

To Juna, these garments were coarse. Her people's outfits had much more aplomb, and nowhere resembled anything rustic. Her people enjoyed appearing fashionable, not mundane or extravagant to a fault.

And these Pixies represented the mundane. Their skin, a somber hue compared to a Fairy and a Sprite, and their dragonfly wings' filaments shown much duller. Interesting enough, none could match the Sprites' lithe butterfly wings, feathery with flowing fluorescent tails. Juna's wings had misplaced a lot of its luminance.

A striking Pixy with piercing black eyes settled towering in front of her. He studied Juna. Was he their representative?

Juna initiated a conversation, prompting weapons pointing at her, hence, engaging her on the defensive.

The Pixy spokesperson had a short black beard and mustache matching his ophthalmic features. "So, you are the insectoid we are meant to fear? Do not attempt to voice a foolhardy excuse for your transgression upon the Ty Desert. You do see your fate?"

His palm caressed the side of her face. "You are the great Lady of the Fairy?"

"Juna. My name is Juna."

"Juna is your name? **Lady** Juna?"

"Flower. I am a Flower."

"A flower? Do any of you see a flower before us?" The entourage laughed.

"No, you are much too pale for you to be any flower I would be interested in."

"'Flower' would be equal to what I would think you call a 'Lady'?"

The Pixy and his entourage broke out in greater laughter.

"What a name to give to one who wishes to rule the Mountaindom with as treacherous an ally as the Giants. A 'Flower'!" He stated, "You have probably been sniffing a lot of those around there."

The entourage guffawed.

147

Juna would not relinquish. "What are you talking about?"

"Do not raise your voice."

"It is Quirm you must fear; not us! Do you not—!"

He slapped her. Juna reeled from the impact, the slap's biting sting streaking across her cheek.

She rebounded, challenging her assaulter. "Your pictures are not on my wall." An arresting light spurted from her clenched palms delineating the anger in her facial muscles. "I am not your **earth**."

The nettings started to sizzle from the contact.

The Pixies, except for the interrogator, receded acknowledging her defiant display. He smirked.

Juna could sense the air become humid. Droplets upon droplets, including her sweat, elevated to culminate in the space between the leader and her forming a whirlpool of briny moisture. The whirlpool lunged at her engulfing her, compromising her posture. Juna yelped as more splashes bombarded her netting and she.

More whirlpools sailed about her interrogator strapping themselves about his abdomen in alternating loops, a divine right indeed. He must be royalty.

"This makes two of us, little flower. When I order you to be silent, you have better be or else my wrath may have been a lot more painful than that; but I can see your 'Lady' behind your mask of contempt. Moreover, you have proven to me that what has been relayed to my **sediments**, my **mineral**, and I is most likely true. Your sediments have—"

"'My sediments'...?"

"Your sediments—your 'more than one'... sediments."

"My roots."

"... I told you to be quiet.

The Giants have proven to master the art of battle, or so legends would have us permit. We really know nothing of the Giants and your sediments, but we will not fail to acknowledge the fact you are dangerous. Your presence here, far from your Cory Mountains, has proven that your sediments are combining forces with the Giants in an attempt to overtake this mountaindom. The Pixies will meet the **end-of-shifts** before we would allow this to pass."

Juna allowed reason to overtake her frustration. "How do you know this is true?"

"…I already told you. Never have the Pixies had a Fairy enter our Ty Desert in our age. Neither have we seen what an actual Fairy looks like, if not for this moment. And, last of all, sediments of great royalty should take up **shifts** in luxury, not battle."

"Shifts?"

"The length you can breathe and thrive."

"Growth, you mean. We say 'growths.' Well, thank you for the compliment, I guess."

"Amazing. I tell her to shut up and she is defiant to the end." The Pixy entourage laughed. "Do not take what I say to you as a compliment, little Lady."

"It seems your information has a little flaw within it. My roots—sediments—have always known the arts of battle, but we are not attacking you."

"Your lies are as deceiving as your plain beauty. If you were so skilled you would not have been so easy to trap."

"I do not lie. What I tell you is all true. If you do not listen to what—"

"So, you admit it?"

"No—"

"Enough!! You have said enough. You are a liar and your presence here must remain. I do not want the enemy to know anything of the Ogres until the moment comes. And, when it does come, your feeble sediments, as well as the Giant's, shall fall before they dare attack. It is unfortunate they will be aware of your long absence and will probably ride out to your aid. By then, the Ogres will be warned and will be as ready as my sediments are."

He made an about face to his entourage barking orders. "Carry her to our **cavern**. I want her caged there until further notice. I am sure my Lady Gasma will be pleased when she sees this 'Flower' arrive."

He stooped toward the frustrated Fairy. "Believe me, she will."

The netting flopped the Fairy queen onto an interior siding with the abrupt vertical tug. A dozen Pixies hoisted the lamp like a novel grain gathered for the ensuing feast.

Without granting Juna a final assessment, the Pixy hoisted himself adjacent to her prior to speeding ahead. And, with importance granted onto any special arrival to his kingdom, "My name is Guisarrio—Lord Guisarrio. Remember that when you go speak to my Lady Gasma, little succulent 'Flower.' So succulent... yet, so plain. Oh, we are going to have some fun with you."

Juna did not tussle with her face compressing against the dowsed netting. Her protracted journey tired her enough... in addition, Guisarrio and his people's bronze complexion fascinated her, quite mesmerizing. Even more so, she could not comprehend what the eccentric markings were on their bodies.

CHAPTER 22: Thalla

gazed at her and could not regain a stoppage. Did she not notice that her mate had teleported from a beast's lair, from certain end-of-seasons, to come and rescue her from Xurchon's wrath? I doubted that. Magic did acquire many wonders. I just wished a better situation than this would be one.

I stayed observing her throughout the moonday since her owner never returned. She slept upon a bundle of burlap sacks on the floor in the corner using one as a blanket. When the sunday begun, with faith, she proceeded with her sweeping. A step toward her would have been sufficient, but I sensed she must make the first move. But she kept on sweeping with the occasional dusting of various articles and weaponry she would bypass down the aisle in front of me. She did not acknowledge my arrival at all.

The elegant olive dress she wore at our Spring Celebration tore in different places exposing various marks from previous beatings. The more I stared at those marks, the angrier I got. My anger changed to a dire need of killing anyone who dared lay such hands upon my mate.

But I could say little for myself as well. My bloodbrother and our royal blood had been taken away from me. Welbern had been acquired by this evil empire along with my new companions and that mysterious lamp. And, my Steadfast, my beautiful loyal Steadfast, my unipegon had disappeared from me forever. A bundle of rags upon myself, my sole property.

Swen... why did I just think of you?

Thalla, we must share our wounds together as loved ones should always do, but I would have expected our reunion in a different arena. The moment to speak must be now before your soulless master, Aman, entered within and witnessed an intruder upon his premises.

"Thalla," I whispered in a voice clear enough.

Her broom's oscillating motion stopped. A whimper escaped, but she would not seek the bearer stating her name. She remained motionless with her head's droop unveiling her wits still in possession.

"Please, my love, turn and see your mate in his true flesh and blood as you have seen him hence. Long separation has made us look different from before; nevertheless, I have recognized you as you should me."

"You are with the end-of-seasons. I saw you being driven to the Torture House. If not for Aman, I would have also seen you enter."

My mate placed the broom beside the pine counter to her right. Leaning against the counter, she released her first teardrop upon the dusty surface. A shifty cloud erupted from the teardrop's impact.

Thalla's head still did not turn. I did not need my telepathy to sense a struggle evolving from within her revealing the discord she had been facing at this moment.

My reaching out would make matters worse. This conflict was for her to manage alone.

I felt terrible, but patience had never been my virtue. "It is not true, Thalla. Man's chamber of end-of-seasons and torture could not hold me if not for the aid of Methelo, Rolando, and Sylvia." I swallowed my breath, a solitary impediment within my throat, regretting my error.

Her fingers, once of elegance; now of roughened marks, speared through her hair as her palms attempted to block my words from defining her reasoning.

She wailed a cry I had never heard through the joyful seasons we shared at Lorel. "You lie!" she dared not look at me, trying to gain her composure. "They have met the end-of-seasons and so have you! Leave. Please leave. I have done nothing but loved you. Now, it has all ended. Quirm has won and the Elvin race is finished."

Her words struck me with surprise and pain. "No, you error, my love. There is still hope, I believe, if we only stand upright and fight for it. Hope and the gods are still on our side. Zaendara can still be saved. Now, come, if you do not believe in me, at least allow my fingers to touch your shoulder and prove I am your Ygl in whole."

She paused.

I wished I could believe my very words. Someone needed to. Closer, with hesitance, I approached her bedraggled shape. When upon my mate, her body's heightened tremors verified her nerves getting the better of her, preparing to flee.

I reassured her, "*Thalla, my mate of purity, since when was a spirit of the Interim gifted with the power granted by Achal, our great Lorellian goddess, herself?*"

I touched Thalla's shoulder. She reacted with an enhanced shudder; then, her tremors diminished.

My hold became lasting. "*And since when did a spirit ever resurrect in solid flesh?*"

Soon my fingertips unearthed respective sides of her neck. Her skin's softness, a recurring suppleness accustomed to my pressing lips. The bonding reminded me of our younger seasons. At first sight, we had just met and fell enamored with each other without speaking of such phrases. I felt maybe she wanted to make the initial move, but my brazen behavior outdid her. When my lips engaged this spot, a little sootier because of circumstance...how wonderful her suppleness... a warmth flowed granting me the bond sustaining our original love.

My gentle fingers rubbed her collar's segments. Again, my lips sought toward her neckline's special area, placating her further. "And since when did a spirit ever express love like this?"

I kissed her neck again—a most tender kiss; the third took a bit longer. All the while holding her close.

She moved; I loosened my hold.

She stared through me with dampened eyes examining me to the best of her ability. A bruise on her cheek's upper left side marred a beauty everlasting, "You are... my love," she tried to say. "My Ygl." The words stammered out in small gulps while she cried on my shoulder.

"Yes, it is me."

Another tear rolled. A tress of her hair fell upon her face, veiling her beauty. Pulling her tress behind her pointed ear, I restored her radiance. Her smooth lips, about to gape. A lament would have become obvious, yet, past hardships would not permit this. Thalla wanted to tell me what happened, for her nature was to inform me of any past occurrences during my absence on ventures. An influx of tears streamed from her ducts, washing the dust from her somber lips.

She wanted to tell me, and she did. "Oh, Ygl, it was terrible. These slaughterers have killed our king, our prince, and Sylvia. Great Achal, give us mercy. Our kin did not have to know. They could feel... as I did... in our thoughts. Oh, how we cried. As if our very best possessions had been stripped away from our beings. But you were there, Ygl; that gave us courage. For then, even the legends seemed to come true, but when I saw you enter that unholy hole, my spirit, our spirits, fell... both for our Elvin beliefs of these ridiculous legends and because of my love for you.

And now, you return as if Achal heeded our pleas and sent Steadfast to receive you... to save our kind." Her head fell upon my chest sobbing. "Oh, please tell me, Ygl, is it true? Is there really a god of pure evil? Is there really a Xurchon? Hold me. Hold me, Ygl, as tight as you can. I need your warmth... I am afraid and..."

I embraced her. Not even the rags she wore could block the longing between us we desired. "It is better to have courage, my Thalla, than to cry. Did Lorel ever begin because the races within were of cowardice instead of courage? These past hardships have so weakened your heart and mind. Come, let me depart to you some of my courage if our kind is to win its freedom."

Of course, I lied. How would I know how anything could end? I did not have Advisor Sylvia or my bloodbrother's precognitive ability. I felt just as helpless as my Thalla but would not dare show my true demeanor.

She gazed up at me... so much tenderness... so much pain... we kissed. Our lips did not part, for this may have been our final embrace.

Subdued. Everything in the shop harmonized with the amorous sacrament of our embrace. How long we kissed? I did not know and did not care. My intent needed to soothe her and adore her more as well.

I remembered what she said about Sylvia's foretold legend, the Elvin legends, strange enough. How Sylvia could predict so far into the future baffled me. The Lorellian advisor told me that she experienced moments of intense future clearness. Why did Methelo not have these moments, after all, he was king, the most powerful of all of us? Nonetheless, the unknown appearance of a Xurchon would come to possess Man's emperor into executing the god's bidding. Man's emperor would have the Elves captured and enslaved. An Elf would escape and that Elf...

Could all this be true? Swen evolved from somewhere unknown. Giant spiders and Demons had done the same, and even this small evidence of the legendary Jode had fallen into my hands from my deceased bloodbrother's rib. And yet, Emperor Rondo did not seem at all possessed. I may not know Rondo well, but I did perceive his behavior as sane. He, at least, did not appear petulant when he spoke of the terrible name. He praised his new god.

The trembling of Thalla's body receded along with our embrace.

"Yes, my Thalla, there really is a Xurchon and his power over Zaendara's future is manifesting its effect over all." My voice, no more a whisper as the disclosure flowed true to her ears.

Gentle Thalla did not shake or cry; instead, she peered into me, searching. "What do you mean? Has Xurchon captured another other than us?" She clung closer forcing our bodies to meld.

"Yes, the Dwarves. Soon Khun will come next, but they are arming themselves for the assault. I doubt even this will stop him."

"But why?"

"I do not know. I am sure it is his nature."

"Nature," she stated with a grunt. "Xurchon is of a sour essence. One that I doubt would ever be sweetened. What could be his motive to turn his thoughts toward a peaceful continent as Zaendara? For sure, it must not be something minor."

I rubbed the edgy artifact on my finger. The facetted texture assured my custody valid.

"This is his motive." The angular jodepiece glistened. The distorted planes' colors flowed lucid into one another much like my telepathy's inherent essence occupied against it.

"Why, it is beautiful, but why go after so unusual a ring unless—"

"Unless it is imbued with certain power. This is not a ring. You see it is a piece of what Xurchon is really searching for—a much larger gem called the Jode. Methelo and the rest told me about the magical powers inhabited within it. With it Xurchon could rule all of Inner Earth if the Jode ever came into his possession.

Methelo, Rolando and Sylvia are now merged mentally within this small jodepiece, I think. Without them doing that, I would have found no way to escape the manticora or that hellish pit."

Thalla appeared confused and proceeded toward the booth at the aisle's far end.

"What is wrong? Do you not believe me?"

She turned and waited for me to come closer. "I do believe you. I mean the Demons and even what you tell me is all beginning to make sense. You know, I would never turn away from what you say, but the problem is, why does Xurchon not just come down and search for the Jode himself? He has power enough."

"Maybe it is because he fears the wrath of the other gods and goddesses coming upon him."

"Maybe, but why have the gods not stopped him? They too must know about his evil plan, but they just stand and watch him go through every phase until he gets all of Zaendara beneath his grasp. It is just terrible! Terrible and unbelievable! The legends are coming to season almost as if they were really here. This Jode emerges out of nowhere itself as if ready to fulfill a prophecy, and now... now the gods seem to have met—the end-of-seasons. End-of-seasons to the Elvin kin. End-of-seasons to our pleas."

I held her tight. "I have asked the same questions, but it is important for us to believe in them, my love. For why should Xurchon be a reality, and they do not? They are a reality and they shall always prosper. They brought me to you. Did they not? They shall do the same for our kin. It all takes a matter of moments. Is not there enough?"

"Then, why have they not cleared the skies of his evil essence? If Achal combined her power with Miredo and the rest, they would be many to his one. And what about the Dwarves? Why have not their gods reacted to this?"

Most of what Thalla inquired I did not bother to pause and contemplate, an uncomfortable affair. Where were the gods—all of them? Have we been worshipping beliefs instead of fact?

No. The belief had to initiate somehow. "This is confusing. You are right. They must not be real at all... but they must be because something must be keeping Xurchon at bay. He would not be hesitating to strike if not for something of the sort."

My theorizing did not placate a thought too much to bear, and I knew the subject needed to change before her master arrived. "We have got to get out of here. Do you know when Aman will arrive?"

"I wish he never does."

"Do you have any belongings?"

"Yes, a cloak I made, but—"

"Put it on and let us go. The streets are busy so no one will recognize our departure."

"To where?"

"Chrot, that is where they are holding Kute and his friend, Ding, hostage."

"Wait. You rush too fast. I have something to show you.

Who are Kute and Ding?"

"Plant Kute is a Giant prince and Ding is a Dwarf. They were with me when we were captured along the way to the Ogre estate."

"Good. That is all I wanted to understand, though, I am confused that a Giant looks like a plant... or is named 'Plant'... I have got something for you that I think you will like."

"What is it?"

"Come, you will see." She led me to a long counter where Aman sold his weapons. From behind the booth she brought something wrapped within a thick dingy sheet.

I unraveled it and came across quite a surprise. The first item, a huge club carved from rotund stones. The dense weapon could be mistaken for any other type, except for a particular item—the handle carved into a bear claw's semblance. No other could carry such a weapon but a royalty. Next to the club, a large axe with sharp diamond blades lay. The edges curved like the twin moons at full crescent. Dried blood splattered on the blade's surface as well as the spiked wooden handle.

"Of course. Where else could the weapons be brought to when Rondo would have no need of them?"

"They were brought here by an emissary of someone named Werkle who was interested in their value. Though, I am not specialized in weaponry, like Aman and you, I am sure these are the stripped articles of the prince and his Dwarf friend. Are they not?"

"Yes, Thalla, these are Kute and Ding's weapons."

A smile creased upon her lips. "And, now look at this." She ducked behind the booth and brought out another wrapped item.

"You do not mean...?"

She did not bother verbalizing another word. Her smile expressed enough as she shoved the wrapped article to me.

I unwrapped the item with cautionary excitement. Alas, exposed within was a broad sword with the blade's edges emitting a shiny luster. On the heavy blade's top side, along the fuller, three odd shaped runes terminated at a striated hilt with a sable globular pommel stabilizing the blade. Two dots, equidistant to each other, shown between the second and third rune.

Attached between the thick hilt and the blade, an outcropping of metal, a crossguard similar to a minotaur's horns, exhibited a similar luster. The horns jutted forth as if pointing at the runes, except the tips curved a slight away. Last, an amber gemstone centered itself at the hilt's spectacular cross section. A ruffled wreath of straight tiny blades encircled the gem, encasing the stone. Any blade could have been forged in this way, but none were at all. None, except...

"Why, it is incredible." I gazed at the sword held in my hands. A unity seethed amongst our duet—one the yielder; the other, the eradicator. This sword could not be mistaken. "We are back together, my Welbern; my DemonSlayer."

"Aman saw the weapons later when the emissary left and decided to test each one to find any uniqueness. That is when he came upon Welbern. Not only he, but I too knew your sword when I first glimpsed upon it. He then called a messenger to relay his finding to Emperor Rondo. I heard him mumbling about selling the other two, but he decided to honor his emperor. Afterward, he wrapped Welbern up within this linen and put it behind the counter where none would find it, except for my adamant inquisition. I had planned to escape with it this sunday since he left on some business leisure. I already have a mare out back and, as you notice, I found this cloak by my lonesome so as to conceal my features when I make my escape. It is not the best, but it will work."

The cloak was a bit tattered, but this disguise would have to do.

"And your escape you will make with me accompanying you along the way."

"To save the Dwarf and the Giant Plant prince?"

"For sure we will. They may need their weapons too, you know." I buckled on a back scabbard found on the shelves behind a compartment and slid Welbern snug within. "Well, let us be going before Aman does arrive. Uh, is there another cloak somewhere about here?"

"I am sure Aman—" Her brows furrowed affixing her gaze beyond me.

I reeled and witnessed a row of dusty windows she had not gotten to clean yet, and would never have to clean after our escape. However, through the dust our Elvin gaze traveled. Crowds of Quirmeans mingled about each other with their Elvin slaves carrying, exchanging, or cleaning things.

A man with graying hair did not browse the other businesses but strode to the shop. I recognized him, and so peered closer... of course, the Quirmean who dared lay hands upon my Thalla that sunday.

"So, this is Aman. Well, he will experience more of a surprise than he thinks. Go, Thalla, put on your cloak and grab the weapons in the bundles. Quickly! Before he enters. I have a small repayment to owe our little friend for the obedient ways he has taken care of you on my absence."

"Please, my love, do not hurt him." Thalla slipped through the door closing with a subtle slam. The weapons were taken along with an extra sword stored in the horses' saddle packs.

159

I could never comprehend the rewarding joy I felt mated with someone of the purest Elvin character. She, who would not allow me to harm her punisher... I would entrust the thought of killing you, Aman, but not with Thalla in my conscious. No suspicions must be aroused after our escape, but that did not mean I would not resort to other measures.

A quick psychic call flashed through the piece. The warm bluish-yellow glow enveloped my hand, disseminating throughout me. Nonetheless, I remembered the last incident and mustered an additional psionic thrust to diminish the piece's assault. Was this Methelo, Rolando, and Sylvia?

I remained in command of the jodepiece, using the sentient power to convert my form into that of my mate. My built figure slimmed into elegance as my skin melded into hers... my bones cracked a bit here... and cracked a bit there. I could sense the change most in my face with my cheekbones' painless lengthening.

Moreover, the way I imagined her became an exact replica. Flakes of dirt and dust minced upon me. Remnants of ragged dress replaced my apparel. An extensive entanglement of unruly hair poured down my posterior. When the whole transformation completed, I noticed the glow enveloped me again as before when I teleported into this shop.

The moment Aman plodded in, the glow receded. The seasons had etched on his face a certain toll taken. I would have mistaken him for an aged tree in Lorel stricken with drought. So many wrinkles receded from his semi bald head. He was not much taller than I with a bit of a slouch.

Having taken a quick glimpse of me with nothing in my hands, Aman flew into an outrage. "What are you doing standing there? You are not done with the dusting!"

He stormed toward the register with an energy unlike his age; I did not move. "Well, get started! Including with those windows! I am expecting one of the Emperor's officers here, and I expect this place spotless. Move!"

He bent behind the booth mumbling, maybe reaching for Welbern and the other weapons. "Stupid Elf." Soon he would realize their misplacement and resort to punishment.

I wanted to reach out and grab him before he could react, but I realized I would be too frail to succumb him. I would have to reverse my transformation to my true self. The eerie glow encircled me commanding my former body structure to retain itself. To my dismay, the transformation hastened too quickly for me to handle. Stings, the thrust of hundreds of blades, surged through me. A burning numbness left my head awash. Had the spell backfired?

Aman turned with greater fury, "You-you foolish Elf! W-what have you—?" His anger became horror as he witnessed me reeling in mid-transformation.

I fell against the opposite booth displaying a set of sharp Quirmean knives. I pressed my head's temples to fight the searing pain contemplating whether I had underestimated the jodepiece's power or if this misfortune was my own careless ignorance.

My bones' cracking and my flesh's contracting had at last ended. Subsequent tiredness overcame me. I had strength enough to squint from the ordeal. Then, I remembered Aman. With a quick glance back, I awaited the peril.

He lingered over me with one of his knives well at hand—the blade pointing straight at my posterior. "So, that is what you are. A shapeshifter, eh?" He grimaced. "Well, you will have to do more than change into that Elvin general to scare me, you witch. Now, tell me where you hid that sword or else I'll pry it out of you."

I dared not say a word.

"Tell me!"

Nothing. I waited for the proper moment. My next response must be perfect or else his goring will hinder me.

"Why you filthy low down—" His insult punctuated his blade's ferocious thrust. Rolling from the assault, I angled myself a little to the side.

A spinning Aman pressed another strike; my upraised arms confronted him. The bluish-yellow glow appeared again as if by instinct, but the power emanated about my hands, then jetted forth like a beam of light encasing Aman's upraised weapon... his knife shimmered and disappeared in the air.

The spell forced my hand to engage in the shape of holding a cup. The space between my fingers and thumb began to compact, and a kind of firmness formed. A shimmer glistened about my entrenched palm. The vanished weapon reappeared within my proud grasp.

Aman fell aback.

"Now, tell me, Aman, since when are you granted the right to degrade an Elf whenever you feel fit and since when did you find it pleasing to take Welbern within your possession?" I stepped closer.

I did not need my telepathy to distinguish his fear; anger still overtook him. "Get away from me..." He fell and tried to grab another knife. The knives glowed, then flew away, leaving me satisfied with my apparent mystic apprenticeship.

"Obey me... I am still your master." He tried concealing his fear.

"I believe you misconstrue me. No Man shall ever command nor use me as a slave. None have nor will."

He gasped. "You are not... Ygl."

"I am General Ygl of Lorel, Quirmean. And I do not need this dagger or the magic to prove it." I threw the weapon aside, my other hand squeezing about his throat. His feet no longer touched the ground. My strength may have not rivaled some Quirmean Men, but it did rival most.

"Look how easily you fall into my trap Aman and now even struggle from my grip's unrelenting end-of-seasons. Tell me, does Emperor Rondo know anything about my blade?"

Aman did not answer. A bountiful of tears converged with his sweat. I sneered imagining many more of his kind feeling pain like this. "Does he?"

Aman shook his head as best he could.

I smiled and squeezed harder.

"Ygl!" the gentle whisper was so stern. "Drop him."

Distraught at the rear doorway, Thalla maintained calm indignance. Her cloak exposed her form indicating her debut to have been sudden. She hurried to me and grabbed my arm. "Please, my love, do not kill him."

"You forget the wounds he has placed upon you, Thalla."

"That does not matter. It is your kin and your soul you must worry," she cried.

"I do not understand."

"Do you not see what will happen? If you kill this man without defense, with such malice, it will make you what Xurchon has made them. Fight this fury, Ygl. I know you can. Please... do not kill him." She held my arm tighter.

Enlightened Thalla proved me wrong. I acknowledged my past actions much akin to Aman himself. I know I had anger issues and, if not for Thalla, I would always harbor them. I abhorred my current conduct. For the love of my goddess, Achal, I would not be like the Quirmeans!

I threw Aman upon the floor. He squirmed a bit and then scuttled with all the quickness of a jackal toward the armament I had casted aside. The bluish-yellow glow enveloped him.

Thalla gasped...

His arms straightened against his abdomen; he fell flat on his face. The very air created ropes all about him forcing his limbs from moving... a bandanna materialized to gag his screams.

"Did... did you just do that?"

"I... I am not sure."

"That was magic?"

"Yes. The jodepiece's."

The jodepiece had again come in handy, though, I did not know how long I should rely upon such a gift instead of my skills... instead of faith and belief. This enchantment came so easy, making me leery. Was this accomplishment me? Or the piece?

In truth, Quirm and Xurchon defied me, alone, until all the estates could be warned. However, if the estates were warned would I be confident enough in escaping unscathed from any power? Even from this little artifact?

This jodepiece had protected me thus so far, but I must not rely too much upon such a weapon. The evil within may be greater than even the gods themselves. My gratifying psionics were enough to hold such malevolence at bay... so far.

"Are you ready, Thalla?"

She pretended to clean windows so as not to arouse suspicions. *"As I always am, my heart. The horses out back are saddled and ready. All we have to do is escape."* Thalla stopped scrubbing. *"My love,"* she stared out, *"if my knowledge proves me correct, that must be the captain who is to come and take Welbern."*

I peeked with her. A jail wagon pulled up front, a little different from the prior one that delivered me. Its cart smaller with a few railings bearing the goods within. Maybe meant to make the captive feel more ridiculed.

Thalla gave me a little room, whispering, "But, that does not look like an Elf in the wagon's cart. Is it, Ygl?"

I peered closer to observe the posterior of the unfortunate hostage. Her senses had proven truthful. An Elf had not been stashed away, but a shorter huskier figure of someone else—a Dwarf.

CHAPTER 23: The Captain

O kay, our careful strategy seemed not as feasible as we assumed. With my Dwarven colleague's arrival everything would have to modify again.

Could Xurchon be behind this? Was the God of Evil toying with us? Did he plan to stall us in an effort to get Emperor Rondo's forces down here? If so, my misfortune would be the jodepiece's reuse.

"Who is that?" Thalla inquired.

"Ding."

"Ding? You mean the Dwarf?"

I affirmed with a nod.

Thalla continued, "So that is what a Dwarf looks like, but, Ygl, does that not mean—?"

"I know what that means, my love," I whispered in return.

I accompanied her silence as we observed the Quirmean captain commence to leave his seat to enter the shop. A rather sturdy individual bearing much confidence, his height and build were similar to mine.

In the wagon's rear, a couple of guards situated with Ding. They wore Quirmean steel armor: a midriff breastplate, knickers that rounded their legs above the knees, metal boots protected below the knees, and gauntlets. A fine chainmail constructed their pants for pragmatic reasons protecting the mounts with solid steel safeguarding the groin. Nonetheless, I could not understand why they could not use a similar process for the armor's top portion like the Khunians did. The breastplate must be an uncomfortable affair.

The captain's armor, similar to Spenz's, was different from the two guards. He wore a much shinier one, several badges and medals across the upper left, and a helmet. The helmet interested me most for it would play a part in our escape. Atop the helmet, a strong pinnacle. The visor rose over his nose somewhat like a bird's beak. The bottom of the helmet's anterior stretched along his lower cheekbones. In between the helmet's ends, a minute space permitted the soldiers to see their captain's lips as he barked orders from the teeming spot. I may be projecting a bit, however, yes, this helmet would serve the perfect purpose for concealment. A new plan should now be adopted, "Thalla."

"Yes?" My love prepared to do anything for our exodus.

"Go out there. Delay the captain so that I may get a trap ready."

"As will be done." With a quick kiss, she headed out the door.

When she left, I returned to initiate my part of the daring idea. This would have to take much of the jodepiece's magic in order to outsmart Xurchon.

I grabbed Aman's struggling carcass and dragged him to the shop's storage aisle: large racks and shelves stocked with many armaments stored from public view—a good hiding place. Aman attempted to scream through the gag. Poor old Quirmean. What Xurchon had done to you should be avenged for you, your kin, and for all Zaendara. Xurchon would pay. Your emperor would pay. I swear it by Achal's psionic sword of memory.

I placed my hand onto Aman's face knowing his muffled cries would be acknowledged. I did not want to hurt him. "*I wish you would go to sleep.*"

I seized a bit. A brush of cold swept through my arm; the bluish-yellow glow encapsulated the store owner's features and my hand, then melted within him. Aman shook for a moment; then, slouched.

Wow! Did I just put a spell of sleep on him? Wow!

After settling his head down, I headed to the front window to see how Thalla fared. The Quirmean captain had her in so unholy an embrace that she could do nothing, but, his bidding—she kissed him! No one tried to stop him or anything. People just walked by.

"Look at the new wench!" Someone laughed, acknowledging what the captain had within his power.

Of course, some Lorellians tried to impede him, but whips kept them at bay or some brash Quirmeans beat them with fists.

Ding could not move because of his chains. However, I did not think he would know my mate, or care.

My building anger relieved Welbern from its scabbard. I always found my heightened emotion hard to control no matter the meditations my kin practiced. I charged for the door to do battle with the Quirmean wretch.

Clutching the door's handle, I discovered the artifact producing a different glow... no shadows could be perceived. Was this glow meant for me alone? A figure (a face?) surfaced within the somber brilliance. I could not tell of whom the features belonged. A vague visage with little structure. Was the face female? *"Sylvia? Is that you?"*

No, much power seethed from this new player. Achal? Man's goddess of arts and games, Welna?

A fulfilling voice spoke in static, "DOST NOT PROGRESS, ELVIN GENERAL OF LOREL. XURCHON HAS AGAIN ATTEMPTED TO DIRECT THEE INTO A MURDEROUS FATE HE HAS DESIGNED FOR THEE. LET THY MATE BE REGARDED AS SHE IS. THE TRANGRESSION IS A DECOY. INAUGURATE THY PLANS AND, REMEMBER, IT IS THE JODEPIECE THAT SHALL TETHER THEE TO THE JODE.

CONSIDER, XURCHON'S POWER INFLUENCES EVERYWHERE, INCLUDING, WITHIN THY MIDST. THIS IS WHY I AM UTILIZING THIS UNUSUAL ROUTE VIA THY PIECE... A VENTURE TO TAKE AGAINST SUCH POWER."

What the apparition meant by that hallowed testimony I had no idea, and the resonant voice made me wonder that it may be male. Miredo, the Khunian Elvin god of nature? Man's male god, Istratos, the god of magic personified, could be more appropriate.

The glow vanished, and I realized the strange persona was correct. If I would have stepped out that door I would have met the end-of-seasons. "I abhor you, Xurchon and your desires," I whispered.

Then, I realized something else: why were there no direct attacks from the god of evil? He could have shot knives with ease or picked at my skin with the available spear points, but he had not? Could the gods be sheltering me, and, if so, why had they not put an end to this madness? You were correct, Thalla. Oh, so many questions...

At this point, what did anything matter? Something, someone, of great power just reached out to me. That would be enough to satisfy me for now.

I returned to where I ditched Aman. After examining him, I decided to not transform myself into him for risk of underestimating the jodepiece's power again. This situation required a better imperative without risking Thalla or my season to the Quirmeans. An illusion would be a hopeful best since the risk would hopefully not be a hard spell to cast.

Look at me discussing spells as if born of Man's flesh. Anyway, if any problems aroused, I hoped an illusion spell would not be such a troublesome spell to enact when the moment arrived. At least not as difficult as the transformative one.

Magic seemed to have many limits. If only Swen could be more than a genie. I could have inquired her assistance, but now...

I casted the glow upon my form once again and focused a brief while upon the shopkeeper's features. Every little line, every little etch, every little stale whisker provided me a story of how tired a person he may have been if he had not received such help. We knew the Quirmeans were a prosperous kin. How could he be so tired? Maybe nobody cared to bother helping his business? Maybe he drove kin away with his bad attitude?

I thought the spell had expired, but I felt a lot more comfortable than prior. When I aroused from it, I witnessed the glow still emanating about me.

Welbern protruded from its sheath, my blade's shiny fuller being used as a mirror. A weathered Aman's face reflected upon the fuller; none other. This wonderment amazed me. I took another astonished glance to witness my own face revealed upon the shiny side. How incredible! Could this jodepiece's power be relinquished already? No, this could not be.

I dug deep. My straining memory attempted to retrieve Aman's face again—every little line, every little etch; every little worn-out whisker. A graying initiated to my hair's color. Aman's face reappeared... unbelievable. The very moment I thought of Aman, the illusion would return altogether. No wonder the mystic radiance continued enveloping me, but would the Quirmean captain acknowledge the glow?

I hurried to the door and swung it open. The captain still kissed my mate with such madness. He had her trapped between the wagon's side and himself.

"Uh, excuse me, Captain, but when I sent my servant out to bring you in, I did not mean for you to keep her out here for your own leisure. She has work to do as well as you do." I did my best to maintain a proper posture and keep myself from gagging. My voice did sound somewhat like Aman's.

The twisting captain glowered straight into my eyes. "One more remark like that, old man, and you will feel my leisure taken upon you," he rubbed his sword hilt, "But, you are correct. I have to take this weapon to the emperor that you request must be a secret for only the good emperor's honor to see Come, let us go in and retrieve this weapon you've authenticated."

I allowed him to proceed past me, relieved the jodepiece's glow remained undetectable. Thalla positioned near the door behind us.

I proceeded past him near Aman's area. "It is of really high value, Captain, but I did notice something unusual about it that I think our emperor would find most pleasing. Would you not agree, sir?"

The captain did not reply, prompting me to investigate: there he persisted with Thalla again in his embrace, his lips pressing harder against hers.

The apparition's advice kept my anger at bay. "Really, Captain, you are here on business."

My disturbance distracted his gluttony. He glared at me again, allowing my mate permission to break from his embrace. She snatched the cloak she left on the counter.

"Now, Thalla, go behind the shop and finish cleaning those other weapons. Do not forget to put the cloak back after you're done wearing it." She raced out the rear door without a stutter. "And clean off some of those shelves afterward!"

The captain laughed. "Really, old man. You certainly have a way with that slut. You are the only one I have seen that has not had any problems with these stupid Elves. By the way, you don't mind I take her away from you for a couple of days? She is quite attractive, you know, except for those damn ears."

At last, a discussion! Maybe I could get more information out of him before he noticed this trickery. I proceeded to the rear aisle with the captain following. I did not dare come close to the shopkeeper until I retrieved the information I needed to know.

"I see what you mean, Captain, but it is just that I am so scared of the way everyone has been acting lately since Emperor Rondo has made these sudden conquests upon all these strange estates. I mean, I would allow you to take Thalla—that is her name—out with you, but what do you think would happen to her when she is with you? I mean, I really need her returned of sound mind if I'm to get any work out of her.

We are not the peaceful race we used to be, you know. It frightens me to even think of it." A satisfactory performance, I must admit.

The captain gave me frank "once over," then he tapped my shoulder. "Cheer up, old man! There is nothing to fear here in Quirm. With Emperor Rondo at the height of his new power, there is nothing in all Zaendara that can stop Quirm and his wishes. Give it all to the mighty Xurchon."

I would need more than this. "Why Xurchon?"

"Why? Where have you been, old man? Xurchon has shown our emperor the way to rule power. He has made our emperor more loved by his people than ever before. We feel freer than ever. An ecstasy fills us to do things we have never done before at such a level—steal, fight, lust, destroy, and conquer. It is incredible. Never have we felt like this before. " He turned to admire the large encasement of swords on display. Some swords plundered from Lorel and maybe the Dwarf Grand Diamondom. "Tell me, old man, do you remember the way the emperor felt before this?"

"No, I do not. My mind is old and weary... I do not remember things well. It was long ago, though, was it not?"

"Oh, not exactly. Maybe for you. Here, let me remind you. Two or three months ago was when the populace started to notice a growing change come upon our emperor. Now, you must remember that everyone loved him very much even back then, don't you? He is a good ruler and let us not forget it, but, of course, let's not also forget the disappearance of our wonderful princess nearly six months prior and the assassination of our Empress Maxis about a year ago... I'm quite positive those events had a negative effect on him. Interim, it affected us all… well, everyone tried to reach out to him, tried to uplift him, but no one got anything out of him.

One day, his advisor, Werkle, attempted what none could. At first, it seemed Werkle had accomplished well, for he left the emperor's private chambers very much pleased but it seemed nothing was resolute because the emperor still alienated himself from the Quirmean populace.

Then, one day, Emperor Rondo did appear before the royal court and asked for an urgent assembly—and, an assembly he did have. From all parts of the empire everyone arrived to fill the streets of Gablen; not even those streets could contain such a congregation. Miles upon miles were gorged with Quirmean citizens there to listen to what our beloved emperor had to deliver. He told all of us about Xurchon. He told us about how Xurchon would make everyone fortunate and more prosperous by conquering all of Zaendara in the name of Quirm and our ancestors.

The people were at first shocked by Emperor Rondo's denouncement of the true gods, Istratos and Welna, but decided to believe in Xurchon to appease our emperor. Eventually, everyone began to worship Xurchon as our new true god and Emperor Rondo initiated his promise. Thousands upon thousands began to recruit into the Quirmean army in search of conquest.

Not only that, but unfortunate rumors began to circulate about many witnesses seeing the emperor wield a magic—magic unlike what he has done on prior occasions, potent magic. Many did not believe in the rumors until the day we attacked the Dwarf Empire with this, as the emperor called it, Death Mist, he conjured. The emperor then ordered us to search all over the place for some gem that looks like the one he wears around his neck, but is larger.

Now, people are spreading rumors about him having Demons in the palace at Gablen. What fools!

The great thing is we have now captured these dratted Lorellian Elves, and soon those little pip squeaks from Khun will follow. And, the people still love him! You see why everyone worships Xurchon, old man?"

"Old man"… heh-heh… By Achal, did I have a surprise for you, Captain, since at this juncture you could not witness the jodepiece's sole power.

A remarkable little artifact. Almost too remarkable. You should not be in Emperor Rondo and Xurchon's possession. Or could the ideal be Xurchon's possession alone? Rondo could be acting as an agent for the God of Evil's needs. A pawn expecting to win riches for himself as a reward.

On the other hand, my theory could be wrong altogether. Maybe Rondo did not realize what havoc he unraveled, but his unfortunate engagements these past moondays demonstrated his behavior as justified. Amazing how such a good ruler could become insidious in such a short period. However, I wondered if his advisor, Werkle, had anything to do with this radical change. As the captain stated, Werkle did leave Rondo elated. And what about the missing princess? Who assassinated Empress Maxis? Why did I not know anything about this?

Oh, I would never figure this out! So many things were still out of place. Werkle could have been behind Rondo's judgements, but why did Rondo make such decisions? Did he not know the consequences he would have to pay to Xurchon in the future? He must, or else he would not be praising a name of such filth. Somehow, Emperor Rondo wanted something more than Zaendara beneath his grasp and—the Jode.

I did not, and could not, know. "True. We worship a new deity, but tell me have we ever seen Xurchon in true form as Istratos did, himself, when he became god of all Quirmeans?"

"If you have been to the temples, old man, you would see the many statues there that simulate what he looks like."

"Who? Istratos?"

"No, Xurchon. All statues of Istratos and Welna should've been destroyed long ago."

"Yes, but do we know his purpose here in Quirm? Xurchon's? Do we still have the peace we had once held when our former gods were our deities? I thought not. Our emperor must be told to deliberate with our new god, and if our emperor chooses not to, then we... the people, should use force. Why should the people of Quirm worship a god they do not know anything about? Everyone has changed because—"

His astonishment never prepared to erupt from his lips, my ploy had worked. "How dare you speak against the beloved emperor and Xurchon?

You speak treason and those who dare speak such words should and will be killed!" He reached toward his belt for his weapon.

My precise withdrawal placed me near Aman. "W-wait! You forget the sword."

"That can wait until I am done with you. Then, it will be my men and I who will seek and bring it to our beloved emperor."

Closer and closer he gauged toward me with a gleaming, hungry blade wavering ahead on clutched hands angling for my neck. My ploy worked to my benefit... he lunged expecting my feeble form to not react well.

How wrong he was. I dodged his blade and obliged a spectacular nimble kick to his rear. Down the captain fell, aghast at the genuine Aman bound upon the well swept floor. "What is this?"

He squinted at a willing Welbern thirsty for a nice battle. "You are... you are an imposter. And now try to impersonate that filthy Elvin general."

"If you peer closely, you will see that this skin is true and not fake as before. How do you like the blade?" I kept my guard.

He arose with his sword still at hand. His brows furrowed providing a closer scrutiny of his disbelief. They popped up for a moment, then furrowed together again. "You are dead!" His anger shaped with fear's touch.

The space between us shrunk, his sword aimed for my waist. "And by Xurchon, you shall stay dead!" His sword slanted toward the intended.

Welbern blocked the blow with ease. "You did not expect you could defeat a general, did you?"

"I would do more than that to your ungracious kind. After I am done with you, you will be dismembered and then fed to the manticora."

"That is odd. I thought I already killed that a while ago."

"No." The captain tried to aim for other slashes.

Stepping upon the balls of my feet, I jumped aside from the next swing and charged in blocking. "If this is how well you can fight, I would be very remiss to parry with your general."

The despising captain retaliated trying to take me by surprise with upraised sword. He took me by surprise, but not by much. In a short while

Welbern switched from my main sword arm to the other parrying the captain's sword before he could press any closer to me.

Taking advantage of this ambidextrous swordplay, I punched the captain's neck. He fell, reeling against the adjacent shelves; clinging onto them. The dazed captain gawked up at me before flopping over.

Welbern slid back into my scabbard. I knew the attack I had delivered him meant to rid him of consciousness, a part of my new escape plan.

His apparel was all I required. Placing my hand upon his helmet would initiate the worst concentration I would ever experience. Nevertheless, the concentration must happen. The instinctive bizarre glow had already enveloped both our forms. The captain's armor disappeared, but must reappear upon me as unfortunate as the situation may seem. The challenge was that my clothes had to disappear in order for the transformation to work.

Therefore, this mystical action required additional magical assistance to prevail. I concentrated a little more to keep the armor from appearing again upon the captain. I focused and clenched my teeth for a tougher concentration—a deeper telepathic concentration.

Oh, Swen, where were you? I needed a real magician. Painful. I fought to emit an extra surge of magic upon myself. The magic seemed to resist, but I would need to rise above this hardship.

With slight relent, I weakened my hold upon the primary spell. Alas, the menthol magic flooded all over me. My garments vanished from my view, however, I still struggled with the interchanging spells.

Deeper within my mind's murkiness I searched with one eye. My other eye peered downward as if assisting with the intersecting of, and the splitting of the disputing spells. The blackness' edges became lax and then swayed with psychic turbulence blustering from everywhere, shifting into an image much like Rondo's Death Mist. By Achal, the Death Mist! Was that horror within my mind?

A scene emerged within this bleakness of another blooming murkiness. Rich vague images of mountains, forests, and such could not escape my mystic stare. A female materialized from the surrounding's meshing, adorned within a gown of gases foaming about her, a rapid trundling toward me.

"*Master Ygl,*" Swen soothed. Her timbre, a slight tremble, yet the softness persisted. "*Listen and listen well, for the rhyme of the Jode I must tell. A rhyme to Flower Juna which became a lure that unfortunately led to her capture by the Ogres.*"

"*Uhm... Swen...*" Too much information overwhelmed me. I had not wanted to communicate with her, yet if I did the spells could diminish.

And so, her rhyme began:

> "*Across the sea of sand,*
> *In a hidden green,*
> *Lies the powerful Jode*
> *Of unusual entity.*
>
> *Power to rule a world.*
> *Maybe even more.*
> *Thou may possess it*
> *If thee only cross the shore.*
>
> *Some seek it for strength*
> *To do what they think is right.*
> *No matter the possessor*
> *Many will feel its might.*
>
> *Seek the danger and*
> *Savior of the land;*
> *Reveal the secret*
> *Of the treachery of Man.*

The rhyme ends for thee to mend. Do not let thy mind go to rest. It is not the end of the test. Leave I must now, and leave fast for my call has come to past."

My peculiar genie transformed into a ball of pure light. The light divided into two colors: blue and yellow. The two balls' luminance could not alleviate the bleak experience's gloominess. The energy balls faded into a pair of garments' embodiments: the captain's (blue) and mine (yellow). In mid-transformation, the balls rose to each other, the garments acting as a source of attraction. In contrast, the energy balls' withdrawal from each other intensified with equal strength. Repulsion and attraction in an instance.

From my yellow garment, a soft radiance directed itself toward the epicenter of the captain's blue armor culminating into a familiar yellowish-blue mixture. When enough of my garment's yellow radiance had permeated within, a hesitancy occurred. The invading mixture retained a penchant to transform into a type of focal point for the armor's receptive blue. This focal point's envelope began to grow and push the blue energy's inner walls farther and farther apart. Thus, a bluish-yellow hub altered the captain's armor into a rather large hole.

In response to this exchange, the remnants of my garment's glow condensed and stretched rendering itself into an arrow's shape. The arrow shaped image shot through the bluish-yellow hole taking the radiant focal point along the way.

The hole compacted upon itself to reform into a bluish glow. The blue glow pulsated brighter and brighter saturating my mystical vision, compelling me to continue witnessing this blinding event. The blue brilliance continued with pervasion throughout my vision refusing to halt until the moment the pervasion attained my pupils' membrane. My mind coursed with an immediate searing of never ending pain. I gritted refuting any screams.

Within the blackness the bluish glow folded like a rose meeting the end-of-seasons. Was I going blind?

My eyelids fluttered open to allow any amount of natural light to penetrate... but the light never arrived. From my pupils' perimeter, a dawning glistening was born inhibiting the sunday's arrival. When the special dawning dissolved, it welcomed quite a surprise: the captain still sprawled upon the ground with my clothes appearing upon him.

I evaluated myself. The air felt heavier as the captain's armor made a metallic debut. Heavier and heavier, layer by layer, polished weight built upon me. Alas, the spell had worked. What joy! What euphoria to have experienced the Quirmean royalty's divine right. However, joy would be an unfortunate brief exchange, for rapture could not be realized until Xurchon and Rondo's evil plans were halted—and, if needed be, their end-of-seasons.

I relieved Welbern and its scabbard from the unconscious captain and hustled to peer out the rear door. My mate awaited outside wrapped in her cloak patting her horse's belly.

"Thalla," I whispered.

"Yes, Ygl." She smiled. "Oh, wonderful! Everything is going so well. Do we escape now?"

I motioned her to speak lower. "Can you see the end of the jail wagon from where you are positioned at?"

"Yes. Sorry."

"That is okay. The very moment you see it move, begin to follow it. I should be at the reins. Here, take Welbern." I slid my occupied scabbard to her.

"All right."

I knew she would be just as elated free from Man's bonds, but liberty required a source of escape. The carriage's front door opened, and I strode toward the guard resting upon the wagon.

Ding glared at me as if he recognized the personage being me within this mystical guise. I did not blame him. From what I understood tales had been related that Dwarves, too, possessed the power of infravision within their sight and probably better infravision because of their environment. Nevertheless, my ploy must be against the two guards; not him.

"Soldiers." My voice matched as close to the captain's as I could acquire. Our similar heights blessed my bad improvising.

"Yes, sir?" They harmonized. A concerned look crossed their faces.

The soldier closest spoke first. "Captain, sir, is there something the matter. I mean your voice—"

"If there is anything wrong with my voice, then it has to do with the duel I had with that imposter in there. Yes, I said an imposter. Now, get in there and awaken him. I want him placed into the jail wagon with this lowlife."

I did well, but they both seemed hesitant. "Go!"

They hurried in amazement. When they dispatched through the door, I retained the driver's seat. Pulling the reins, I observed as the burgeoning crowd separated to allow me secure passage.

Thalla followed upon her steed from the shop's rearmost alley. A bundle I knew well coddled within her cloak. The cloak, a large one indeed, she made sure shielded every part of her, except for her gloved hands.

Which street laid before me would steer me toward Skavir's south main gate? The impulse to wander within the direction of the crowd's main flow proved difficult. True, many visitors carried bundles of personal treasures about the place, but could some visitors be buying or selling or could some be heading home or to either the main gates? The typical task left to do was to harness the horses about the city until I attained the southern gates, but if I did find those main gates, would I beat the captain's guards to that destination?

A horse's hooves cantered beside the jail wagon. Uneasy Thalla glimpsed toward me. "What is the matter?" she whispered from the hood.

"I do not know where to find the south main gate."

"That is such a silly thing to say. You have the Jode's power bound around your finger—speak to the horses."

I always loved Thalla around when I dealt with problems. I felt stupid contemplating without her logic, no matter how absurd. A good balance, we comprised for each other. Not only did I share my problems with her, but we shared them with each other. I guess the secret behind love... caring, was it not?

My mind cleared of any past thoughts to prepare my psychic call. To one of these Quirmean creatures the call would transmit, and maybe not to the other. This juncture would be when the jodepiece must come into play.

Within my gauntlets, I let the rigid jodepiece glow, permitting power extraordinaire to emit forth and blend with my psychic call's force. A fullness pervaded my mind with an enigmatic compliance; the transfer completed.

Far into the horses' minds I lunged to tap the intelligible cord that would respond. The horses' heads unsettled with a little snort probing to obtain the person who had disrupted their privacy.

"It is I, the driver, who speaks to you, oh, great mares. I am in need of finding the south main gate that will lead me to the road toward Chrot. Would you care to help me out?"

"We would love to, but only under one condition."

"What is it?"

"That you allow us to have food when we get there. We have been pulling this cart for days and have not had a bite to eat."

"It is a deal."

Contact broke. The skillful horses trotted down the shortest route possible toward the main gate progressing amongst the crowd with such ease avoiding every impediment whatsoever. I gladdened I requested these mares' assistance because I could not devise a plan past all these constant interweaving streets. Kin would need to visit often to figure out a proper path within such an artsy city.

The main gate was attained. Although I had been delivered through the gateway once as a prisoner, the construction's immense size and grandeur still amazed me. The main gate stood out larger than the buildings themselves, twenty to thirty foot construct's embodying the greatest of oak trees with crisscrossed iron bars running up and down a cumbersome length. On the left door's epicenter suspended a ten foot gold mask of their emperor with a smooth border encircling. The right door flaunted another huge golden mask replicating another handsome notable. Rough sharp edges hewed that mask. On the forehead, an image of the gallows.

"That is the face of Xurchon, or who they believe is Xurchon. Even in the churches there are statues of him with the exact features upon it," Steady Thalla whispered beside the wagon.

I glimpsed, witnessing Ding staring at her with disdain. The Dwarven hatred knew no bounds.

"My love, communicate via telepathy. We do not want Quirmeans suspicious of anything. Now, we must hold our thoughts for this slight passing moment. The gate's opening stands near."

A small tract of land separated the wall of parallel spiked logs encompassing Skavir. Attached to the brazen wall suspended the southern gates—periodic portals discharging visiting throngs from the city endorsing such fierce callousness and murder.

Upon closer scrutiny of Xurchon's mask, intertwined whips comprised the encircling border. The whips' firm tassels made sure they grasped the preceding handle. Whip to handle... whip to handle...

The silliness of it all. To imagine, the emperor wanted his kin to love him more than their new god. I guess I would have to agree with the claim. Why would I love a being that embodied such pain?

We surpassed the junction with the artsy crowd's flow when I noticed a sentinel acknowledge me from a midlevel platform. "Captain? I thought you said that dung was to go to the Torture House. What's the matter?"

"A messenger of the emperor himself gave notice to me not to bring him this day since my men were searching for a certain article in Skavir's weaponry shop." A terrible feeling churned within my gut. Another lie and one just as worse as the prior but was I not inhabiting an empire diseased with evil in every crooked corner? I felt more at ease believing such a theory true.

"Oh..." The lead guard may have been confused; nevertheless, the guards allowed us passage.

After all, a Quirmean captain headed down an extensive road to Chrot, the slave city, where a promising final objective awaited. The twin suns shined bright upon high for this route. If we maintained a steady pace, we should arrive there before the moonday.

CHAPTER 24: A Wish

Gablen, Quirm's capital.

The taciturn throne chamber once again communed with Rondo's apparent compulsion to brooding. Three vacant thrones' reappearance compounded the divergent worlds' merger. He couldn't make them disappear for long. He couldn't.

The guards abided preparing to protect their Emperor from whatsoever else would dispatch through cumbersome doors.

The table bedecked with refreshments still mounted in one side of the well decorated room; from the stands, an assemblage of goblets with a threesome misplaced. By all appearances, everything appeared intact as if a tussle never occurred in the area.

Rugged wool carpets, expansive imports from the artistic town of Wyp, lathered the floor with their picturesque designs. One displayed a grand hunt authorized in the Forest of Lorel's northern region when the two races were in better terms. A pound of hounds and straddling hunters pursued a large stag racing around the boundary. A relief of the stag's affixed head dominated the rug's center. Another carpet displayed a bear's affixed head with an analogous scenario supplementing a fight to the death. Farther over, accompanying rugs exhibited men participating in sports like archery and sword fighting representing the athletic town of Vante. A trophy or medal spotted those rugs here and there. Additional rugs displayed theatrical pageants of people singing or acting on a stage. Dancers, musical notes, and masks dotted each rug representing Wyp's other talents. Strippers swinging on poles or performing lap dances, prostitution, or gambling represented another of Wyp's facades. Gold trinkets dotted these rugs. Chrot, the current slave city, represented with images of cattle, pigs and other farm life with flourishing speckles of wheat and corn included. Rondoville's main church dominated another rug. Skavir's Torture House, with its uninviting paraphernalia adorned yet another, never revealing Wyp's many parcels that maintained the city's economy.

Amongst these rugs, a modern pairing trekked up the four steps to the emperor and his estranged empress' thrones like bookends. Streams of gray radiated from the perimeter, embodying the handsome image of a face many had come to acknowledge at any city's gateway—Xurchon, their new god; their true god. No treading upon these hoary rugs.

Anyone could tell Rondo's displeasure if they stepped closer to him upon his dais. Muffled sounds could be gleamed teeming from his throat's solemn depths, a mumble of intense unease both for his people and... himself. Over and over, he imparted the impression to dictate to himself his sudden grief's source. "They must love me..." His yearning akin to a prayer. "I-I have done all I could for them, have I not? Now, you are the final accomplishment I can enact to win their love."

The repetitive mantra's meaning to the guards, if they bothered to listen, would be vague. To Rondo, they rung ominous and proper in the early morning.

A rapping came from the oaken doors prompting the guards to point their lengthy spears.

"Who is it?" A slight echo carried Rondo's voice.

"It is I, Werkle. One of your disciples has come to bring you good news of great secrecy."

A deep elation cleansed the Quirmean emperor's ruminating with other matters at hand. "Allow the disciple to enter, then stay and protect my throne from outside."

Werkle waltzed in with his emperor's secret disciple. Rondo adored his disciples when they beared good news. Who wouldn't? Quite larger than Werkle and taller, the disciple wore a thin russet robe with a begrimed hood ensconcing the messenger's face.

"Well, what is it?" The emperor maintained a rough tone disguising his respect.

183

"It is about Juna, the Fairy Queen. She has been captured yesterday outside the walls of the Ogrean Kingdom." The messenger's voice: a monotonous gravel—like a stone traveling upwind against an avalanche.

"What!" Rondo preferred a disclosure, like this, would never arise, but at this moment the issue had. If the Pixies captured Juna, then the Giants' threat must be worsening.

Stepping down from the throne, Rondo sauntered toward his balcony's ashen hickory doors. "This is impossible. Only days ago, I found out from that meddlesome Giant prince that his people knew nothing of my threat. How can this be?"

"She could be a spy for them," Werkle advised.

"Yes, you are right. That has to be it." Rondo hesitated, contemplating.

"The Pixies have already been persuaded to follow your loyalty, but ... the Ogres have not," the cumbersome disciple stated with uneasiness.

"Then, have them persuaded by the so-called threat of war the Giants are preparing to forge against them. Tell them the Quirmean Empire will aid them since we are under the same threat. We need opportunity before we can strike out again."

"But we must not strike out too fast," Werkle interrupted, "for the Giants and the Ogres along with their winged allies will be wary of our cause."

Rondo turned to his advisor with resentment upon his lips. "You speak wise words, Werkle. Words that I know I must trust and must not turn away from. Let wild fantasies, and frustrations, and fear tear into the souls of the Ogres. When they are done, the Ogres will rally and will start warring with the Giants. They will be expecting the Quirmean Empire's aid and aid they will get.

The Giants must be eliminated! I am in need of what I still search for. The Giants will not block me from receiving it.

Now go, my disciple. I want this war waged quickly!" Accidental bluish-yellow sparks exploded from the emperor's hands.

The disciple receded, cowering in the begrimed cloak like a deer hiding from the lion, struggling to speak. "P-please, my emperor, allow me to speak one other thing."

"Quickly. What is it? You know my patience grows short."

"Found with the queen was a… a lamp. I do not know how such an article could come into her possession, but—"

"What does this lamp look like?" Rondo could not conceal his surprise with this new information.

"Well, it's certainly large compared to the Fairy's size. It's boxlike and made of a yellow tannish metal. A clear one forms its spout…"

The disciple trailed on with further description, but Rondo already knew the answer. How the treasure got into a Fairy's hands, he did not know. However, a retrieval was of the highest urgency.

"Get it," the Emperor demanded, "and do not return until it is safely in my possession."

"Yes, sire." The disciple cowered scuttling its cumbrous form out of the throne room.

At the door's closing, Emperor Rondo turned around to peer through the balcony doors' glass panels succumbing to worry. He had not intended the Giants to become an early player in his game, but now they must be hindered from going any further. The Death Mist would not dare enter the Cory Mountains, home of the Giants' estate. Why? Rondo could not comprehend; however, he knew the Ogres and Pixies would be the selected pawns to do his handiwork, his unwitting familiars dedicated to the Quirmean forces. Then, the Ogrean kingdom would collapse as well.

"Is there anything you would like for me do, sire?" Werkle asked.

"No, nothing at this moment." He dangled the amulet from his neck admiring his prize. Silence thrived again spreading its odorless breath about the room.

Rondo's behavior these past days disturbed Werkle. Had the emperor become unwell or just impatient? However, to Werkle, this did not matter. He appreciated why he advised his brother to worship Xurchon. The adviser relished his advice as his moment ticked closer and closer.

A voice, deep and sullen, resounded in the room. "RONDO."

The calm emperor regarded the overture while frightened Werkle jumped clear from the floor.

"What is it you want, great Xurchon?" Though he maintained an air of strength, the emperor's voice conveyed a minute shudder.

"COME QUICKLY TO RYKON TOWER THROUGH MY HOLY MATRIX." A pale amorphous medium appeared propelling a precipitous chill through everyone present from its formlessness. "THESE ARE SECRET MATTERS THEE AND I MUST SHARE ALONE."

Rondo proceeded to his temple via the pale matrix. The swift atmosphere enveloped him without a sound bequeathing the selfsame stillness again in a shivering phenomenon's wake.

CHAPTER 25: Chrot

Solitary travelers, Thalla, Ding and I made our way down the lengthy road toward the slave city. Beforehand, I navigated the jail wagon so that the Skavir crowd's remnants could continue past us to their journeys elsewhere. Their passage allotted us privacy on a sunday's crossing point with the moonday towards the southeast. We encountered a nice woodland with much underbrush along the way, a thankful blessing. The horses' flaring nostrils and heavy panting alarmed me to provide them sustenance somewhere along the route despite the coverage.

A speck could be seen over the pebbled road's horizon. The speck could be none other than the slave city of Chrot. There had been no other target seen on this tenuous route except the sky's blue stretch dotted with slight gray clouds. Brave Los and Num, the twin suns, peeked through the fluffy foliage to squint at our horrid experience while offering a faint golden silhouette to their neighbors.

I surveilled the remaining countryside, becoming aware the scenery was not unlike the major cities. Some did have Quirmeans bargaining for goods, even though those goods were food. Moreover, all houses erected on proud fields of cultured green. Many farms lay about like a blanket of food and trade for both types of environments.

Lorellians did little farming, enjoying the fruits of what nature had to provide; however, witnessing Elves cultivating the fields for their unlawful masters made the irony quite evident.

Every length my companions and I traveled, not a single area of land was left without a residential colony. Even in the farmlands, where the farmers resided on the brink of such settlement, centralized homes flourished. The centralized homes' inhabitants thrived on the advantages they received for helping the farmers in the fields.

These fields I remembered from my past visits before the ruckus. I realized nothing had changed. Nothing! These citizens still toiled over the fields; little frolicking could be seen from the Quirmean bloodchild who slaved in this supposed peaceful land.

I would have tolerated such a scene if not for a current fault I kept revisiting. Everywhere, I saw more and more Elvin slaves. But, the faults did not conclude there. From the fields, I witnessed robbers stealing food which prompted me to wonder how much unfairness fostered within such a "prosperous" estate. The female Lorellians were being used for more than the reason of farming. Of course, the bloodchildren frolicking were not Lorellians who performed labors they found quite difficult.

The woodland tapered the closer we arrived to our destination. Grateful groves of trees still flanked the road's sides. Giant oaks, sycamores and maples, along with numerous shrubbery, acted as barriers against the suns' rays and this ungrateful public's scrutiny—and my fostering anger.

I recounted how multiethnic Quirmeans were compared to us more homogenous Elves after acknowledging the innumerable Fumians milling about. Predominant in the empire's south thrived the Fumian aspect of their ethnicity, darker skinned Quirmeans, hardworking and very loyal. In the north and along the coast, thrived the more intellectual Vantenians. They did have more of a slant to their eyes, but nothing like Elves. The lighter skinned citizens, settling in the middle of the empire's beltway, were known as Gablenians, the most devout. As my bloodfather, Scall, related to me, Quirmean blood mixed among these ethnicities. To this sunday, no ethnicity ever referred to themselves as that ethnicity but as Quirmeans. Empress Maxis was Fumian.

"Ygl," my mate's sweet voice called. Her tone felt almost as soothing as Swen.

"What is it, my love?" My attention never averted from the surroundings through the trees.

"We have been traveling down this road for a whole sunday, including, the sunday before. Should we not rest? As you can see, the horses already begin to tire and we are not even far away from our next destination."

I did not want to stop because I knew the vengeful captain and his men followed behind us. We had to reach the slave city soon before Plant Kute's deliverance to the Torture House. However, a whole bewildering sunday surpassed without leisure, and no sign of a jail wagon carrying a Giant prince had been seen at all.

Could the fact be that they took him another way? If so, then Thalla and my ruse would have failed and Chrot's reinforcements would recapture us. Kute must be in there.

"We will stop, Thalla. Come help me unshackle my Dwarven friend from his bonds."

The reins were pulled. The wagon slowed onto the road's side with the heavy trotting's immediate halting.

Thalla's horse arrived by my side. She leapt off leaving the three horses to graze on the fresh grass. I would need to provide water later.

Thalla placed her lap's bundle onto my driver's seat. "What about the kin around us?" She leapt with the lightest grace only an Elf could attain. "Will any of them see us?"

"There are too many trees and brushes along the passage for anyone to peer through. It would only take Elvin vision to pierce through the substantial shade these trees' branches throw."

"And, how do you presume to unshackle him?"

"With this." From within a gauntlet I produced a key. "I felt it rubbing against my wrist."

We proceeded to the jail wagon's tail end where we witnessed Ding had moved away from his spot near the driver's seat. The closer we approached, his mood became more apprehensive.

A sneer escaped his knotty beard. "Take your slimy Elvin paws off me. I do not need the aid from a race as low as yours to come help me. Get away from me."

Stunning. Never had Ding acted in this manner before... well, not exactly in this manner. He did have a grudge against me, but not one such as this.

189

He should be grateful we saved him from his end-of-seasons. Why would he not want us to extract him from the chains?

"This Dwarf does not seem to like our help, Ygl." Thalla moved closer to him with the key.

"Come, Ding. That is your name?" She kneeled beside him.

He edged away.

Unbothered, she proceeded. "Let us help you."

"No. Get away from me." A pair of shackled feet swung up to assault her. Thalla receded with a leap, but she fell over the railing from the limited spacing.

In effect, my jodepiece's menthol cool vigor coursed through my veins. Bluish-yellow energy burst forward from my hand closest and enveloped Thalla before she could touch the ground. Her weight, a slight nudge on the burst's other side.

She stiffened and turned around in the air. Her levitated landing punctuated her smooth floating. My mate waited beside the jail wagon diagonal from the Dwarven thief, her cloak still enveloping her.

The formidable glow emanating about my hands diminished.

"H-how did you do that? Where did you get such power?"

I chuckled. Maybe this spectacle would get him to change his mind. "It is a jodepiece cut from its original source—the Jode."

Ding's brows furrowed creating thick ridges on his nose's broad bridge.

I continued, "From within comes an extraordinary power known as magic which can be wielded in a variety of different proportions and instances. Remember the emperor used it on us in his throne room? It depends, I guess, on the purpose and strength of the wielder.

Now, if you will allow me. I will free you from your chains using its gifts." Startled, Ding hunkered. "No."

I hesitated. "Ding it's not the same piece. Rondo has his own piece."

Thalla climbed onto the jail wagon and approached Ding again, but I motioned her to stand down. If I had not, her recklessness would have been her demise somehow. *"Do you really think he could hurt me, Ygl?"*

"Well…"

"Yes, if true, Dwarves may be stronger than Elves by a great deal, but we are more agile."

"Wait, Thalla."

"Elf, if you think you are going to unshackle me then you are more unfortunate than the female."

"Is that so, my friend?"

"I am not your friend."

"Thalla, go get the bundle where I sat, and please show Ding a surprise."

She obliged and opened the bundle.

"I warn you, Elves. Do not think you will be able to touch me. I will—" Thalla revealed Ding's beloved axe. "What? How did you get Gore? Hand it over to me!"

"Can we keep the noise down a little, please? If you want your beloved blade you must be willing enough to allow me to free you from your chains."

Ding squatted upon his spot undecided. His eyes shifted from Gore; then, to me. He frowned knowing that he would feel helpless if he did not have his axe returned. "Go ahead..."

Ding lifted himself on his knees and turned his back, presenting the dratted chains shackling his wrists and ankles together.

"That must have hurt your shoulders a lot throwing that kick."

"Just get it over with."

His face's expression prior to his turn conveyed more than indecision. By instinct, I linked a psychic rapport to his muddled mind. An emotion I knew well bounded too many of his incomprehensible thoughts—anger. I could not decipher any words; however, I could almost distinguish a misunderstanding derived from this psionic nexus.

Swen was the empath; not me. Only she could help me out with this. I did know that anger alone would make someone so complicated to understand. Methelo and my bloodfather, would be embarrassed by my intrusion.

I touched Ding's chains. I shuddered with the passage of my piece's potency releasing from my telepathic interference.

The bluish-yellow glow enveloped both hands and chains. To my surprise, this magical meddling assisted me in understanding my unconventional ally further: I saw images of Rondo, Werkle, and a pale smog surrounding a nondescript being... and me.

"Magic. Are you using magic, Elf? Do not use this magic on me!"

"No. No. No magic." My meddling subsided with my embarrassment.

"Trust is not easy to come by with this one." Thalla slid the key to me.

I commenced to unlock the five locks.

"Ygl, you could have so easily made his chains immaterial and vanish them from our existence leaving him with freedom, yet he fears this power more than us."

"His estate and kin were captured by the Quirmeans already. I am sure he has been through enough."

"...Poor creature."

Clickity-clack. Clickity-clack. The chains fell. The Dwarven thief stood snatching his axe from Thalla with a simultaneous stare of mixed feelings at me. Wow! He did not know what to think of Thalla and me. He sneered and turned to leave.

"Do not go anywhere, Dwarf, please. You know they are after us."

Ding hesitated, knelt and spat on his dingy shirt's hem to clean the dry blood off Gore. "I know, female Elf," he answered with a smugness. "Tell me, Elf, why did you not use this magic before? You could have saved all of us from this trouble."

"Because, Ding, my friend—"

"I am not your friend."

"We have gone through enough together at this point for you not to be, Ding. You came all this way with Kute and Juna certainly not to be my enemy.

I did not get this small piece of the Jode, this jodepiece, if you will, until... my bloodbrother, King Methelo, gave it to me."

Ding stopped rubbing his blade's surface, never distracted from the double-headed blade's fine craftsmanship. "I thought your Grand Diamond met the **end-of-rings**?"

"Grand Diamond? What is he talking about, Ygl?"

"It means the same as 'king,' Thalla. And if the 'end-of-rings' means the end of existence, then you are correct, Ding."

"Yes, Elf. So be it."

"Yes, that is true, but it was more like his essence that I spoke to via telepathy, I think."

"You think? Either you spoke to a spirit or you did not. I am an atheist, you know."

"I know. Anyway, what we are to do, at this point, is get Plant Kute and ourselves out of here so we can renew our expedition of the magic jewel called the Jode. I already told you this is just a piece of it—"

"That you will not use on me."

"Yes. I strongly believe I must use the attraction between this piece and the Jode to lead us to the point of origin." I made sure not tell him of the psychic rapport between Swen and I. My suspicions of what I gleaned from his mind did not leave me.

Ding grumbled, "Well, I will warn you just one thing; that is, you better not dare use that stone's power upon me because if there are such a thing as legends coming true, then we Dwarves are unaffected by magic and you would not like what I will do with you if you ever did project magic toward me."

His bravado did not shock me as much as it shocked Thalla. My hefty companion's disrespect was simply uncalled for. Something more than just hatred toward my kin dwelled within this Dwarven thief; I aimed to find out. "I agree with you, Ding, but it may be important to remember what happened to you at the castle and take that into consideration. And, was your grand diamondom not captured by magic?"

Ding paused, then grunted. I did not feel so bad knocking him down a peg or two just to entice his return to reality. We needed all the help we could get.

Thalla pulled me away. "Tell me, my love," she was stern, "you have been around this Dwarf longer than I. Tell me, do Dwarves have feelings to anything besides themselves?"

"Your guess is as good as mine. It is hard to comprehend their kind, Thalla."

"We must watch our every step with him." Thalla shook a little, then she froze with one ear pointed upward.

"What is it, Thalla?"

I noticed it also; not as clear as our Khunian neighbors would, but I did. Iron's clashing upon the surface. Four thumps sounded after one another with a brief interpose between each set following the exact rhythmic pattern as the one before.

"Hooves."

"Horse hooves," I specified, *"too many; maybe enough to slow us down and overpower us."*

Ding, we are in earnest need of your skills. Can you help tell us how far the enemy now rides?"

Our Dwarven survivor produced another faltering grumble as his sole answer. Grabbing a hold of the rear rail, Ding sauntered onto the other side. He knelt upon the ground and placed his hands parallel to each other.

His ear hovered closer to the ground accompanied with a deep carefulness. Ding stayed in that pose for a short while.

"Seriously, Ygl, you are having this Dwarf listen for a sound we can hear perfectly well."

"Being mountain dwellers, I feel Dwarves can gauge the sounds better than we can since they thrive within that environment. They had no choice in the matter considering. I could not fathom them having better vision, but better hearing is a better bet. Plus, I think Ding needs to feel important. I do not have a problem helping him out with that."

"You are funny, my love. I understand. I could not imagine thriving in such closed quarters."

"I agree."

"No more than five miles away, Elf. There are five or six of them."

"Well, he is rather grateful after all." Thalla peered with all her Elvin vision down the road. "I can barely see them, but they are coming. That poor captain still wears your garments, Ygl, but he still leads them."

"The horses are coming faster," Ding added.

"Then we must be going. Quickly, both of you sit diagonal from one another with your hands behind your backs."

194

Ding plopped himself at the wagon's far left corner, and Thalla sat opposite closer to me.

"Thalla, place the bundle right in the center of you two beneath the hay." I leapt off the wagon and went to her horse.

During the reined horses' sending to me, the jodepiece's instinctive glow commenced. *"What are you doing? Leave the mare brother alone, and let us be on our way,"* the first demanded.

"Just wait a moment. I have to hold the enemy back, so we may go," I responded.

"All right, but please hurry. We still thirst," called the other.

My glowing hand hovered above her horse's saddle. I shot a quick glance toward Thalla who gave her approval.

A chilled intensity saturated my skull; I wavered.

"Ygl...?"

I gathered my wits allowing the unwelcoming heat to surpass, "I... I am fine. Just hold on..."

In the air, above the horse's saddle, swirled a faint mist I could perceive. The mist stretched and expanded until a vague image in a cloak and long tangled tresses made a graceful appearance. My mate's replica stared down at me, sword in firm grasp.

"Are you ready?" I asked.

"Yes." The illusion's voice, as soft and humbling as my mate's.

I directed the horse into a northern route, slapped its posterior, and let the mare race toward our pursuers.

"Ygl, are you okay?"

"I am fine, Thalla." I gathered my composure and hurried upon the wagon's driver seat, shaking the reins. The horses relented racing off at a full gallop.

"You are not fine, Ygl. We will do little telepathy. You need to regain your strength against that thing."

"Okay."

The chase was on. Kute, my friend, hold on.

CHAPTER 26: Expectations

The fraught Quirmean captain realized he had been shepherded into a sham, humiliated in battle, and left in embarrassment wearing an Elvin recidivist's ragged garments. His men almost misidentified him for an impostor until they noticed the jail wagon's departure.

A touch of fear tinged the captain's anger. Fear in wondering how his emperor would react upon realizing the Elf had escaped and defeated one of the emperor's best warriors. If luck hadn't favored the witnesses in Skavir who observed the jail wagon's departure, he wouldn't have been able to track the emperor's enemies thus far.

The jail wagon came into view not more than four miles away. The captain grimaced at what a snare the emperor's enemies led themselves into. The thick foliage of bushes, trees, and expansive farmland constrained the pursuant from absconding the route. The wagon was of old structure and the horses had gone for three days without much of anything for sustenance. For sure, these factors would slacken the enemy down.

He had four well-armed warriors against an exhausted Elvin general, an Elvin whore, and a shackled Dwarf. Yes, reprisal should be more than sought against that dratted general.

The captain and his men lessened the gap with their quarry—no more than three miles left to go.

"Captain!" yelled a squad member.

Too immersed in thought, he acknowledged a brutish horse galloping their direction at full speed. A cloaked and hooded figure upon the horse's dorsum was poised with a sword upraised.

The hood slid off revealing the Elvin female. Hatred stirred upon her visage.

"Captain!"

"I know," he remained cool, "I can see the whore approaching. Oh, so she thinks she can wield a sword, eh?

Roel, get up in front and shoot an arrow at her quick. Teach the whore a lesson."

"Yes, Captain." Roel rode forth as the others relinquished.

"We will not have such a fool block us from capturing that Elvin general scum."

Two miles outstanding. Many crossroads had been exceeded leading elsewhere. The slave city's magnificent walls hailed not far away.

Zealous Roel notched his arrow aligning the slender steel shaft to aid his focus via the sight window. The devoted arrow whistled from the bow's rest like a fowl swooping to seize an unwary quarry.

The stalwart Elvin rider charged forward absent of fear. The well-behaved arrow struck her midsection. An excellent shot! The female rider screamed and exploded in a burst of light. Her stallion, frightened by this occurrence, sped on.

A scream pitched from Roel's throat. An arrow's apex—his devoted arrow—pierced through his posterior via his midsection. As the arrow's fletching exited, the feathers reaped a gushing accolade, ensanguining Roel's regalia and his saddle. He wavered upon his mount squandering his grip, plummeting.

A lifeless shell, Roel became an impediment thwarting the other mounts' paths. One horse tripped over him knocking its master off. The other two horses reared, startled, both forelegs kicking high in the dust. Another warrior tumbled off.

Thalla's riderless steed careened down the road, a frightful abandonment, not caring about anything attempting to block a crazed mare's path.

The second fallen warrior rose upon his knees, dazed, failing to acknowledge the anxious equine's lethal incursion. The hapless warrior emitted one scream, one scream alone, as the horse's powerful hooves trampled over him. His body rocked with gentleness upon the ground.

Blood oozed from the fallen warrior's ajar lips—a sordid labial homage to the jodepiece.

The Quirmean captain's befouled endeavor baffled him. Already two of his men laid deceased from a notched arrow's consummate stroke and... and... those scum known as Elves.

"Captain." A survivor staggered toward the horse faltering over Roel's body.

"Quickly! Get upon your horse! We must warn the sentinels at Chrot's gates! The enemy must not get into the city's walls!"

CHAPTER 27: The Chase

We broke free from the foliage's safety. A stretch of grazed grassland separated the remaining course from the local housing, a more defined panorama of what had lain hidden beyond the foliage's refuge.

Chrot emerged proud at the pathway's end. I observed the red oaken gates with triumph. We, at last, reached our goal. Along the fenced perimeter, a stony rampart lined. However, another contrast amazed me. The first large gate exploited a large golden mask resembling Emperor Rondo's other mask on Skavir's south gate, but the second mask appeared quite dissimilar to Xurchon's mask. The border encircling this emblem held ringlets, not curvy lines of intertwined whips; and, not as roughly hewed. Upon that mask's forehead, the image of a bound Elf kneeling upon his shins with his head drooped.

Rickity-rick...

rickity-rack...

The jail wagon jolted upon a rock on the ground. The wagon, not built for such high speeds, held its balance.

"*Thalla, do you see the gates?*" The wagon's balance being maintained and my anger kept me a little preoccupied.

"*I already have seen the gates. Why would one city have a mask so different from that of the other?*"

"*I do not know myself why it is either, but I do remember a stray remark that that captain said about the statues simulating what Xurchon looked like. Now, I comprehend what he meant.*"

The jail wagon jolted again. I held onto the reins; the horses sped on.

Rickity-rick...

rickity-rack...

I continued, *"Who knew this wagon was this bad!*

Every city seems to have their own image of what Xurchon looks like, but none really knows."

"It is almost as if they are worshipping a nothing," Thalla concluded.

"A nothing that we know nothing about, except as a being of ultimate power, hatred and evil."

Another jolt struck the wagon!

Rickity-rick...

rickity-rock...

rockity... rockity...

The old structure began to wobble a bit.

"The enemy approaches closer." Restless Ding alarmed from the rear. "And we are no more than halfway there."

Rockity-rockity-rockity...

Ding shuffled a bit, but kept his arms behind him. "It does not matter now! Come on, nasty Quirmeans! Come taste Gore!"

"I must admit, I admire how stalwart he is." Thalla stated, *"We need to lessen the telepathy."*

"Prudency is of priority. You cannot hear me over the clatter."

"All right..."

The reins were given a harder shake; my orders became louder. The horses responded with a greater rush of hooves.

Behind us, the captain and his squad's horses galloped with greater speed. My Lorellian cloak billowed about him like a flag of abhorrence.

In the naked countryside, Quirmeans and **kin** stared in awe and ran through the fertile fields to speculate. The twin suns' rays dispersed behind a line of trees. The moonday generated a slow descent upon the Quirmean Empire allowing the sunday to slip away...

The alarmed guardians at Chrot's gates acknowledged the occurrence below them with apprehensive shouts. The mighty oaken gates fluctuated for new visitors.

******

"Captain, they are opening the gates!"

The anxious captain shared his surviving warrior's dismay, ascertaining the emperor's desirable dominance. He also recognized the carriage wheel's hub had iron bearings whose efficacy wasn't of the utmost performance, the spokes would attain an eventual misgiving.

"Fool! You think I do not know that?! Ride faster! Faster!" The captain's heels jolted his horse harder and harder.

Onward, the mounts galloped.

******

Our jail wagon halted in front of a band of guardians at Chrot's entrance. A spoke popped off.

"Captain! What is the matter?" inquired a befuddled warrior, his lesser medals inferred him as a lower ranking officer than I. His dark-skinned commander approached with much intent.

I exaggerated my panting. "Sent to take slaves back… with the prisoner dung… when attacked by bandits—"

"Bandits!"

******

Indignant, the captain observed the dialogue at the slave city's entrance. He witnessed as a warrior mob proceeded to broaden their ranks across the stony summit of Chrot's Great Wall.

He glanced toward his last two warriors. The warriors' panoply disappeared replaced by garments only a bandit could wear. Static horror flounced through the captain's mind.

"We have failed," he muttered. The scum had led them into another scheme.

"What, Captain?" Asked one warrior unaware of the illusion garnering upon his visage.

"Never mind! Quickly, turn your horse around and let us get out of here! Quickly!"

The reins pulled.

******

"Don't go after them… till night. That… is… is when the other… bandits may come out." I did my best to maintain the captain's vocal tone.

Thalla and Ding kept their heads unseen.

"Don't worry, Captain. You are within Chrot's walls now. Just enter in with the captive. We shall take care of the problem. After all, this is just one of the few things that has been happening around here."

I trotted the horses into the city's haven. The dirt road trailed past the gates' opening, terminating a short distance away. The faithful mares delivered a psychic sigh.

We made it at last. Kute, we have arrived.

"Fire!" Chrot's commander roared.

As the gates closed, arrows shot off into the air like a maddening flock of birds. Many of them aimed at the three escapees' course.

The gates almost shut. A good number of shafts struck both horses and riders while others secured the ground about the bogus bandits who lumped off, motionless. One horse stumbled forward as the others galloped toward the resulting moonday's mauve horizon.

The gates were barred with thick logs pulled into place from a side wing.

CHAPTER 28: Hay

After being admitted into the dirty town, I hastened the wagon's steering away from the busy guards at the main gate. At Chrot, the beechen edifices' shapes sharpened and appeared rather quaint with worn colors on the faded wood unlike vibrant Skavir's less angular cityscape. Many of the grandiose beech trees were cleared out to make way for the farmlands. These Quirmeans here had no desire to maintain beauty compared to good bargains.

No doubt more soldiers would be within immediate range since Fumi, the military township farther east upland, stationed nearby. After all, Chrot was a food bastion. Morro Ascension, the massive fort based at Fumi, loomed high above all as if nothing could be concealed from its high stony turrets. Gablen possessed stony perimeter walls, as well.

Into the Chrotian mass we ventured with a populace almost as great as the prior. Our accurate horses chose their route and turned sharply around a corner. The citizenry meandered about the streets in the selling and buying of items from the various auctions held within, but these items in the arena were my kin—Lorellians—a slave city in the absolute and the town exploited the bonus title.

During my few past visits to Quirm, Methelo referred to Chrot as a consortium. I often wondered why a city would want to sell consorts. Upon my first visit, I realized Chrot was an actual marketplace, not for whores, but for the farmers from the surrounding lands to sell their stock. They all consorted, as such, to sell to any visitor. Funny how things evolved.

Soon we passed through the town's section where the citizenry inhabited. We raced by large edifices exhibiting many Quirmeans peering out of their windows at the new arrivals brought for auction. Ladders hoisted against some of these buildings with Lorellian slaves utilizing wet rags in attempts to clean the grime while their masters supervised.

The knot of citizenry began to grow tighter and tighter as we rode deeper into the municipal core. My guess appeared incorrect. Stables, large stables, came into sight. Many of them contained animals for sale.

An absurd instinct overcame me triggering my interest about these stalls. The dimness in some, the farther ones, may have been too oblique for my normal Elvin vision. I switched to my infravision. My kin's inherited sight pierced through the dimness with prospects of acknowledging any forms concealed. Red images, representing warm blooded beings, formed. Heavy chains strapped horse-like creatures grazing in earnest within their limited area. Their anterior resembled any raptor with restrained wings taut to their sides.

Hippogriffs! The Lorellian bloodfamily's steeds! I assumed they would be sold later or maybe killed. Moreover, maybe we would find Stonecrusher, and Crater, and Redfang someplace... and maybe my Steadfast, though, I would find it hard to believe my faithful steed would allow himself subjugated in such a manner... No, my Steadfast would not be here.

A mental interference... within proximity... the horses. My mind surrendered allowing present thoughts to dissolve. One of the horses' head appeared. "*Food and water! In those stables. Please allow us to eat now.*"

"*Not yet.*" These brave tired mares. "*Wait until we have passed through those gates.*"

Contact broke.

The rigid jodepiece rubbed against the gauntlet's interior. Why had the jodepiece not shined at all at this juncture? After all these telepathic sendings between the horses and I? The artifact would glow when magic played, but why was the glow not evident during the telepathic sendings?

Amazement pressed upon me. The answer: the enchantment placed upon the captain's armor. That enchantment seemed to absorb the artifact's light. I could fathom this engagement would then diminish the glow's shine since the enchantment also worked its effects upon the Quirmean armor. And, after all, my divine right handled most of the battle.

Or the combined might of Methelo, Rolando, and Sylvia's psionic essences could still be playing a huge part in keeping everything at bay. Thank you, my bloodfamily. And thank you, Achal, for giving us the strength to move forward against such an adversary.

The crowd's pressure grew tighter; soon the mass separated as they took sight of the jail wagon. My infrared vision kept surveying within the stalls.

The jail wagon headed toward the smaller oaken walls in Chrot's heart which could be the main holding area. There were several other structures surrounding. My infravision found no difficulty discerning these structures as occupying Lorellian slaves in them for a future sunday's auction. The slaves farther within this urban outrage must be more immediate sales.

Before we arrived through the lengthy entrance to spy a spacious grassy field of auction stages, I noticed red pulsating images in a stable not far away in the square, two nervous horses meandered about, larger than Man's horses. Near them, in the background, a wolf's rigid image lay. We finally found the three steeds!

The crowd's flow gradually modified. Many Quirmeans strutted through the broad wooden archway with dusk's approach. Passing through the archway, I witnessed many Lorellian slaves being marched off and out from the auction area to their quarters in penitentiaries beyond the inner gate, deserting the platforms. Businesses closed their doors in the idling commonwealth.

The destined structures erected like external pillars with my Lorellian kin staring out from windows with despair. I hoped my kin could distinguish my personage within this damned helmet's shade. Maybe that could give them a glimmer of some confidence. Hope was all we had. I... I must believe.

The kin inside the main auction area's walls dwindled as the Lorellian slaves stationed in their quarters. I scanned back to Thalla. She returned a fatigued look sympathizing with the horses.

Ding glared. I knew he did not care either way.

Rockity-rock...

                    rockity...

I directed the unstable wagon down another street in haste. The squeaking wheels blended little with the moonday air and the horses' measured trotting. Maybe the loyal equines understood the issue at hand. This predicament would have been easier if Rungna-Olivia came along. Her divine right far surpassed my tepid rapport with them.

I steered us down a deserted alley into an empty stall a building away from the main auction platform where a satiated encirclement of companies encompassed a bulwark stage. We configured ourselves near this intersection's epicenter embodying a different borough within the city.

I leaped off my seat. *"We must hide ourselves from the guards who patrol the streets this moonday."*

My hands raised feeling the jodepiece's relentless coldness pulsate through me. I must have let my guard down! Ugh, the power! Such numbing power like ice... colder than ice!

Where were you, Methelo, Rolando, and Sylvia?

My instincts fended off the sneaky entity. The undesirable heat, in response, returned keeping the entity at bay... keeping me safe for now. Keeping us safe, by Achal. We were safe.

I pulled my right gauntlet off. The glow resumed. I feared this glow of immeasurable power. I had no right to this power. Methelo had no right to such power. He had no right to conceal it neither, yet, he did. Somehow we shared this power with Man. Why did Methelo not tell any of us about this jodepiece? Or maybe he chose not to tell me. Why?

The thought of crates crossed my mind—large heavy bulky crates. The image endured with the accompanying encompassing glow. I broke from the reverie... box upon box, a large wall of crates loomed blocking the shut stall doors—another illusion worked.

Thalla crossed over to comfort the horses. The initial horse surveyed her, their bulging orbs held such sadness. The misery the poor beasts must be feeling. I did not need our psychic rapport to understand.

"Ygl..." Sympathetic Thalla affected me so.

My hands gestured toward the area in front of the horses' hooves.

I concentrated. Far into my mind I searched for a reality other than illusion... there the reality flourished, a brighter light in the bluish-yellow, waiting. Thoughts, demands, directed at the light. The light evolved to take shape with the edges commencing to swell and contour... gaining color—a faint brown... a tan... a picture formed. A picture of hay, vegetables, and a hefty basin of water.

The vision flashed to a blur...

I focused as best I could downward. There I witnessed the horses munching on a large pack of healthy food at their hooves with a brimming basin nearby.

Someone would have thought I had become quite the expert. Satisfied, I climbed upon the wagon to discuss the plan to rescue Kute as the group huddled absent the piece's unnatural glow.

CHAPTER 29: The Brand

Across the streets' cover, we crept within the organizations' indistinct perimeter. Ding and Gore remained shrouded underneath Thalla's lengthy cloak. I made use of the shadows to shroud myself since I had no cloak to blend with my surroundings. I guess I could have casted an invisibility spell, but I feared using the jodepiece too often.

Our silent procession led to the structure across from ours, sneaking with the moonday's stealth. So far we had not been caught. The relief I felt knowing Mitral's archeornyx, Jinx, did not accompany us... immeasurable.

An enormous stage's emergence engorged the nearby locale, a good marker. Steps sprouted from all sides of the platform.

"That is the main square and main platform where a majority of your disgusting race is being sold at, Elf," Ding whispered from the rear beneath Thalla's cloak. He had promised to assist in Kute's rescue.

"Now, are you sure it is that building holding Kute?" I pointed toward a two-story blackened outfit a block away from our hiding place.

"Of course, I am sure, fool, that is where I was held at, but be aware that this building is guarded the most." He pointed. "See?"

Down an abandoned street from where we proceeded, a red cloaked figure could be detected.

Ding continued, "Come on. There may still be many more, but we still have to hurry."

Silent, we traversed the avenue. Footsteps fell soft with our eager scanning. The twin moons' brilliance almost uncovered our advance's surprise upon the hulking windowless outfit.

Then we made our journey to the door. After a brief telepathic affirming of the interior, I grabbed the handle and gave it a slow twist... the knob turned... then stopped, locked.

Ding rolled his eyes with his signature glare. He knew what I needed, and only he could provide the service. His rough fingers fiddled within his beard's knots. When they completed their arduous search, they pulled out what many thieves always concealed—a pick. He handed the small device to me.

"No, you do it. It would be a lot more expeditious from an expert like you."

Ding grumbled and took over. "Just remember, I only tagged along to show you where Kute was and nothing else. The Plant is my race's ally... you are not."

click... clickity... click... click... the correct "click" rapped his ears.

Ding absorbed his triumph for a moment. "There it is. Done. Now, let us get in before we are caught, and quit speaking to me with such big words." Cautious, he opened the door inward to the shadowy foyer.

We crept in, closing the door with the selfsame caution. Ding, the best equipped for this pallid scenario, lead the way down toward a corridor. Frantic, Thalla and I searched.

The bare floor led us far down the corridor until Ding stopped us at a dull wall's corner where a few feeble torches tilted, adding some character to the otherwise gloomy surroundings.

Ding peeped over the corner's edge down the corridor. "I see no one," he whispered.

"Ding, I think it is best that we communicate via telepathy, all right?"

"Like he expects me to know what that is..."

"This is exactly what it is, Ding."

Ding paused, grumbled, then we continued to creep farther. I knew if I enacted telepathy it would bother my mate, but common sense was of importance.

Our surroundings got murkier the farther we searched. Thalla and I employed our infravision as best we could preparing for any cloaked figure's surprising arrival.

"Ding, do your kin not have infravision?" I kept alert.

He did not answer. However, the Dwarven thief did stop, hissed, and raised his hand gesturing us to proceed slower. He whispered, "The ground—"

"Head voice, please, Ding."

"Humph... I am not used to this."

"It is important to be right now."

"The... the ground begins to rise a little here."

The Dwarves' grateful trait: the knack to find weaknesses and strongpoints in the earth itself, values useful in practice. They could somehow tell where secret passages hid or even surmise the land's rise and fall much better than anyone. Maybe this trait evolved after thriving so long underground as miners.

First Ding, then I; then Thalla climbed until Ding stopped again. *"Watch... watch your footfalls, Elves."* Even his telepathy retained certain gruffness. *"We are at the stairs."*

To my confoundment, no torches abounded. He was good at his craft to our benefit. We ascended each sturdy wooden step with deliberate attentiveness.

"Anyone of these steps could be fake, Elves."

And, what danger could occur if we did not know which... careful footfalls... careful... the climb seemed almost endless until my Dwarven friend's hand touched my shoulder. I witnessed as he stretched his bulky leg out into the preceding blackness.

I reached to the rear, touching my mate's shoulder. *"Thalla, pay attention to me. Ding believes the step ahead is fake."*

"Okay."

My hands pressed the wall on either side; I followed suit behind Ding.

A light shimmered above; Ding motioned to halt.

Two lean shadows elongated toward the opposite wall from a room to our left with an ajar door.

"Guards..." I must admit my contempt. My hand felt my leg for the small pipe and darts held there. Gone! How easy I could forget their change in ownership. The pipe must have been left at Aman's weaponry shop with my small dagger and the other leg scabbard. *"...Ding. Thalla listen in."*

"Okay, Ygl."

"What, Elf?"

"Yell at the guards to come your direction. When they do, throw Gore at them. That should grant me a chance to run up and kill the other before he can realize what is wrong."

"That is a plan?"

"That is the best we have."

*"Sounds like you are heading into your own **end-of-rings,** fool."*

"We have no other objective."

"I am with you, my mate." Thalla entered.

"Let us do it."

The bedazzled axe emerged from its concealment. A wail of gruff terror emitted from Ding's rough lips.

The two guards leapt up startled from their posts, each staring down the staircase.

My Dwarven friend wailed again.

The guards descended in a rush, accustomed to their footsteps in the blackness. Their glowing vibrant figures approached like bumbling metal beans.

I angled to Ding's left, minding how he twirled his axe; letting Gore take flight.

THUNK!

ClAnG… cLaNG…

ClAnKiTy ClAnG

The armor's clanking hit the stairs absorbing the subdued guard's yelp. I hurdled forward, gaining upon the other fleeing guard. Maybe they had a warning system that needs impeding.

The guard arrived ahead of me to the top. My plan underestimated his reflexes. The guard went around the side, but his silhouette gave away his readied attack. His sword's pointed outline barred my purposeful path as I hit my mark on the pinnacle floor.

A fast swish sliced through the air. His blade, aimed at injuring my midsection, connected to nothing when I rolled beneath the fuller. The guard howled in anger. Rushing footfalls proved that other guards on this top floor heeded their comrades' calls.

I unsheathed Welbern from its resting place, having rolled to the wall opposite the entrance,

The guard charged me, chance must not be wasted. Kute must be saved. The guard's blade sliced through the air aiming to find a resolute connection upon me.

Welbern blocked the attack. I could sense an impulsive glee explode from my blade... Glee? Glee? I had never felt such a feeling emit from Welbern, my Demonslayer... What was I saying? I had never sensed anything coming from my blade at all!

Was Welbern mystic after all? According to legend, my blade did slay Demons. This act was demonstrated to me when the Death Mist invaded my kin's spring dance; however, I never witnessed such an act until then. Plus, Thalla's blade did just as well. The legends also stated, moreover, that the mark Welbern left on a Demon dispensed a worse penance than the end-of-seasons. I never witnessed a mark, nor got afforded the opportunity.

Nonetheless, my blade's eerie impression seemed to attempt to disclose more to me—something more than the mysterious curse its rumored mark granted upon branding. Did Demonslayer want me know?

I conceded... and gasped... The milieu about me transformed. At once, I found myself located in a world of ever shifting gloom and flimsiness. The fluxes, subtle but not rapid.

A mist, perhaps? A gas? Swen? Swen... Was she trying to communicate with me through this mystic vision?

Vague rolling valleys unfurled everywhere from the precipice I found myself upon. Jagged treetops poked through the disseminating gloom and lightness. Harmonious horror's sinuous screams blended with the bleakness. Figures, indescribable, tumbled in the deeper misty below.

In front of me floated Welbern. An amber energy erupted from my quivering blade. The glow intensified consuming the surrounding phenomenon.

Welbern swung in a full abrupt arc permitting the energy to transform into a blast of frazzled, energetic light dispersing into the vacuous skyways... a speck in the horizon.

Welbern hesitated and swung into another, yet reverse, arc imparting a vast spread of ambient light. Images of somber creatures uncovered not too far above me, decrepit creatures, smelly creatures crawling and scratching upon each other, spitting decay upon each other, cursing upon each other, flailing upon each other—Demons!

I almost regurgitated... okay, I regurgitated a little...

Were the Demons falling from existence? An anguished soul rose...

or dangled... howling from the apparent writhing corpses.

Another Demonic corpse lay, or floated... smirking? On the decrepit forehead, a mark resembling my blade pointed downwards... the Demon smiled ... the mark flashed... the Demon turned to ash.

Other Demons recoiled from the corpse with more disdain as if stumbling to break free of a curse. The shifting haze shrouded the same brand on each fiend.

Demonslayer halted the images and rotated round and round and round. The subsequent emissions built and built brighter and brighter...

Everything flashed out –

The Quirmean blade hacked down at me, the razor sharp edge hunting for meat. Welbern caught the blow, then parried the guard's blade against the wall.

I kicked him back inside the room. Four guards streamed in from one side of the extensive hall. I fell upon my defenseless opponent. His season oozed well from his heart.

I poised for the next assault. The first guard, entering to my left, rushed with sword already raised. I twisted, my conclusive vomit completed my cycle onto the guard's face. I chopped off his sword arm's wrist, then followed with his head.

The two guards to my right were unprepared for my rush across the room. The initial guard collapsed.

I charged the second guard to my right to defeat him before the final guard to my left could catch up. My opponent must have been scared of me, for he lashed out with shattering blows directing me away from the doorway.

A pair of footsteps arrived behind me...

I lunged deep beneath the path of his blade, my feet catching ground, Demonslayer shot up striking him through the vulnerable gut. His scream, an obvious answer to my murderous blow as I dodged aside for the final confrontation.

As a matter of fact, two screams emitted... Ding glowered at me with a bloodied Gore. Thalla stood beside him. Upon the floor strew the final guard—a profound crescent dent implanted in his breastplate's posterior. For Dwarven pride, Ding jabbed Gore's iron endpoint into the base of the corpse's skull. This final kill added to a wonderful décor of six slain guards dispersed about us. I gave Ding a satisfying smile; in good form, he glared a little more.

I sheathed Welbern. "You know, Ding, I still like you." I could have dispensed these opponents with easy psionic blasts, but I erred on Thalla's advice. Simple telepathy would do for now.

More footsteps rushed up the stairs. Ding hastened past me out the door to the hall's other end toward an opposite cornered door. He searched into his burly beard and pulled out something small, the pick.

...tippitty-tap... tippitty-tap... tap-tap...

There must be something important within the room... The reassuring "click."... We rushed in escaping vengeful declarations supplementing clamoring footsteps.

"Kute?" I whispered into the dim musky room. Weary slaves were confined about the tight room huddling together. "Kute?" I raised my whisper's volume.

No answer. I took off my helmet and decided to enact a panoramic sending. *"It is I, Ygl."*

"Oh great general," a wizened voice answered, *"It is you."* The withered elder I encountered earlier crawled up to me with his mate. I bended down to him. *"Oh, great general, it is we, Lyp and Bolanda who tried to save you from your end-of-seasons."*

Bolanda spoke, *"We are so happy you escaped, for everyone in this cell is ready to rise with you and fight back. We know what happened to King Methelo, Prince Rolando, and Advisor Sylvia."*

"Thank you. I felt their end-of-seasons myself, but we cannot rise and strike. Not now.

I remember you, Lyp. You were one of my bloodfather's captains. You are too tired. Wait and rest until I can return with help. Try to formulate a rebellion later. I know how our kin has been scattered all over this empire, but try dispatching messengers. You can do this. Steal arms from Man until you have enough to rebel. All this takes some planning and strategizing, but I know you can do it."

"We will try our best, sir."

I disseminated my tentative telepathy again to include everyone in the confinement. Sad minds, weary minds touched mine. Kin's minds missing their bloodfamilies and yearning for Lorel, yet a calmness culminated amongst them. Meditation did my kin well; I never understood why I never cared for the practice.

"Do you or anyone here know where I can find a very large person, a Giant?"

"I am here." From the room's other side, a large figure loomed. Within his cadence, a shorter person assisted him—Ding.

"Kute, is that you?"

"It is I, General." He emulated a pinch of cheerfulness. *"I am a bit fatigued from starvation like anyone else here, but I am still able. I am ready when you are."*

"You look like you lost a lot of weight."

"I am sure I will get it all back."

His bearskin jacket's threads severed through the middle exposing his sweaty muscled body despite the loss. His leather slacks were torn while his deer skin boots withheld further damage. A small blond beard, a bit thicker than his unruly hair, blended with his bristling mustache. *"Let us be on our way."*

Outside, we could detect the cries of "Clear!" arriving more proximal to our room. I knew Kute could not have stated truer words.

The twin moons' light shot through an adjacent window. *"Captain Lyp, do you know where the window leads?"*

"To the rear of the jail, sir."

"Here, Ygl." Thalla relayed a rope produced from a side satchel Ding carried within his cloak.

"All right, listen. We are going to climb out the building, but we need those who are awake to hold the rope at the other end. When we make it out, keep the rope so that some of those you send as messengers can use this for their escape."

"Hurry, fool," Annoyed Ding whispered.

"Head voices, Ding," I insisted.

"HMPH! I do not want to be caught in here when they enter."

"We will not be, Ding, my friend," Kute responded. *"General, it is best I will go second. I think I can hold you up, but, I do not think I could, Ding."*

"That is fine, Plant Kute."

Several Lorellians rose up from their slumber to assist with our escape. Many held the other end of the rope. Other elves pressed upon the unattended door in a last ditched attempt of defense.

I climbed down first taking as much of the rope as possible. Reaching the bottom, I looked up to see Kute climb down next.

"Captain?" A voice behind me. A cloaked figure stood within the businesses' outline and peered up to see the truth of the matter jostling into view. "Y-you are not the Captain! Fiend, what have you done to him?"

The cloaked guard attacked, throwing me off balance—his blade, an invisible assailant in the moonday shade. Lunar, gossamer beams flashed upon his blade, too quick for my visual adjustment to follow.

I reached for Welbern, but I knew I would be too late. I fell against the building's side as Kute held onto the rope. The guard came at me again. Ducking, I welcomed his misguided blade striking brick. The guard renewed his desperate attack. I rolled to the side and swung my leg out tripping him. His abdomen jutted forward in a bloody splurge to Welbern's inevitable disembowelment. The Chrotian guard rolled to the ground. His expanded cloak exposed a blob of red wetness permeating the fabric.

"Well, General, it seems you did not need my help at all. Glory."

Thalla roped down the wall.

"Glory what?"

"Why glory to war, General."

"War."

"Yes, we are at war and Lolung-Cor is my roots' god of war. We celebrate this moment as ours."

"I think this moment is everyone's."

Thalla completed her descent wrapping her arms around my breastplate, her head nuzzled my shoulder. "I wish for us to make it out of this."

"What matters is that we are together, Thalla."

"Yes, we are."

Kute beamed. "So you are his beautiful **earth**. You are just as beautiful as he is. What a match."

Ding hurried out the window and jumped the rest of the way down. He shook the rope once signaling for the Lorellians to redraw their escape route.

"Earth?"

"I think he means you are my mate."

"Yes. Yes. Mate: earth."

The guards would inspect the room and, to no avail, find us gone; never realizing how we escaped. Soon we would route ourselves through the large arc entry and seclude ourselves within our steeds' stable.

"Yes. Yes." Thalla teared up. "I am your earth, your sky, your heart, and your soul."

"I love you, Thalla."

"And I, you, Ygl."

This moonday we rested after I created a simple meal for everyone to my worried mate's disappointment and Kute's confoundment. This magic was necessary ever so often despite the shortcomings, preparing me to make the sacrifice needed to move us forward.

CHAPTER 30: Piggy Piggy

The Chrotian Captain commanded his caravan of six guards to the three expired bodies. The night's unflappable breeze whipped past their faces as the horses ambled toward their objective. The trio of cadavers, punctured with numerous arrows, reminiscent of roasted pigs prepared for a party.

And a party indeed. These bandits' death pleased Chrot's captain, for they would have created quite a problem for the empire. This new god—Xurchon—and religion seemed so new to the populace; maybe this epiphany changed everyone for the good.

But then why had they forsaken Istratos and Welna, the former god and goddess, so easily? To please a beloved emperor? And why capture all these estates for a jewel Emperor Rondo would exhibit in his gem collection? At this juncture, the captain needed to perform as ordered with no disobedience. He had no issue with this directive.

The captain kicked a lifeless transgressor's perforating arrow. These punctured carcasses would be scrumptious treats for the manticora. The effrontery of such people to chase the captain of captains to Chrot's gates.

The Chrotian captain stooped toward a covered figure. The other guards straddled their horses awaiting. He kicked the cadaver over to witness a man's impassive pupils he obliged and befriended for many years gawping at him.

He gasped imbibing his pride, "Impostors..."

CHAPTER 31: A decision

The Majestic Treehouse's underpinning was not as pervasive as the abundance of other trees in Lorel. However, three solitary sequoias, the only massive sequoias, comprising a particular triangular establishment, presented the magnanimous treehouse as an omnipresent dimension. A paradox within and of the wilderness. Age upon age of construction established a structure that built upon itself to grand unassuming heights in the arboreous landscape. Heights that overlooked Lake Ban's western bank not too far in the vastness. Yet, the jagged tree line did obscure the lake's bank, unless a tenant visited the treehouse's pinnacle.

Wooden bridges: the road map to a network of humble dwellings within the treehouse's branches. The bridges originated from a massive tenement spanning all three sequoias' base. This resilient tenement created a primary tier the suspension bridges connected from to the next similar tier until concluding at the third tier atop. Robust roped railings constructed the bridges, hung to taut support towers. These support towers were unmistakable with signage for each level. The first level, a massive meditation room with wide open windows provided a peaceful panoramic view. A spiral of broad stairs from each sequoia's base led to this primary tier. The second tier serviced a dining area with fewer windows. The final tier, harboring the fewest windows, supplied a gathering area for the royal family: King Scall and Queen Rarle with their children, Princes Methelo and Ygl. Of course, other individuals could visit, but not on this particular day.

Methelo suspended his little brother in a horizontal telekinetic wrap shrouding Ygl's outraged mouth. The younger prince's struggles became painted with a disappointment unmatched by King Scall's.

"What did Ygl do now, Methelo?"

"He got into a fight with Spenz."

"Spenz?"

"Yes, Bloodfather. I do not understand why he acts this way. Rolando gets along with Spenz fine."

Calm King Scall adjusted his tunic while sipping water from a small goblet. "I know you need to get involved with your studies. It is important to maintain a good relationship with Quirm's new emperor. He is close to your age, you know."

"Yes, I know, bloodfather. I am more close to his."

"He is in the nearby tenement with his bloodfamily awaiting my salutation. I need to apologize to him for Ygl's behavior. After that, you may continue to see him on my behalf."

"Are you not king?"

"Yes, but, my existence in this plane will end much like Emperor Rykon II."

Little Ygl halted his squirming permitting a simultaneous expression of shock matching his older brother's.

Queen Rarle did not move from her split reed chair across the way. She observed the situation with crossed legs protruding from a diaphanous red dress not regarding the leaf tumbling upon it—a probable endowment from the Sprites. The dress' top stretched wide from shoulder to shoulder with a small clasp securing the middle dip together.

"You can release your bloodbrother, Methelo. I need to speak to him privately."

"You cannot provide me with such information, bloodfather, and expect for me to walk away."

Queen Rarle intervened. "Just do as your bloodfather asks, Methelo. This is of great importance."

With much care, Methelo turned Prince Ygl upright unravelling the telekinetic wrap allowing his little brother to run to their father's arms. He glanced toward his stoic mother for an answer he knew she would not provide before his departure.

"Bloodfather, please do not meet the end-of-seasons! Please do not!" Ygl would not let go.

"There, there, my little bloodchild. I did not mean to alarm you. That was very wrong of me to state. I will not leave any moment soon. Now, tell me. Why did you hit Prince Spenz?"

"Because he cheated."

"He cheated?"

"Yes."

"At what?"

"At hiding and seeking."

"Hiding and seeking? How do you cheat at that game?"

"He poked his head from behind a boulder and stuck his tongue out at me."

"So, he let you find him?"

"Yes, he was cheating. He was supposed to hide so I could go seeking for him?"

"Ygl. Ygl, do you not see he wanted to make it easier so he could go seeking you? You hit him over that? My little prince, he likes you and you hurt his feelings. *It took you that long to find him, huh*?"

King Scall's psychic sending caught Ygl unaware, *"Yes."*

"Now, Ygl, you retain the gift of telepathy and not once did you utilize it while your bloodbrother muffled you in his telekinetic wrap. Why?"

"Because you do not want me invading kin's minds."

"But you would not be doing that."

"It would feel like that."

"So you are being fair minded."

"I... I like to be fair, bloodfather, if that is what you mean."

"Good. Then be fair with your friend, Spenz, and apologize to him. It is important to care for kin before judgment. He meant to only have fun with you and that was all. Can you do that for your bloodfather?"

Ygl paused with a little embarrassment. *"Yes."*

"Good. That is my good little bloodson. I will meet him and you later to make sure he is all right. Remember we must be a caring race, especially with Man. They are our next-door neighbors—"

"So is Khun."

"Yes, but, we deal mostly with Quirm and one sunday we will need each other, and I need you strong for that sunday for both races. Can you do that for me?"

"Empress Maxis will bear him a new bloodchild in the next term. Such a shame... Tell him, Scall." Queen Rarle retained the psionic gift of retrocognition, past sight. As queen, hers was a divine right unlike the many her husband wielded.

"I am getting there, Rarle."

"What is wrong, bloodfather?"

"Oh, nothing, Ygl. You like Khun a lot, do you not?"

"Oh, yes, I like it a lot there. It is such a beautiful forest and the Khunians are a lot of fun."

"They like to do a lot of combating with each other."

"Yes, it is fun to watch."

"I have spoken to Blasmle and Rungna-Olivia of the Protectors, Ygl. I want you to go to Khun."

"Really?"

"Yes. I want you to go there for five seasons."

"Five seasons? Why?"

"Because I want you as my little general. I want you to learn their art of warcraft and perfect it. Can you do that for me?"

"But, we have never had a general."

"I know. That is why I need one now. With your passion and love, I know you can be a great one for me while your bloodbrother will be groomed to be my presumptive king."

"I... I do not know..."

"Come on. Do this for your bloodfather, bloodmother, and your kin. We all need your cooperation."

A female, a couple years older than Ygl and a little unkempt, bounded into the room wearing an amalgam of wood shavings and dirt on her short-sleeved shirt. A hammer with a satchel of nails attached to her belt. "Oh, I am sorry, King Scall. Queen Rarle. Prince Ygl. I was looking for my bloodfather."

"He must be down the hall making the new window." Scall noticed his son embarking a novel interest onto their visitor.

"Thank you, King Scall." She granted Ygl a slight twinkle from her eyes.

"Hey!" Ygl did not want her to go; she bided. "You want to come with me to Khun? I am going for five seasons. My name is Ygl."

"I know who you are, Prince Ygl. I already addressed you," she giggled, "I am sorry I cannot come with you to Khun."

"Why? We could have fun."

"... I have a female mate."

"Oh..."

"That does not bother you, right? It does not bother my bloodfather."

"No. No. That does not bother me. I do not really know anything about relationships."

"Okay," the smaller bloodchild studied him enamored by his innocence. "I will tell you something. I will wait for you. Would you like that?"

"Yes. Yes. I would like that a lot."

"Okay. It is a deal." With a hand crossed behind her withholding her hammer, the female held out her other for an obliged shaking before scampering to her work site.

"Wait! I do not know your name!"

"Thalla." She hustled off. Her satchel's jingling diminished the farther she ventured down the hall. "My name is Thalla!"

CHAPTER 32: Growth

On this new sunday, our eagerness to escape this bedlam of an empire attained feverish heights deeper than the Interim's depths.

Thalla had awoken brandishing her weapon with leftover hay. "Did you have a dream?"

"A dream? No... it was more like a memory. A missing memory I had forgotten so long ago. Why? Why now?"

Ding rested a little farther away, massaging Redfang's coat. "Information."

"What?"

The robber remained stoic, "Your parable about the gold locked away in the chest given to your friend. The gold is information. The chest is the trust you gain with it while the lock is the faith you secure with that trust. Information is valuable."

"I am amazed, Ding. You just said a mouthful. Any ideas?"

He registered an unusual composure. "What are you fools doing? Do you not realize word of an impostor has already been rumored? That Emperor Rondo will no sooner get an army out here before we know it?"

"Ding is correct, by no means, dear General," Kute advocated. Astonishing how a prince could be friends with a thief. A story worth telling. Kute peered out the stable door hidden behind the jodepiece's simulated wall. "This early cloudnoon the Quirmean guards would be congregated in the central auction area of Chrot. If we are to leave, pragmatism must be now."

"I understand," I replied. "We are to escape to the south where the Fendor River runs no matter what is in our way. That is our best strategy at this stage."

Plant Kute mounted his gigantic horse, Crater, underneath the lofty ceiling. "But, General, the city wall will block our escape. How are we to pass through that? I am grateful you were able to destroy my bracelets with the little jodepiece, but I do not think I would be able to use my divine right here. Not yet." I noticed Kute's relaxed composure as well—almost as if testing me.

"Well, I do not know what your gift is, but if you feel it will not be of current help, then it will not. Just remember, my telepathic control on this jodepiece is limited and tiring. My hold on this artifact is very tenuous and I can only do one spell at a moment. I am not a magician like Man's royalty is. It is already taking a lot for me to keep this illusion up." That rib I found the jodepiece on must have been Methelo's. Only he could have had the strength to endure this power. But how? How did this artifact even get there? He never told any of us about this irregular loop. Was this piece the meaning behind his stomach pains?

I proceeded to the wearied horses who risked their seasons to deliver us here. Pieces of hay dripped from their munching maws.

My hand patted the nearest horse's hindquarter. The horse looked at me. *"Thank you."* A sudden psionic snap between us signified our connection would be final.

"Ygl," Thalla's voice stayed steady and soft, "I wish us all luck. Let us hope we are all safe... I-I fear for us."

"We will be fine, Thalla."

"I have faith you are right." Her pulsating lips caressed mine, striving to hold the bond between us forever.

"Whoa-ho-ho, I would say 'Get a room, you two,' but," Kute hugged both of us, "I would not mind sharing... Whoa, we all need to bathe soon."

"Whaaa?" Thalla's confusion made me giggle.

I did not struggle. "That is alright, Kute."

"Hey, I do not mind sharing. Either one of you will do."

"We do mind, my friend, we do." I shook my head, chuckling.

"This Giant prince is quite a character, Ygl."

"If you think he is, wait till you get to meet his friend, Juna, the Fairy queen."

"A Fairy? You actually met a Fairy. Are they like Sprites?"

"Well, I do not feel much resistance here," Kute interceded.

Nervous, Thalla and I let go, keeping our chuckles low. "Okay, let us get going. I need to take down this illusion to reserve my strength."

"I must admit, General, Emperor Rondo has not made an appearance to block us. Maybe he is not so omniscient?"

"Maybe."

Thalla and I leapt upon Stonecrusher's winged spine in synch with everyone else. "Remember we must move fast, swift, and low since it would be hard to hide you, Kute. Practicality is of the highest order. My strength must be reserved for this. Is the way clear?"

Kute peered out, "Yes."

"Let us begin." The illusion dissolved, the sunday's bright radiance peeking through. Crater tore down the stable door with his mighty hooves, leaving a wooden aftermath upon the break's wake. Stonecrusher cleared the path further permitting an easier breach for Redfang to pass through.

Familiar with the Quirmean city's layout, I took the lead. Our departure's alarm had already carried as we steered our mounts through the slave pens' locale. To our luck, not many Quirmeans traversed the thoroughfares, however, the few passersby's cries obliged the guards to consider our escape.

Onward the mounts galloped. Redfang and Ding followed behind. Thalla hung on tight. Not far away, a cavalry emerged with many foot soldiers; however, too late. We had made our clear exit from the city's main auction area.

Next, the wall. The mounts sped through the bordering city streets. Stonecrusher and Crater's strong legs gave strident leaps between gallops. Quirmeans ducked for cover leaving behind screams of anger or terror. More Quirmean warriors answered the ruckus. A small platoon dared block our escape.

"Weapons!!" I commanded. Club, ax, and swords whipped out with the kicking and trampling of hooves, and gnashing of canine teeth. Through the thriving barrage of armory we bore slashing and bashing away at those who dared impede us.

The vengeful warriors' responses resounded quick and deliberate. However, their attacks were nothing compared to my faithful allies. Kute bashed through with his mighty club of stones fracturing armored helmets, partaking big red gashes on their heads. His intimidating presence made many an enemy balk. Gore swung low in large arcs consigning many without the use of legs or season in the aftermath.

Again and again, Chrot's protectors pressed toward me, the Lorellian general they loathed for whatever reason. The Elf that must meet the end-of-seasons.

Thalla lashed out from one end while Welbern's silver tooth scoffed away at twofold the amount on the other. A good team she and I made since before our marriage.

So close the lot of us came. So close to the end-of-seasons as the Quirmean band attempted to press in on us, but the pounding of Stonecrusher, Crater, and my tempered telepathic blasts held them at bay. Soon, more warriors joined in on the fray. A few wounds scathed me. I knew my allies must have suffered some injuries as well.

"There he is! The impostor! Onward!" The captain of Chrot made sure I acknowledged his presence. He must be frustrated from the lethal predicament I induced upon someone of his ranking. His horse's hooves came thundering closer.

My telepathy meandered within the synapses of the Chrotian captain's mind, disabling his personal pursuit, a proper delay to his group. A telepathic blast like that must be measurable considering the power I harbored that could affect even me.

My psionic assault almost left me blindsided to a couple of sword attacks my instincts volleyed. "*Kute!*" mass telepathy became an easier matter that deserved credence. "*We do not have enough luck, and I doubt we will be standing much longer. We must escape before it is too late.*"

Crater and Stonecrusher's exuberant neighs echoed the Giant Plant's boisterous cry. "All right!!"

The mounts tore into the band with an equine high kick, a gnashing of lupine fangs and a boisterous spread of powerful wings. Other pursuing warriors overrode the trampled bodies, proceeding with the chase; ignoring what stood in their way.

Again, through the city streets we raced hoping to deceive the enemy into going another direction, but everywhere we rode other warriors popped out to block us. Always south we raced until we saw a looming red structure at the grassy field's perimeter: Chrot's Great Wall! Faster and faster we raced kicking our steeds' sides harder and harder.

We broke into the field, light green and serene compared to our setting. The grasses, short and fluffy, almost reminded me of home. A butterfly flitted by undaunted. The insect's spirit, so free—so uplifting. This was the Lorellian way, including cherishing one another. Caring for Man became an obvious hindrance we learned too late.

Our pursuers poured out of the city into the field marring the image. Fortunate for us, they advanced too far away to continue battle.

"General!" Kute bellowed from behind. "Upon the wall! Bows!" The ledges teemed with immediate archers notching arrows for a valuable target practice.

Without falter, my hand upraised. Psychic energies coalesced within the jodepiece in tremendous waves despite prior reluctances.

Nothing happened—no energy spurts; no trinkets of power. The jodepiece was fighting me? The piece must have sensed our escape and did not desire for us to succeed! Rolando warned me about its evil essence needing a challenger. I trembled on my saddle as two forces tugged with relentlessness to gain dominion over each other.

Arrows volleyed...

The desperate mounts tried to steer out of the barrage's way. Kute's massive form got nipped on the hip and right leg. He bellowed such a deep bellow, but not out of pain. He actually enjoyed the barrage! I had to give credit where credit deserved due.

Fortuitous Ding remained safeguarded behind Stonecrusher and Crater's bulky romps, except for the few shafts almost skinning him.

More arrows pocketed the ground, warning shots or just plain luck. Or, maybe Jinx flew overhead.

pock!

229

pock!

pock!

I yelped! An arrow's shaft embedded itself into my right shoulder. I had dealt with worse pain than this practicing warfare with the ferocious Khunian Elves. Pain: a way of existence as a general.

"Ygl!" Thalla pulled the intrepid arrow out, tore off a rag, and bandaged the profuse wound.

With jagged movements, Stonecrusher struggled to gain more ground as the forces within me pushed and pulled—strained and struggled. My body irked. My head ached.

Two soft hands impressed my head's temples. An inducement of telepathic waves entered my mind piercing the shuffling barrier between good and evil. Thalla may not be gifted, but she and I shared a strong rapport she had become accustomed. I collapsed from the psychic trance and allowed my mate's love to embolden me.

Advancing warriors hesitated in awe as the bluish-yellow radiance blossomed about my hand—immense power I could never comprehend. Thalla and my combined psionic waves must have flowed in too forceful. The power erupting from my hand shed such immense luminance, an expiring star dazzling everything and everyone. Regardless, I could still perceive the archers reaching into their quivers.

The piece's power coursed through my arm akin to the iciest of shards. My forefingers flexed once; out flew the most primal spell I ever casted.

A beam of power dashed through the air in a flash. An explosion resounded from the rampart's summit the beam caressed. A number of archers tumbled to the ground accompanying the unfortunate minimal debris, but not enough welcomed the end-of-seasons. My blast was errant and befouled—the jodepiece tricked me?

"Oh-ho-ho, General, you said you wanted to reserve your strength. You have a funny way of showing it! Here, let me help as best I can.

Crater, kneel!"

Crater performed as commanded and lowered himself to allow the Giant Plant a chance to leap-frog in front. Kute took immense strides in short bouncing sprints—the red wall loomed not far away.

Amazing! With each booming stride, Kute grew bigger and bigger... and bigger than—maybe as large as the Majestic Treehouse! His royal gift manifested with not a rupture to his paraphernalia. Lorellians had believed the Giants' natural height the size of mountains. Who knew this legend developed into a divine gift for a select, his divine right? I could understand why Kute decided not to reveal his divine right until the moment fit. He would have been too much of an easy target against Man's magic.

His thickened skin repelled a meager barrage of arrows with ease; the unexpected backlash knocked the confused archers off their balance. Enough structural loss to the wall provided Kute a chance to kick down the destabilized area, thereafter slamming his immense fists upon the fresh rift's new edges. The reverse strike produced aftershocks along the weakened obstacle knocking more archers off balance.

We passed through the damage on toward the deep rushing river, Fendor. Beyond the river, a towering beast of marvel loomed, the Great Wall of Quirm, belittling all the cities' walls as brick and mortar stretched from Lake Ban in the west toward the eastern Zaendaran shores. The archers there, few and too distant to affect our exodus much like Fumi's copious military farther east upland. Man's ego played well to our advantage.

... A tingle seethed my body.

Misfortune complemented more arrows volleying from behind. The warriors renewed their attack at a faster rate, but our goal arrived closer. The disappointment they must be feeling—their prospective bounty humiliating them—fueled their courage to stand against my little jodepiece. Or maybe they feared their emperor's wrath more?

"Ygl, your clothes! They have reappeared!" Thalla observed, hence, the answer to the tingle.

"I must have used so much power in that first spell. There was no way I could hold this one.

Prepare for the second phase of our escape. Hold tight!" I swung my hand up again; not as elevated as prior, focusing upon the Fendor River.

"Ygl, it took too much out of you."

"I-I have no choice." The magic returned, except not as forceful since I enacted a lot less effort. Why was the jodepiece not attacking me? Or

struggling against me? What trickery. Never would I try another spell like that again. I should never possess so much unyielding power.

A familiar glow emanated from the Fendor.

Kute retained his normal size mounting upon Crater, vanguard to our trio. "General, what is happening? Has the emperor found us? The river emits a glow."

Oops... I forgot to disclose this part of the plan. The jodepiece's bitter coldness flushed through me in an instant. I irked from the pain.

"Ygl!"

The burning heat within me surged in response, "The jodepiece is trying to control me."

Kute twisted Crater around to witness my struggle. "General?"

Thalla held onto me as I struggled to maintain myself. "Kute, just go! He will explain later."

"I will not until I am told what it is. You never know if Xurchon is attempting to stop us!"

Impatient Thalla yelled, "Can you not see the Quirmeans are almost upon us? Enter!"

Embarrassed, noble Kute refused a retort. Hasty Ding raced past Kute, holding tight upon Redfang's furry spine. The overpowering Fendor, Quirm's strong natural defense, could not impede his Dwarven friend's smooth entry.

"Oh-ho-ho! I will not be humiliated twice in one cloudnoon!" Kute joked, enjoying the moment. Onward Crater tore into the biting currents, his master relieved the shimmering shaft did not lead to the end-of-seasons.

The Quirmean warriors advanced close enough to delay Thalla and my elusion. If they succeeded, there would be no way to control this already difficult spell.

Thalla's lips pressed upon my neck with all the strength she mustered.

"*Thalla...*"

"*Let my kiss be a mark of my admiration and blessing to you, my love.*" She pulled out her sword. "*Good luck on your mission. I will love you beyond forever.*"

"Thalla, do not!"

She leapt off Stonecrusher with a banshee's scream, her curly wavy hair flailing everywhere as she attacked our unprepared pursuers. The seasons of our climbing upon Lorellian trees aided her elegant dodges of the most proximal blades, returning faster deadlier blows than prior. I trained her well. Five Quirmeans succumbed beneath her well wielded blade until, alas, they surrounded her. Thalla fought away from me, aiding my exodus into the Fendor.

I could not help her. I did not have the skill to channel the jodepiece's power in a binary when my telepathy struggles against the piece's constant assault.

"No." I am a general! A Lorellian warrior! I would not be forsaken! You would not kill my mate! You would not take her away from me again!

I bounded off Stonecrusher before entry, racing upon the naked space to rescue my Thalla, "No!"

The lead guardian rode upon me swinging his blade. He had never met a warrior like me. I hurdled up kicking his blade, running nimbly along its fuller as if it was a tree branch, granting the blade's originator Welbern's answer… The spray of blood and sweat mixed with the cool spring air.

… I must maintain the jodepiece's control … I must not hinder Kute and Ding's escape.

I charged the fallen guardian's horse into the throng surrounding Thalla slewing them with broad strong sweeps combined with bounds upon bounds upon their mares. These Quirmeans never expected one trained by Khunian fierceness. One trained for battle. One trained for war.

They thought every Lorellian a complacent meditator. They were wrong… and I was too late. Thalla draped upon the ground with little movement. Her skin, darker than her olive wreath at the dance, tinged with crimson spots reflecting the crimson puddle underneath.

My helplessness could not overshadow her logic. The mission's importance superseded everything. More warriors attempted to seize me.

An abrupt neighing from behind… with a grunting and a gnashing, Stonecrusher's teeth snatched my cloak's collar. Hefty gray wings spanned to obstruct any adversary; heaving me toward the watery portal.

"No!"

… Bubbles rushed passed me… and past me… and past me…

233

CHAPTER 33: Epilogue

Quirm's southwest region beheld a plenteous farmland where laborious farmers sowed their crops since winter's conclusion. However, they weren't independent in the striated fields. An abundance of Lorellians slaved away in a foreign landscape neighboring a beloved forest.

The Forest of Lorel's new inhabitants dressed different nowadays perusing through sporting their Quirmean steel, sword in hand and clopping hooves would procure any fugitives if need be. As the soldiers hacked through, away amongst the firs, near a solitary pond, rested a fledgling willow. Songbirds alighted upon the willow warbling sweet songs, but if a bystander attended close enough a weeping could be heard amid the melodic joy.

The adventure continues in
"THE JODE: Part 2: Awakenings Reckoning"

Corey McNaught's amazing art:

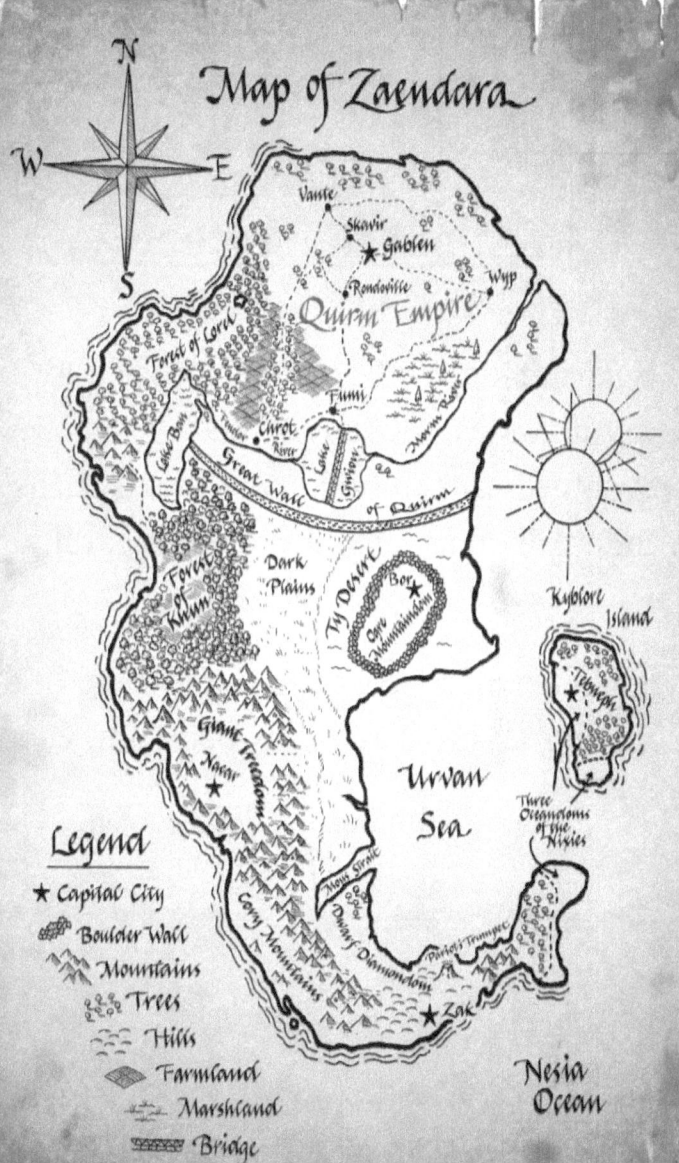

About the Author

PJ Selarom, an Air Force veteran, is a lover of mythologies, inclusivity and comics. He ventures to combine these ideals in his wonderfully dark adventure of love, religion, and politics.

He resides in a treehouse somewhere in the country taking care of his baby unipegon.

He can be reached at PJSELAROM.COM